THE DARKEST GIFT

A novel

by

LEN HANDELAND

Our guide from yesterday turned up, the one who showed us first the Procope and then the rooms I was letting. For a few *sous*, he showed me some of the sights of Paris. Despite my exhaustion yesterday, we walked as far as the Ile de la Cité to see the Cathedral of Nôtre Dame and climbed the bell tower to see the city of Paris before us. It is hard to describe how I, a farm boy who had never seen anything higher than the roof of the parish church, felt when I saw the full magnificence of Paris.

When we got back to the café, I paid and dismissed my guide, and, giving up for today on my gentleman in blue, I was ready to climb the stairs to my attic. The sun had gone down about an hour ago, and I thought I would have a brandy before going home. I turned to look for a waiter, and there he was, wearing the same blue breeches and vest, the same lavender coat, the long brown wig, and the lace at his neck that was as white as the first snow. And he was looking at me with those bright blue eyes, staring. Not to be intimidated, I stared back. Finally, he smiled. With one hand, he indicated a table with a chessboard set up upon it. I took a chair, and we sat down opposite each other.

"I am a habitué here. You are the guest and must take the white" were the first words he ever said to me.

Since I was young, I thought myself to be an excellent chess player, ready to match my skills with the best the capital had to offer. I often played against my sisters and brother and beat them all. However, my father would never take me on, which should have told me something.

This gentleman checkmated me in two moves. He did not laugh at me, but he did smile out of the corner of his mouth. We played another game, and this time he checkmated me in three moves.

"Sir, I perceive I am out of my class," I said. "I thought myself a good player at home, but I had only my family to play against me, and I see now that what we called chess was very different from the game you play. I am not worthy of playing against you, sir."

It was clear that the gentleman had enjoyed dominating me game after game. He was pleased by my tribute and smiled at me now more indulgently. "I suppose you must learn from me, then," and he proceeded to show me a series of maneuvers. I would have felt foolish except that he so obviously enjoyed instructing me.

A waiter stopped at our table and said, "Milord?"

"Two tankards of ale," my lord, answered without raising his eyes from the chessboard.

Now, assuredly, I would learn his name.

"If you buy me an ale, you must know my name," I said boldly. "I am Fabien Levesque." I waited.

"Stefan, Baron of Vitré."

There, it was on the table: if he were an aristocrat, he would have heard the name, Levesque. Although I was no better dressed than a tradesman, and Stefan was a member of the court, we were both members of the aristocracy. Things between us were now put on a new footing. We could associate openly. We might even visit each other without risking suspicion from anyone. It was a significant step forward, and I hoped to see Stefan again after this night.

When our ale arrived, we drank to the health of the king. I drank freely while Stefan sipped. When I reached the bottom of my tankard, I could feel my face getting warm, the ale was strong. Notably, however, Stefan's face remained that uncanny white. I wondered if he were ill.

We lingered over the chessboard long into the night. Other men joined us to watch and learn from Stefan. I gave up my seat to a man who wanted to play, and Stefan finished him in minutes. I couldn't help observing that Stefan had given me much more leeway, had allowed me to lose much more slowly, as if he had enjoyed my company and wanted to keep it. He beat several other gentlemen. By then, it was pretty late.

"Come, let me take you back to your rooms," Stefan said. "Are they far from here?"

"No, just around the corner," I said.

"Nonetheless, it is pitch dark, and you do not know how dangerous Paris can be at night. My carriage is waiting." He made a gesture to a servant who was sitting on the sidewalk outside of the café.

I did not want to look like some effeminate coward who could not be trusted to walk around the corner by himself, so I protested.

Stefan ignored my protest and repeated, "You do not know Paris. Come." He put down his tankard, and I noticed, with considerable surprise, that it was full. Those sips had been pretend; he had drunk nothing.

Stefan brushed the servant cruelly aside and helped me into his carriage himself. He lifted me as effortlessly as if I had been a cat. When he got in, he brushed his knee against mine. An accident, no doubt. However, the carriage was big, and he did not need to sit so close to me.

"This is it," I said when we came to the sign of the mortar and pestle.

"Did the apothecary give you a key?" Stefan asked, and I had to admit I had not thought to ask.

"Here, give me that lantern," he said to his coachman; and by its light, we picked up dirt clods from the street and threw them at every window we could reach. After a time, my landlord, the apothecary, appeared in his dressing gown, rubbing his eyes.

"Good night, my friend," said Stefan, and he tipped his hat to me and was gone.

The apothecary had taken Stefan's measure, so he scolded me very little for waking him up. "I will have a key made for your lordship," he said.

"I'm not a lord. But I will be obliged."

I ought to have gone to visit my cousin d'Amboise the next day, but I could not pull myself away from the Procope. I knew I was making an idiot of myself, but there I stayed, as fixed as if I had planned a meeting. I played chess. I played cards. I listened to men talk politics, which was all new to me; at first, the only name I recognized was that of the king, Louis XIV.

At last, as the sun waned, I ordered a brandy. What a jackass I had been to suppose that that fine gentleman, Baron Vitré, had nothing better to do with his time than to hang around in a café with an infatuated young man! Didn't I have more important things to do? I asked myself angrily as I drank another brandy. If he showed up, he would know I had been waiting for him, and the power imbalance between us would weigh even more heavily on his side. I didn't even know if he had these feelings for other men. I suddenly felt foolish!

Thus I spoke to myself as I consumed my third large brandy. When it was empty, I sat the glass down and stood up, and the next thing I knew, I was grabbing at the table, and there was a crash as the dishes hit the floor. Everybody looked at me, of course.

"Don't worry; I'll take care of it," said a voice in my ear; it was Stefan's voice. I turned quickly, and our faces were so close that we could have kissed. For a long moment, neither of us moved. I was staring into his blue eyes and seeing thoughts and images I had only imagined.

The proprietor came forward, and Stefan moved his face away from mine, circled my bicep with his hand, and told the proprietor he would pay for everything. He brought a gold coin that would have paid for everything many times. The proprietor smiled and took it, and the café swirled back into its customary amusements. Stefan was still holding my arm. I was as still as a statue, afraid that my knees would buckle if I attempted any movement.

At last, Stefan dropped my arm and moved away. He smiled in a pretty ordinary way and said in a relatively common voice, "Did you do your duty and visit your cousin today?"

I blushed. "No, I'm afraid Cousin Geoffrey will have to wait one more day."

"And who is this Cousin Geoffrey? Is he a Levesque?"

"No, Geoffrey d'Amboise."

"The Vicomte?" Stefan said in surprise. "I know him well. Let us call on him together."

"You mean tomorrow?"

"I mean tonight. He keeps late hours. Lately, he has said he dislikes crowds, so now he sits at home for an evening with no more company than his silly niece. He's decided that he's going to read all the books in his library, which is an exceptionally dull one, so he's probably nodding into a volume of Euclid right now. He'll be glad to see us."

We got into Stefan's carriage, and he held my hand as if this were the most natural thing in the world to do. It was as cold as milk on a winter morning, but I decided I did not care. There had to be an explanation, some rare disorder, and Stefan would explain when the time was right. I laid my head on his broad, muscular shoulder.

CHAPTER 2

The transformation of Fabien

(FABIEN NARRATES)

Stefan was right; Geoffrey was glad to see us. He sent his niece to her room, put down his book, and asked the servant to bring cordials. "Stefan never drinks anything, but you."

"I have come to pay my respects to you, Vicomte; I am your cousin Fabien Levesque, just arrived in Paris."

"Little Fabien? The last time I saw you, you were—well, let us not go into the number of years that have passed. Suffice it to say you have done a good job of growing up. You were always pleasing to the eye, but now, you could get into any trouble you liked."

I was shocked by his forthright immorality, but I could hardly say it displeased me.

"Yes, that's what Fabien has come to Paris for, trouble," said Stefan. "We must steer him in the right direction, mustn't we?"

"It seems to me that if he's met you, he's in sufficient trouble already," said the baron.

Stefan laughed uncontrollably. He seemed pleased to be cast as someone who would corrupt youth.

The servant came in with a tray of cordials. The baron poured me a tiny glass of what turned out to be elderberry cordial, the same as we made at home.

"Yes, your dear mother sends me a bottle every year," the baron said when I remarked on this.

From then on, the conversation dealt with all the new marvels of Paris; the opera, the ballet, the musical gatherings, the public dances, and the galleries where you could see fine paintings. Paris quickly became a center for the arts, and the baron was glad about it.

"So much of the time, the city has been just like the country, only muddier. You've done well to come in the summer," the baron said as he caught me looking at my boots. "This new Paris will have the world flocking to it. It will be a city like no other."

"There's already the university," Stefan said.

"The university! A bunch of drunken, penniless would-be priests who would duel each other to the death for a bottle of cheap red wine! The university has not brought us any glory, and it never will. I don't hold with priests. I don't hold with the Church."

"And our precious Notre Dame de Paris, said to be the finest cathedral in Europe?" Said, Stefan.

"Notre Dame is a thing of beauty in its own right," said the baron, and then he changed his subject to the opera. He planned to go tomorrow night, and would we care to go with him?

I had never heard any music beyond the pipes and guitars that the peasants on our estate played on feast days. Before Stefan could answer, I said, "We would love to go with you!"

"They're putting on a new opera by Lully, called Persée, at the Palais Royal. The king will be there, which means everyone will be there. Shall I meet you in my carriage at?"

"Call for us at the Procope," said Stefan.

As we left, I thought life in Paris would be more magnificent than I had imagined. Tomorrow night I would hear an opera for the first time, witness the new art of ballet, and perhaps even see the king. As for tonight, I did not dare look ahead to what would happen when Stefan and I were alone. I was sure it would be the fulfillment of my dreams.

Stefan handed me into his carriage once again with those enormously powerful arms. I must admit I was growing to like it. His strength made me feel delicate and treasured. I wanted to give in to that strength and see where it would take me.

Stefan got in and called out to the coachman to start, and I heard the sound of the whip cracking at the horses.

The Paris night was so dark that Stefan did not bother to close the curtains before he took me in his arms and kissed me.

"What is wrong? Are my lips too cold for you?" he asked a moment later.

That made me draw back, despite all my desire for him.

"I have a rare circulatory disease. The blood does not flow properly. Do you wish me not to kiss you?"

"Oh, no, Stefan, I want nothing more in the world than for you to kiss me again and again."

Which he did, with his strong arms tightening me against him. I have no idea how long the drive was to the apothecary's, but I know I was surprised when we stopped there. Stefan withdrew his lips from mine. I tried to think what to say so that he would come upstairs with me. I wanted him so much I could hardly speak for confusion. He had a word with his coachman, who drove off into the night, and then I let us into the building.

It was just as dark inside as out. With Stefan holding onto my coattails, I had to feel my way up to the attic stairs. Outside my room was a small table where a candle and a tinderbox always stood. I tried to strike a fire, but my usual skill had evaporated along with my nerves. Stefan took the flint and steel from me, and in a moment, the candlewick shone a muddy light. I was embarrassed that I had not bought a beeswax candle, being able to afford only tallow.

Stefan asked me if he was invited in. I glanced at him with a confused look and said, "Yes" We only needed enough light to show us to the bed. Closing the door, we pulled the curtains closed, and then we were alone, as I had wanted to be with Stefan since I first saw him. We stood face to face, suddenly leaning forward to kiss me deeply, passionately, our tongues wrestling with one another. He picked me up as if I were light as a feather and carried me over to the bed. He threw me on the bed and then slowly nuzzled up to me, growling a bit as he got closer and closer to me. He undressed and stood before me. I could tell he was aroused. His body reminded me of a marble statue; even though Stefan was well-to-do, his body was not soft as a woman's. No, every muscle was defined, his veins protruding, and his skin as white as the winter snow.

"Undress!" he commanded me. I did as I was told; I had longed and dreamed about an encounter like this for as long as I could remember.

At once, he was at my neck, licking it, smelling it as I heard myself groan with pleasure. Stefan continued making sexual advances along with licking and smelling my neck, which quickly led him to caressing both of my thighs with his large hands inching higher and higher until they had found their way to my buttocks, giving them a slight squeeze. Then using his tongue, he licked every inch of my body, returning from time to time, kissing me deep and passionately. I experienced various emotions and anxiousness, as I had not been intimate with anyone before, man or woman. Feeling such incredible passion, as if I were about to burst out of my skin, and fear I could somehow not point my finger on. I had the feeling of being entirely under his control, feeling powerless to prevent anything that I might not desire from happening.

I will not try to describe the ecstasy of that night, even though it was all about to change. Stefan took even more pleasure in dominating me than I had guessed he would. I became his possession; I belonged to him entirely before the small hours came. As we rested on the pillows, Stefan stroked my hair away from my forehead and called me tender names.

"You have made me hungry, Fabien," he said. "It's been a long time since I was with someone of your energy, your passion. However, now I must get up and go out to nourish myself." "Shall I come with you, Stefan?" I asked, feeling confused. "No, this is something I need to do alone; soon, you will join me," he said.

I thought to myself, there were times when I felt I understood Stefan, and there were many times when his mood would change so quickly from a momentary display of tenderness to outright cruelty, as in this moment. "But, when will I see you again?" I asked, feeling weak and timid and suddenly very aware of my nakedness. "We shall meet again at the café" Perhaps in a day or two. I cannot say for sure," he said coldly. "Good night Fabien," he said. "Good night Stefan." I watched him leave feeling confused and empty. While we were physically exploring each other's bodies, I felt as if I was his and he was mine, then suddenly everything changed.

Perhaps the handsome gentleman I had recently met at the café had suddenly lost interest in me as if I were merely some conquest? The thought of finally having experienced a physical encounter with another man and possibly losing him, or instead, him losing interest in me. I knew I had to return to the café and win him over again.

The following day came, and my mind again became fixated on Stefan. All that mattered was to reignite the passion and tenderness we had shared before his sudden departure the night before. I made my way over to the café, hoping to see him sitting there, perhaps enjoying breakfast, and maybe he would be willing to have me join him. Instead, I arrived not seeing him, thinking perhaps he was trying to avoid me.

I ate my breakfast alone, asking myself, would I ever see him again? I decided I would return to the café that evening, and perhaps I would see him again and that my luck would return to me. Later that evening, I returned to the café to see him seated with another man in the back, engaged in a chess game. I walked over to where he was sitting and asked if I could pull up a chair to observe the match. He glanced at me and returned his attention to the game, easily defeating his opponent. The man got up to leave and offered me his chair as I nodded my gratitude to the stranger.

"Stefan, I don't understand why you left so abruptly last night," I said as I watched his expression. He looked at me and glanced away, saying, "I told you Fabien, I needed to satisfy my hunger," as he appeared to dismiss my question with a simple answer. "Stefan, I have spent the entire day thinking of only one thing; you, thinking I must have done something wrong?" I said, practically pleading with him. I hated that he had such a hold over my emotions and loathed myself even more for allowing it.

"When can we be together as we were last evening? I long for you?" I asked suggestively. "Well, I am feeling a bit tired," he said, indicating he was willing to return to my room at this very moment. He looked at me and grinned. I felt tremendous relief all at once; he hadn't lost interest in me, and we were about to become once more intimate, my last night as a human. I was about to learn everything about this handsome and cunning creature.

We returned to my room above the apothecary, and once again, as before, Stefan asked me if he could enter. I replied, "Yes, with pleasure," as we laughed. "Will your servant be in?" Stefan asked softly.

"No, I let him go for the evening. He'll be at some whorehouse, no doubt, drinking watered wine by the quart and disporting himself with the ladies. He'll stumble in at dawn." "Shall we go upstairs, then?" Stefan asked even more softly. We made our way and entered my room. As soon as the door closed, we entered a world of ecstasy and passion. Our bodies clung together tightly with soft caresses and deep passionate kisses. We walked over to my bed hand in hand; despite his icy cold touch, the passion flames had ignited again. We undressed each other and lay on the bed. As our first physical encounter had been, exploring each other's bodies yet again, Stefan suddenly froze; he stopped talking. He was listening.

Unfortunately, I had heard the same sounds. They came from the bottom of the house, from the front door. I realized that I had forgotten to re-lock the door behind us in offering myself to Stefan a second time. So, whoever it was had no difficulty gaining access to the house and only the difficulty of darkness in finding the stairs. Whoever it was, stumbling and singing bits of a popular song as he climbed. It was my servant Jacques. Near panic, I told Stefan.

Stefan's reaction was one I could not have anticipated. He was not embarrassed in the least. "Your servant, eh? Tonight, he'll serve me better than he has ever served you."

I could not imagine what Stefan meant by this. Indeed Jacques was about to provide the most scandalous of interruptions. I racked my brain for solutions to the problem as Jacques's footsteps sounded closer and closer. At the same time, I wondered at Stefan's actions. He had found the tinderbox next to the bed and was kindling a spark and then a fire. A stick from the fireplace smoldered at the end, first red and then yellow. Did he want Jacques to see us?

No, that was not it at all. It was Stefan who wanted to see Jacques.

"Monsieur, monsieur, I am so sorry to be so late," Jacques said through the door. "I found the front door unlocked, maybe you have the key? I will go down and lock it."

With these words, Jacques opened the door to my room. Jacques stopped in his tracks when faced with the tall, powerful, naked stranger who seemed more like an animal about to spring at his prey than a human being.

"Monsieur?" was all he had time to say before the horror began. I was too afraid to close my eyes to it, I was so scared of Stefan at this point that I was fearful I might be his next victim. But I was not the one chosen. Stefan seized Jacques by the shoulders, pulled him close, and bent his head to one side. No, no, this could not be happening, not to Jacques! But as I watched, Stefan pierced Jacques's neck with those extraordinarily long incisors, and began to drink Jacques's blood. Perhaps the greatest horror was that Jacques was still alive—and worse, that his terrified eyes caught mine. I read in his gaze the belief that I would do anything to save him, just as he would have done anything to save me.

How could I have looked on as Stefan murdered him? How could I have stood there and watched and done nothing to stop the carnage?

I have often thought about this, and I still do not understand it. I was paralyzed by fear; I felt there was nothing I could do, nor anyone on this earth that could have done anything to prevent this attack. I felt as if I had betrayed my servant, who felt more like a member of the family, my Jacques.

At last, after what seemed like a very long time, the light in Jacques's eyes dimmed and then went out. My good servant Jacques was dead, and I had watched passively. My lover, Stefan, who had overwhelmed me with pleasure, now overwhelmed me with grief and terror. He turned toward me, his face was that of an animal still seeking more prey. I shrank into the bedclothes, but that did no good. I had to fight him. His physical dominance, which had appealed to me so much when looking forward to being sexually overpowered, now took on a new and threatening aspect. There was no way I could crush this man, who was no ordinary man.

He saw my fear and began to laugh. He was delighted that he had terrified me. For a moment, I thought that my terror alone would afford him sufficient pleasure, but I might as well have expected a wild boar to lose interest in a newborn lamb. I was at his mercy and was nothing more than food to Stefan. His appetite for sex was just that, another appetite. He experienced no tenderness, no passion, nothing that made an encounter human.

I crouched in the corner, waiting for him to do whatever he wanted. I could not think of a single way to defend myself.

He threw his massive body on mine, crushing me into the mattress, and put his hands around my neck. Now no other part of my body interested him.

"Are you going to kill me?" I asked faintly.

"Oh, no, not you," said Stefan: "I have other plans for you."

His hands grabbed me and tightened on my throat. I noticed that, for the first time, his hands were warm.

"What are you going to do to me?" I insisted.

"I will make you one of my kind, a creature of the night, a vampire."

I had never heard the word before, and he did not elaborate on the meaning of the word saying only, "You will learn over time, but for now," he menacingly said as Stefan bit into my neck and drew my first blood. He drank for a long time as I got weaker and weaker. It did not matter very much to me whether I lived or died. I thought I had found love, the love I had unknowingly longed for all my life—and that love had turned to degradation and horror!

Stefan did not kill me; true to his word, I was about to be transformed into the same creature he was, a vampire. "You are very weak now: you must be strengthened, or you will die" he bit his wrist till the blood flowed, and then he held his wrist up to my mouth and ordered me to drink. "Our blood combined will make you as I am."

"Go on, drink. It will not seem unnatural to you now." He commanded.

He was right. I was now as thirsty for his blood as he had been for mine. I clutched his wrist ever tighter. Once I had drunk enough, I sat there and thought about what I had just done. Shortly after that, the convulsions started as I began to panic. "What is happening?" I looked at Stefan looking, confused, as I pleaded for an explanation. "You are dying a mortal death. Soon you will be reborn as one of the living dead, a vampire."

He said. No sooner had he said that than the light in my eyes dimmed as I lost consciousness. I awakened and immediately felt different, stronger, and somehow invincible. I looked at Stefan, who sat there waiting for my transformation. There was a clarity to my vision and hearing that hadn't existed before. I somehow found the courage to ask him, "What is a vampire?" Stefan said mockingly, "A vampire has the best of life, never needing to work, having nothing to do but go to parties and all these fashionable new amusements, the opera, and the ballet, and mixing with the best of society." Stefan continued to educate me, giving me even greater clarity. A vampire could change shapes at will into any number of animals, whether bat, wolf, or rodent, that a vampire could turn into mist or fog. That there was no longer a need for food or alcohol. If consumed by the vampire, it might generate extreme nausea. That the tears we shed are not the salt tears of mortals but rather made of the same substance we needed to consume to survive blood. A vampire could levitate, fly through the sky and move incredibly fast, so fast that a mortal's eye could not detect it. That the vampire was free from sickness and death or, instead, the traditional end which befell mortals; that the vampire was neither living nor altogether dead. In addition to the word vampire, there were other descriptions, such as the undead. And lastly, that vampires were not entirely invincible as immortal beings. That sunlight would disintegrate a vampire. That fire could destroy us as well as a wooden stake through the heart.

"And killing innocent people to stay alive."

"Jacques? He was nothing. He was a mere servant. There are always more servants to replace him." He said cruelly.

"I think he was more than a mere servant to his mother," I said.

"Why are you so sentimental? I expected better of you. You seemed to enjoy the kind of life I lead."

"Jacques was not simply a mere servant' to me, either. I knew him all my life," I said.

Felling enraged, it was at that moment I began to loath and distrust him. I realized he was diabolical, who not only took delight in luring me with his charm and good looks but also took great pleasure in destroying me as well as Jacques or anyone he chose to. "I still feel the hunger," Stefan said as he told me I would soon experience the thrill of the hunt, Stefan said mysteriously. "Come."

We got dressed and went out into the pitch-black street. I had an idea Stefan would be looking for another victim to satisfy his cravings; however, I was under his spell and would do whatever he told me to do.

Remarkably, we encountered someone right outside my building. No sooner had we left than a man approached us from the darkness carrying a dagger and a lantern. He demanded we hand over all money we had. Stefan's reaction was not that of any mortal man; he began to laugh uncontrollably, almost doubling over. The thief became enraged and took the dagger and stabbed Stefan in the stomach, and that was when the attacker realized that Stefan was no mere mortal: he stopped laughing and removed the blade from the thief's hand and threw it on the ground, there was no blood coming from where the knife had been thrust.

The thief stood there quite motionless, undoubtedly shocked.

"Shall we dine, Fabien?" Stefan asked, and with that, he took the thief by the neck with his powerful hands and ripped open the thief's shirt, lunging toward his neck. I noticed what I had missed before, but how had I missed it? Stefan's incisors were much larger than those of any human being. They were more like the fangs of a rabid dog. Baring these large incisors, he bit into the man's throat. Blood spurted on the dirt below.

In a muffled voice, Stefan commanded me to join him. "Here, bite into his wrist," he said. I knew I was powerless to resist, although I did not yet understand why. I only knew he had made me into the same unholy creature as he. I followed his command, for now, Stefan was my lover and my maker and master. All my instincts told me to obey. In the time it took to blink an eye, I had taken the man's wrist and bit into it. All the while, the thief was screaming. No one cared if you yelled, nor would anyone come to your rescue in lawless Paris. We drained every drop of blood from this man and left the body propped up against a building as if the corpse were some poor marionette with its strings cut.

"How do you feel, Fabien?" Stefan asked. He had hold of the lantern and held it up to my face.

"I feel as if an unquenchable thirst has, for the moment, been satisfied." I wiped the blood from my lips with my handkerchief, which I then handed Stefan to use.

Stefan wiped his mouth as if he had just finished a long and sumptuous supper. He spoke quietly as his sensuality returned. "Shall we go back to your room?"

CHAPTER 3

Parting is such sweet sorrow

(FABIEN NARRATES)

The following morning, I woke alone. Stefan had left in the night, and mercifully he had taken Jacques's corpse with him. But as soon as I felt that gratitude that I would not have to get rid of the body, I felt remorse for having had such a thought. How could I think of Jacques, who had always been kind to me and like a family member, as merely "the body"? Jacques had looked out for me since I was a tiny child with a talent for falling into water butts, finding patches of nettles to get lost in, and angering the ill-tempered ram. I had a flash of memory now of Jacques throwing me up in the air and laughing as he made me laugh. Jacques passionately loved to fish—notably when he was supposed to be doing something else—and taught me all the ways of angling. He loved girls, too. It sometimes seemed to me that there was not a girl in the world that Jacques did not think was pretty and had winning ways of complimenting them. Someday I would be grown up, and I would admire girls just like he did. It came to me now that my brother had not chosen at random when he sent Jacques with me to Paris. No, indeed. Jacques's family had worked alongside our family since before anyone could remember, and Jacques himself had been looking out for me my whole life.

And now, because of me, Jacques was dead. For a night of pleasure, my pleasure, Jacques had given his life. Instead of being glad about the removal of the body, I became anxious about what Stefan had done with it. It seemed doubtful that Jacques would get the Christian burial he deserved. How would Stefan explain to a priest his possession of a dead body?"

No, Jacques's body would have been consigned to the Seine hours ago. As I thought of this, I wept; as my tears fell on the white bed sheet, I was startled to see that they were red, and in a flash, I remembered Stefan's words about creatures such as us not shedding mere mortal salt tears. And how white my hands were! My whole body was as white as Stefan's. And my heart, which should have been thumping, was silent. I put my hand to my chest; nothing. With this thought, I became more frightened than ever, but the worst had yet to happen. As the sun rose higher and the light in the room grew stronger, my skin began to burn as if I were in the Sahara Desert.

I quickly sought refuge in an empty trunk I had bought to store valuables. The bare chest would be used instead to provide me an escape from the blinding and blistering sun, which only a short time ago had provided pleasure and warmth, was now and forever more my enemy.

I fell into a deep slumber, and awakened as soon as the sun had set, as I climbed out of my chest. Stefan was sitting on my bed.

"Why did you leave me?" I asked him in an agitated voice.

"I had every confidence that you would put that empty trunk to good use, and I was not mistaken," he said and laughed.

"You will come and live with me and give up this ridiculous room you have called home. Perhaps now you understand why I was a bit secretive with you?" His mood had abruptly changed; he now looked at me tenderly. He seemed to switch from cold and cruel to loving and caring instantly. I didn't know exactly how I should feel about the man who was now my master since he was the one who had made me into a vampire, but I stayed with him for a hundred years. I felt powerless to leave; I felt like his prisoner. Though he continued to be cruel, he also continued, at times, to be tender. After each incidence of cruelty, he lured me back with the hope of physical affection and lust.

I could see that he enjoyed having power over me; he delighted in controlling me and forcing me to kill uncontrollably, commanding me, cheering me on as I unwillingly stalked my victims alongside him. I felt that I had no choice but to remain with him.

Our nights were spent pillaging the city of Paris and the countryside, feasting on the blood of human beings. We strolled through the parks or the darkened streets of Paris looking for victims. Sometimes we would happen on a robber. Other times we would observe a patron from the café going out into the blackened streets of the city, and we would ambush him as he went around the corner and into the darkness, where no one would hear the screams for help. It felt as if Stefan and I were unstoppable since the police were powerless, they had no idea what was causing this endless list of casualties.

There were brief, enjoyable outings during this time, as they were very much in keeping with Stefan's personality. We attended dances and the opera, and the theater. However, every night invariably ended in slaughter. I recall one instance involving an entire family, a father, a mother, their children, and their coachman, who had enjoyed a picnic outside in the Luxembourg gardens.

Stefan and I arrived just after sunset as the family began to board their carriage. There were no other onlookers around except for the coach's driver, who would be included in the killing of the family. Stefan felt it was the perfect opportunity to drain each of them, including the two small children. I remember hearing the screams from the coachman, the husband, and the wife to take their lives and spare the children. Stefan merely laughed a deep, sinister laugh. I shuddered inside, knowing what he and I were about to do.

The first victim was the coachman, who pleaded for his own life to no avail. He tried to run away but was tackled by Stefan's muscular frame. He was drained of blood in an instant.

Next came the father, who bravely held his screams to himself, eyes fixed on his wife and his children as if offering an unspoken final goodbye. He appeared stoic, finally uttering a sound more like a whimper, until his lifeblood flowed out of his jugular vein like a stream during heavy rain, with Stefan lapping and sucking until the man was nothing more than a corpse. Next came the mother, huddled with terror in the carriage, trying desperately to protect her children. She screamed, "No, please, for the love of God, spare my children and me!" But it was useless.

Under Stefan's command, Stefan and I attacked and killed her within a few minutes.

All the while, I heard the screams of the two small children, who appeared to be five or six and had wild-looking eyes that spoke of the panic and terror they were seeing. Taking the lives of the children left me feeling hollow inside as if everything inside of me was empty. It felt like Stefan had destroyed my innocence and ripped out the last vestige of my soul.

I felt numb, and guilty for existing. My hopes would be dashed when I would begin to think that some normality might be possible in our otherwise damned existence. So many times, I pleaded with Stefan to spare the lives of our victims. An inhuman and uncaring laughter answered my desperate pleas. Stefan was mocking me; worse, I was questioning my sanity. Because my actions were not freely willed but forced, I felt as if I were a mere witness to them. It felt like an out-of-body experience. I did not want to grasp the horror that I was helping Stefan to inflict on so many people; I did not want to look at their faces or see the terror in their eyes; I did not want to hear their cries for help or pleading for their lives. On more than one occasion, I broke down and cried blood tears, cursing Stefan and myself.

My actions caused me to loathe more and more what I had become. As Stefan's accomplice, I had become what he was— a bloodthirsty animal. Even though I tried to maintain such human emotions as love and tenderness, I felt those emotions had slipped away during the endless nights under the command of Stefan's diabolical killing sprees.

Stefan knew that my feelings for him were changing. When I met him at the café, believing him to be a man, I had become consumed with visions of passion and wanted to be with him forever. But he had become my tormentor. What was once lust and then love was turning to contempt and hatred. Over time, I grew defiant, and on more than one occasion, I shouted out loud to Stefan how much I loathed him. There was not a trace of love for him left in my heart.

I could tell that he, too, was growing increasingly miserable: he would curse me and say, "You ungrateful bastard! I gave you a new existence, resurrected you, gave you powers beyond your wildest imagination, gave you immortality, and now you're unhappy! I wish I had never transformed you. I wish I had never given you my dark gift!"

Two things kept me by Stefan's side; the power he held over me, the power of the vampire maker over the fledgling, and the fear of never finding another male lover. Was I destined to spend my life alone if I dared leave Stefan? I didn't know. But in the end, I had to go. I could not bear to be tied forever to this feral beast.

There were countless times when I begged Stefan to release me, but each time he would laugh and say, "You are mine for all eternity!" But then, one day, abruptly, without any apparent reason—Stefan did allow my freedom. All I could guess was a slight trace of human feeling was left inside him, perhaps a tinge of pity. Or maybe there was a part of him that did love me. Whatever it was, he did free me. But it came with a price, with a command he made to me. He warned me never to make a fledgling vampire of my own. If I did, he would infallibly learn of it, and would come to destroy my creation.

I believed him.

I agreed to his demands but knew that they would be impossible to abide by. I would not be able to spend eternity on my own.

In my hundred years with Stefan, I realized he was one of those beings capable of existing independently, not needing to be close to anyone nor needing companionship. I had been merely an apprentice of sorts.

I wanted to be more than that, and although I loathed the creature I had become, I had not given up on finding someone who loved me and could love in return. I was not going to inflict the cruelty my maker inflicted on me on another man; that was a rule I had firmly established for myself. I felt that I could find a soul mate by following this rule.

CHAPTER 4

Laurent and Fabien

(LAURENT NARRATES)

I'll never forget the first time I saw Fabien. It was a warm spring evening in May; the year was seventeen hundred and eighty-two. We met at the Parc Monceau. I was there for an evening of festivities celebrating the king's visit. There would be a fireworks display. Fortunately for all the attendees, the sky was lit with a full moon, making it appear as if daylight combined with the dark of night. Looking around the park, I noticed an exciting mixture of people from various social classes. Families were present, and the children were running around; there were jugglers and acrobats to delight and entertain us. The park created a casual atmosphere because everyone spoke to one another, regardless of social status.

One stood out from the rest of the crowd, a man wearing a most elegant blood-red brocade suit that emphasized his extraordinary pallor. I found him incredibly handsome. He appeared to be having a passionate discussion with an equally distinctively dressed man, who was accompanied by a young woman around seventeen. This elegant man finally turned to meet my gaze, and I froze. His gaze was prolonged. It felt as if he were looking right through me. Finally, I managed a smile. He smiled back at me.

I hesitated at first, but then I walked in his direction; something was drawing me toward him. His smile was warm and inviting. As I got close, I observed that he had a very peculiar skin coloring. He was the color of milk. I tried not to stare at his skin and instead concentrated on listening to the discussion. "My apologies. I hope I'm not interrupting?" I said, however, awkwardly. The man with oddly colored skin turned towards me to smile again. I was assured by the handsome gentleman who had smiled at me twice that I wasn't bothersome; however, sensing that neither gentleman wanted to lose focus on their discussion.

I stood there smiling at the young woman who accompanied them, waiting for them to finish. But eventually, the other well-dressed man became so enraged that he took hold of the young woman's arm, abruptly said goodbye, and left for another area in the park. The handsome man with the pallid complexion laughed, shook his head slightly at the other gentleman's abrupt departure and refocused his attention on me. He asked, "What are your thoughts on the latest Lully?" Taken by surprise, I said, "I'm afraid I didn't hear enough to contribute to the discussion. What is it you seek my opinion on?"

"The latest opera by Lully," he answered. "Whether it was as good as his last. My friend who abruptly left is, I am afraid, one of those enthusiastic souls who cannot admit that his idol ever falls short in the smallest way. In contrast, I was saying that I thought the arias, in general, were somewhat inferior to those in the earlier works. Not an earth-shaking discussion, I will admit. I quite forgive you if you have no opinion on the matter."

"I am afraid I have not been to the opera lately," I said. "Tennis matches have much engaged my attention."

"Oh, dear, yes, tennis. All the rage among those who count. The king is trying to ban it, saying it detracts from the practice of religion. Which is odd because monks invented it."

I named various well-known people, courtiers, some of them, whom I had seen playing, and I admitted that I wanted to play myself. I was looking for someone to instruct me.

"I may be able to help you out," said the pale gentleman. "I am no champion, but on the other hand, I don't think you'd call me a novice at tennis, either. Do you have a racquet? Pardon my rudeness. I didn't properly introduce myself; my name is Fabien Levesque." I introduced myself as Laurent Richelieu.

"Well, Monsieur Richelieu, I know where you can get an excellent racquet if you don't have one. I do have to warn you of one eccentricity of mine. I only play tennis at night. There's a sort of romance to it. If you have enough fellows with torches, it's no more difficult than playing tennis by day."

Despite his deathly pallor, I thought this must be the most handsome man in Paris. His eyes were so blue they looked like jewels as they gleamed and danced with the light of the nearby candles.

"I take it you have been to this park before?" he asked.

"No, in fact, this is my first time. I came here to attend the festivities in honor of the king," I replied. I noticed that Monsieur Levesque merely nodded and didn't seem too excited about the events about to take place. "I take it you are not an admirer of the king?" I asked.

"Without getting into a lengthy discussion, no, I am not," he replied. "I came here this evening mostly for entertainment. Look around you, jugglers, dancers, and children running around wildly; it is entertaining, wouldn't you agree?" I nodded my reply. We talked more about tennis, and then it was back to Lully, and somehow, we ended up talking about the American war on everybody's lips. Could the Americans succeed in establishing a real democracy, or were they too hidebound in their English ways?

As Fabien asked this, his hand touched my shoulder. An accident? No doubt it was. I had never met another man as excited by the male touch as I was. But there, his hand again took hold of my shoulder, and this time he looked me in the eye. My heart bounded. Was I at last meeting a man of my kind?

It is one of the peculiarities of humanity that often, when we meet with what we have been looking for all our lives, our nerves overcome us, and we turn and run. It's what happened to me. I could not say goodbye quickly enough, but before I left, Monsieur Levesque and I had agreed to meet again.

"Must you leave so quickly?" he said, slightly disappointed.

"Yes, I must," I said.

"I would like to see you again if that is possible," he asked.

I hesitated at first but answered him with the words, "I frequent a café; maybe we could meet there."

"Which one? Hopefully, not the Procope. I used to frequent it in the past; I am trying to avoid running into someone from my past," he said mysteriously.

"No, the café Alexandre," I replied.

"Excellent. Are you free tomorrow evening, shall we say seven?" Fabien said.

"Yes, I will look forward to it, Monsieur Levesque."

Did I see the shadow of a smile on his face as he bade goodbye to me? Did he know what was going on with me? I could not stop myself from blushing as I turned to leave. Involuntarily I looked back.

Monsieur Levesque was still looking at me, and yes, he was smiling.

I wondered who else he would talk to and how late he would stay. Somehow I had a feeling that he would not leave the park any time soon.

All the way home, I kicked myself. I had learned very little about Monsieur Fabien Levesque beyond his name and that he wanted to avoid running into someone from his past at the Procope. However, I would find out more about him when we met at the Alexandre café. I was grateful that I had a follow-up meeting with him.

I went to the café the following day, and, thinking I might see him before our evening rendezvous, I ordered coffee and breakfast and stayed all day. I ate lunch. Disappointed that he had not shown up, I drank more and more coffee. I ate pastries that were fresh from the bakery down the street. The hours ticked by beyond the agreed-upon time of seven, and doubt began to fill my mind. I kept telling myself I was making a fool of myself and should leave, but I could not do it. Who was ever in love that did not make a fool of himself? I consoled myself by saying this in my mind repeatedly. And still, Monsieur Levesque did not appear. Indeed I was the most stupid fool who had ever lived.

I gave up. I had been sitting at that café for eight or nine hours. I have to say that no one remarked on my continued presence; some men had been there almost as long as I had, playing chess and talking politics. Nonetheless, I felt foolish. I was getting up to leave when suddenly, Monsieur Levesque appeared right in front of me. I had not seen him approach, though I was sitting in the front of the café and keeping an eye on all who entered and left. I did not understand how he could have shown up out of nowhere like that, but I was in no mood to raise questions; I was just glad to see him. I did not even try to disguise my pleasure.

"I thought you would never come!" were the first words out of my mouth.

"Poor Monsieur Richelieu!" he said teasingly. "Have you been waiting long?"

"All day. I had to see you. Please call me Laurent."

"Certainly, if you will call me Fabien. Why all day? We agreed to meet at seven."

I reached into my pocket for my watch and said, "It is eight o'clock, Fabien."

"I am so sorry. I was completely famished and realized I hadn't dined for quite a while; I thought it best to take care of my hunger, as I am not pleasant company to be around without any nourishment," Fabien said.

I looked at him with bewilderment, thinking *they serve food here at the café. Could he not have had something to eat here with me?* Nevertheless, I feigned laughter and said, "Apology accepted," as I observed a bit of a rosiness to his usually white complexion.

"I was thinking we might take in one of the sights tonight," Fabien said. "What do you say to a trip to the Palais Royal? There are all kinds of new shops there."

I agreed most readily, of course.

We hailed a closed carriage for hire, and as soon as we set off, Fabien took my hand and held it in his. My excitement was tempered by apprehension, as I had never held hands with a man before; nonetheless, it felt good, and his touch felt warm and comforting. I tried to appear confident and would not allow my thoughts to ruin the mood. He was, after all, holding my hand.

At the Palais Royal, we found a covered place, an arcade, filled with small shops with glass windows, which I had never seen before. There was pavement underfoot, also a new thing for Paris. You could walk up and down the blessedly dry ground and look in all the windows without going inside to buy an item. The goods sold were costly; cloth, furniture, paintings, books, and sculptures all had their place. Around the arcade, there were gardens and theaters, too. All of Paris, both middle and upper class, seemed to be abroad in this safe and convenient arcade. No one was in a hurry; everybody stopped to chat with their friends or to sit down at a café and have coffee with them. It was elegant and gay.

We spent the entire evening walking from shop-to-shop marveling at the beautiful things for sale. Against my protests, Fabien insisted on purchasing a beautiful silk scarf. It was blood red, like the suit he had been wearing the evening before. "For you," he said as he stood behind me, tying the scarf around my neck, his face only inches away from mine. I felt his warm breath on my neck.

After that, we stopped at a shop that sold chocolate, and I drank some. Fabien, once again, consumed nothing. It had become evident that he never ate or drank anything; if he did, it was in private.

Of course, I did not mention this because it had also become evident that I was never supposed to remark on it. I noticed and wondered silently.

Gradually, the crowds began to disperse, and another group, much less elegant, began to come out of the woodwork; soldiers, thieves, and prostitutes. Fabien and I hired another carriage and took ourselves away.

"Do you enjoy the theater, Laurent?" Fabien asked.

"Yes, I adore it," I replied.

"Wonderful! Then would you give me the pleasure of your company tomorrow night? There is a wonderful show at the Grands-Danseurs du Roi. I want to take you."

As I agreed, I tried not to sound too excited.

We were silent as the carriage drove us back to my room; there was no sound but the dull thud of the horses' hooves on the dried mud of the streets.

When the carriage stopped, I looked out the window and saw we were at my building. I looked at Fabien, uncertain of how to say goodbye.

Fabien took my head in both hands and kissed me tenderly. I had never felt anything like this before. Passion consumed every bone in my body; I felt like I would burst.

Just as abruptly, Fabien pulled away from me. Formally, we said our good nights. As I knocked on the door for the servant to open it, I was so overcome with ecstasy at having been kissed by this handsome man that I could barely keep my hands from shaking. I was relieved when the front door opened and the carriage left because I was afraid I would turn around again and, seeing Fabien, would rush back to him for another kiss.

Alone in my bedroom, I had fantasies about Fabien as I undressed, leaving on only the blood-red silk scarf he had purchased for me earlier that evening. As I stroked the soft silk scarf, I closed my eyes and pictured us in bed together, our naked bodies writhing around each other.

The following day came faster than I expected. I awakened suddenly at the first cockcrow. I was still reeling from Fabien's kiss; I could not put the sensation out of my head. Collecting my thoughts, I got dressed and went to the café. I wasn't hungry; all I could think about was coffee, which I was beginning to feel the need for several times a day. What a strange substance it was, bitter, yet so delicious and so revitalizing to the mind!

More than coffee, though, I was there for Fabien. I did not yet know where he lived, so going to the café was the only way to see him.

As I sat there emptying my pot of coffee, the sun rose. Fabien was absent. What would I do, spend another day waiting for him? I had the arrangement to meet him that evening to see the danseurs. I would find a more profitable way to spend the day.

After a breakfast of soup and bread, I paid and left.

I meant to do something very sensible and productive, but to tell you the truth; I have no idea how I spent that day. All I remember was that after supper, I got dressed in the most fashionable clothes I had: a new black velvet suit trimmed with lace, a gold watch, silk stockings, and black shoes with buckles of gold and diamonds. I stood in front of the mirror and powdered my hair, admiring myself, wanting to look perfect for Fabien.

My servant announced the arrival of the carriage. I went downstairs at a dignified pace, preventing myself from running. Fabien was there in the carriage. His skin color was less pale than usual; there was even a bit of rosiness to his complexion, I was glad to see. I realized I had been worrying about his health without even knowing I was worrying.

The coachman held the door open, and I sat opposite Fabien. After all the uncensored thoughts I had been having about him, I felt embarrassed to be in his actual presence. However, his smile put me at ease. Maybe he had been thinking about me, too. He reached out and grasped my hand. As if by instinct, I recoiled, expecting his hand to be icy, but I was pleasantly surprised to discover that it was warm. He must have been sick on those previous occasions; I was sure of it because now he looked as healthy as my reflection in the mirror upstairs. I was relieved.

How had I come to care about him so much in such a short period? As I glanced over at his handsome face.

"Yes, Laurent?" Fabien said.

"I'm glad to see you looking so much better. I was afraid you were ill."

"My health is very unsteady," Fabien replied. "There are days when I am as well as anybody, and there are other days when my blood does not circulate properly, and I am as cold as a fish. It is a strange condition, but I do have a doctor to look after me. It must be frightening, but I assure you, the situation is not fatal.

I look much worse than I am." He smiled again. "It is kind of you to take an interest in my health. Some people fear and avoid me. I am glad you are not one of those."

We arrived at the Boulevard du Temple. The theater was up ahead, and a parade was going toward it. We were astonished to see that a monkey was leading the march. It turned out that he was the famous Turco we had heard about. We joined the parade, and once Turco got inside the theater, he ran up, jumped on the stage, and began performing. After I had watched for a little while, I realized that he was enacting the news of the day. Turco took the part of a well-known merchant who was known to be trying to get his daughter to marry a man she did not like. The monkey also played the role of the daughter, who was fascinated with an officer who did not pay his debts with cards. Turco next imitated a famous street juggler and juggled as well as he did. Except for those that concerned the royal family, no current events escaped Turco's mockery.

Filled with people, the theater was hot, and I wished I had worn something a little less warm than velvet. I noticed that Fabien was observing me almost as if I were some specimen—and that he had been observing me for some time. I asked him why. I was afraid he had found some fault in me.

He gave me a strange smile and said, "Forgive me, my dear Laurent, but I was just noticing how handsome you are."

I felt a flash of heat come over me, and I realized I was blushing.

Turco hopped off the stage and went up to the boxes to beg the ladies for candies, which they gave him with delight. While everybody was watching this, Fabien leaned over to me and whispered in my ear, "If you think this is amazing, wait till you see what I have in store for you later."

I felt the blood in my cheeks increase again, which caused Fabien to say, "Why, you're blushing!" I laughed and admitted it. I was no longer embarrassed. There was an air of innocence about our flirtation. As if this were a first love—and for me, it was. There was nothing to make me nervous, no suggestion that this was a pickup. Fabien was not looking at me as if I were a piece of meat hanging in a butcher's shop. It was quite the opposite. I felt cherished; I felt that there was no other man on earth he had these feelings for.

When the performance was over, we got into Fabien's carriage. We rode the entire way to my building, consumed with laughter about the monkey's hilarious routine and happy to be in each other's presence. Once, Fabien placed a hand on my thigh, caressing it gently. Despite his gentleness, I could sense his strength. When we weren't engaged in conversation, I again saw his intense gaze out of the corners of my eyes; it was as if my presence had transfixed him.

As we approached my building, I lost my head. I had to get him upstairs with me, but I had no idea what to say to make it happen. I broke the silence by saying that I was feeling a bit tired. As soon as I said it, I knew it was all wrong.

But Fabien answered smoothly, "That is a pity because I was hoping I might see where you live."

"Oh, it's nothing extraordinary," I said, blundering ever deeper.

"On the contrary, I am sure there is much to interest me," Fabien said. "You have taste, and I'm sure you have been exercising it since you came to Paris. Have you not bought any paintings? No Sèvres? No objets d'art?"

This time I successfully picked up his clue and admitted that there was an object or two he might be interested in seeing if he would be so good as to come upstairs to my rooms with me. How he looked at me in that moment made it hard for me to utter the words.

As soon as we stopped, I jumped out of the carriage. I saw Fabien order the coachman to return home, meaning he was planning to stay the night.

I became nervous all over again, worried, and yet profoundly pleased.

It was still quite early in the evening, so the servant who belonged to the building was on hand to let us in. He led us up the stairs with a lit candelabrum to my apartments on the first floor, and then Francois, my manservant, met us with more lit candles. I went in, but oddly, Fabien hesitated on the threshold.

"Are you sure you want me to come in?" he asked.

Why on earth was he asking this? I had made my wishes clear; all too clear, I thought. "Of course," I said. "Come in and see this tapestry I bought yesterday. Francois, some wine."

I wondered if Fabien would refuse, but he said nothing. He was examining the tapestry with interest. Francois served us the wine in two silver goblets that were another recent acquisition of mine, and now I could not help but notice that Fabien looked at the goblet and ignored the wine.

"Who made these for you, Germain?" he asked.

"Yes," I said with some surprise, but luckily I kept myself from saying more. I should have guessed Fabien would know his silver.

"Marvelous, the movement he conveys in a static form." Fabien set down his goblet. "Drink up; don't let me stop you. I am never thirsty or hungry at times; other people are. You must not embarrass me by taking note of it."

I was rather hungry, so, taking Fabien at his word, I told my manservant, Francois to bring us some biscuits, pâté, cheese, and jam and then leave us for the night. *Please let Fabien stay; please let him stay,* I begged some unknown god.

While I ate, Fabien examined the paintings and tapestries on the wall and the trinkets I had in my cabinet. When I was done, he came and sat quite close to me. I looked into his eyes, and his gaze drew me closer and closer. He leaned towards me and kissed me on the lips. I decided not to allow the coldness of his lips and hands to ruin this romantic moment. The kiss drifted from my lips to my neck, which he began smelling and licking, moaning with pleasure as he did so. It was very odd, but if this were what he wanted to do, I would not stop him.

He abruptly pulled away from my neck and stood up as he looked me in the face. His blue eyes clouded over. "Forgive me, Laurent. I was about to do something I do not have the right to do, not unless you will it," he said. "I was overcome with desire. I will only proceed if I have your permission."

"Please, don't stop," I said.

He stepped back and adoringly admired my body with his eyes. I knew he was noticing my arousal. He walked over to where I was seated and took my hand, as I led him to my bedroom. Our lips locked in a passionate kiss as we undressed each other.

Hours passed. I marveled at every part of Fabien's body as he did mine. Afterward, we lay on the bed with our arms around each other. "I never thought I would meet anyone like you, Laurent," Fabien said as he kissed my head.

"I feel the same about you, Fabien. I have always longed to be with another man in this way."

After a time, feeling safe and secure in Fabien's strong arms, I began to fall asleep. Outside, the sky was becoming lighter and lighter; it was nearly dawn. As soon as Fabien noticed this, he underwent a complete change. He leaped out of bed and put on his clothes in a flash. My jaw dropped.

"I'm sorry, but I must leave, Laurent. I didn't realize it had gotten so late!" Fabien said frantically.

"But why?" was all I could say, though I knew he would not answer.

"There will be plenty more of these moments to come, I promise," he said. And with that, he leaned over and kissed me. In an instant, he was gone.

"But when can we see each other again?" I asked an empty bedroom as I heard the door to my apartment open and close.

Who was this man, anyway, and what motivated his often-strange behavior? All my questions began to add up. Why had he left so suddenly? Why had I never seen him eat or drink? Why had he never allowed me to know where he lived? Why did he agree to meet me only after dark? Above all, when would I see him again? I had no control over that since I did not know where to reach him; I could only continue to waste my days at the Café Alexandre, hoping he would show up. Happy as I was, I began to feel a bit irritated. What big secret did he think he had to keep from me, his lover?

I lay in bed thinking I would be able to fall asleep once more, but it was no use: my eyes were wide open, and the sun hitting my face nearly blinded me. No, I decided it was time to rise, wash, and start my day.

I went to Café Alexandre simply because I always went there. There was no chance I would meet Fabien; a man does not rush out of one's room only to go around the corner and sit down and drink coffee. I finished the usual breakfast of soup and bread and then walked. I hired a carriage to take me to the *Jardin du Tuileries,* and spent the entire morning listening to the birds chirping and walking amongst the trees and naturally admiring the vast number of statues. There was one in particular that caught my attention, the statue of *Veturie.* I stood staring at every detail. The figure was made of the purest white marble, similar to Fabien's skin color. The thought of that made me cringe, despite the sun's warmth.

There was no point in continuing to think about Fabien and his unusual pallid complexion. My questions if I dared ask him would have to wait until I saw him again.

I wandered around and saw the most magnificent yellow rose. I bent over to smell the lush aroma and cut my finger on one of the thorns. Suddenly, a droplet of blood appeared on my finger. I could not locate my handkerchief, so I stuck my finger in my mouth, hoping to stop it from bleeding any further. I remember thinking how odd the taste of blood was. I continued to stroll the grounds and marveled at the beautiful assortment of roses a while longer, until dinnertime, and then I had an inspiration.

I had heard people talking about a new institution called a restaurant, where people could pay for a meal. The restaurant I had heard of was the *Grande Taverne de Londres*. It was like the kitchen of some nobleman. Only the chef worked for the restaurant owner, not a member of the nobility; it was open to the public. You could go there and order any one of a significant number of dishes, and the kitchen would make it just for you. There was also a fine wine cellar, and the proprietor, a man by the name of Antoine Beauvilliers, would take the cellar key out of his pocket and get the wine that he felt would go best with your dish.

I decided to try out *La Grande Taverne de Londres*. Some small, spiteful part of me was glad I was going without Fabien. If he were to abandon me at sunrise, I would show him I wasn't dependent on him for entertainment.

I did myself proud at that meal. I ordered every delicacy on the menu that appealed to me and that I had room for. I also drank several different wines at Monsieur Beauvilliers' suggestion. I took my time so I did not get drunk. By the time I finished the meal with a slice of tart of *fraises de bois*, I was so satisfied with the world that I was telling myself that Fabien was sure to turn up in a day or two and that there was no reason for concern.

As it happened, he did show up, and we resumed our love affair. Our bond grew more durable and more reliable with each passing day. We spent time together nearly every evening. We went back to the Palais Royal several times. We went to the opera, which I had never done alone. We were invited to elaborate dinner parties, where Fabien introduced me to the most exciting friends of his. But I never saw him eat anything.

One evening that stood out was a masquerade ball Fabien asked me to attend with him. He had purchased intricately decorated masks for us. Naturally, we each chose a female dance partner when we participated in the dance. However, our gaze was always returning to one another across the ballroom.

We had spent many months together. There were so many unanswered questions and so many mysteries that remained. I found it more and more curious that we never were able to meet during the daylight, much less dine together in a restaurant. However, Fabien always had business to do. Sometimes, I would question him, and sometimes he was short with me. He told me that he felt as if he were being interrogated.

We decided to pause our relationship.

I cannot begin to describe how miserable I felt. I was thrown back into the life I had before I met Fabien, and I now saw a poverty-stricken life.

One evening, weeks after seeing Fabien last, I got home and found him waiting in the lobby for me, seeming agitated. I was much more disturbed than reassured. "Fabien, what is it? What's wrong?" I asked, forgetting to show him I could survive on my own.

"I must speak to you," said Fabien.

"Of course. Come upstairs," I said, and when we reached my front door, I insisted that Fabien go in first and make himself comfortable in one of the upholstered chairs. I was going to get him a brandy before I remembered he would not drink it. I sat down near him and waited for him to talk.

"I have missed you, Laurent. I need you back," Fabien said, but he seemed to find it challenging to go on.

"I have missed you as well, Fabien; I hope you realize that."

He didn't acknowledge that but said, "There is something I need to tell you. It is essential. All-important, you might say."

"Are you going to tell me why you felt we needed to have such a long separation from one another?" I asked with more than a touch of waspishness.

"Yes, I will explain that. Everything will be explained."

"Go on, Fabien," I said more gently. "I'm listening."

Fabien took a long moment to answer.

"Laurent, this is very hard. I have not been truthful with you. At once, a sense of betrayal had come over me, was this handsome Gentleman someone other than he seemed to be? This man that I had spent so much time with and grown to love—someone who consumed my every thought. My head was swimming with doubt, but I was determined to hear his confession. Perhaps it would shed light on the many mysteries surrounding this handsome yet mysterious man with pale skin.

"I'm sure you've found it rather odd that we have never been together during the daylight, which we always meet at night," he said. "And I have never eaten or drunk anything in your presence."

"Yes, I have found that odd," I said, relieved that the matter was coming out into the open. "I'm sure you are ill, perhaps it is an illness I have not yet heard of."

Fabien turned and looked at me. "No, I am not ill. It is something much worse. I hardly know how to tell you, so bizarre will you find it. I am not sure you will believe my story at all."

"And yet you are going to tell me the truth."

"Yes, of course, Laurent. That is why I have such misgivings. Let me say, before I begin, that from the first time I met you in the park, I have begun to feel alive again, for the first time in a very long time. I have enjoyed myself in your company as I have not for many more years than you would find possible. And then there was our first night of intimacy," he said, almost dreamily. "I have never had those feelings with anyone else, Laurent. It was a new thing to me."

By this time, I was all tenderness to Fabien.

"To me, too," I said. "I thought maybe I was the only man in the world to crave another man so intensely. I wondered why I was made so different from other men. Do you feel that, too? Is that what made you want to separate yourself from me?"

"No, I had another reason for fleeing. A much more serious reason." He pulled his chair close to mine and took my hand. Once again, it felt like ice. "I am not the man you take me for. I am not a man at all. I am not mortal."

I could not reply to this since I could not make sense of it. Not mortal? Since Adam sinned, all men have been human. Surely Fabien would not ask me to believe he was a demon or an angel? If so, I would have to try hard, and probably unsuccessfully, not to laugh in his face.

I left my hand in his and stared into his blue eyes, waiting for him to resume talking and explain the unexplainable. My heart began beating faster and faster; it felt like it would burst out of my chest. I stared at him in anticipation. He looked at me and began to explain. "Laurent, I am one of the living dead, more commonly known as a vampire. I was made into one over a hundred years ago by someone I have grown to loathe," he said.

"I don't understand. Living dead? Vampire? I have never heard the word before. What does it mean?"

"I will tell you everything, and I ask that you allow me to talk uninterrupted. Fabien explained in great detail what a vampire was and all of its incredible abilities as it was explained to him by his vampire maker so long ago.

I tell you all of this because you must know the facts to make a free choice to either accept my offer or refuse it."

"What is your offer?" I asked though I suspected I already knew the answer.

"I want to make you a vampire, Laurent, so that you will never die so that we can be together always." Fabien paused. "I know this sounds horrible, and indeed it is horrible in many ways to be a vampire. Not for nothing does everybody fear us. But since I was made a vampire, against my will, it is the only way we can be together. And I need you, Laurent; I love you as I have loved no one else. I am selfish, but perhaps you need me, too. Or perhaps you will pity my love for you."

I reflected on every word he had said and contemplated my life before I met him; there hadn't been much of one that meant anything. I had never met another man who longed for the physical touch of another man, even if he wasn't indeed a man, yet a mysterious creature of the night. I felt anxious and became confused, asking myself, what kind of existence would I experience? I felt apprehensive as I remembered tasting my blood after being pricked by the thorn of the rose in the park. I thought about how this would become my nourishment, blood. A substance that would sustain my existence if I were to join Fabien and evolve as he into one of the undead night creatures.

As he gazed at me tenderly and longingly, I could not have loved him more than I did at that moment. I felt as if Fabien had bared his soul to me and was finally being truthful, yet the dark secret he had shared had frightened and intrigued me.

I looked at him without concealing the love and compassion I felt as I stood up, reflecting deeply on his words. For a brief moment, we said nothing and remained silent. I walked over to the window and looked out at the darkened Paris night, thinking, this is what my reality would become if I were to accept his offer and be transformed into a vampire; endless nights. I finally spoke and gave him my answer.

"Yes, Fabien, I am willing to become a vampire," I said.

He looked at me tenderly and said, "You'll never know exactly how happy you have made me with your decision. You shall come to live with me. I don't want there to be any physical distance between us," Fabien said.

"Nor do I," I replied as he drew nearer.

"Are you ready to begin your journey with me, Laurent?"

"I am, Fabien. Give me the gift of immortality."

"Yes, I have every intention of giving you my gift, but it is a dark one," Fabien replied. "You must be sure this is what you want."

"I have never been so certain of anything in my life, Fabien."

At once, his face turned from a joyful expression and complete happiness to a bloodthirsty and ravenous animal as his face became twisted, and his eyes changed from blue to a crimson red as he opened his mouth to reveal two abnormally large incisors and told me to lean my head over to one side. Then I felt a pain I had never experienced in my life. It was excruciating as he bit into my neck. I felt the warm blood as it ran down my neck. I felt the room as it spun around and heard him sucking the life force out of me. I felt myself growing weaker and barely able to whisper, "am I going to die?"

"Yes, Laurent, you will die a mortal death. Then you will be reborn," he said. With that, I lost all consciousness.

When I awoke, I knew I was near death as Fabien said, "Now that I have drained you almost completely, you must drink my blood. It will resurrect you to eternal life." I saw him bite into his wrist as the blood trickled out. He placed his wrist over my mouth and told me to drink. At first, I felt so weak I struggled to open my mouth, but he put his hand directly over my mouth, and his blood dripped into my mouth as I began to swallow. Immediately I felt a new energy surge, something so powerful it wasn't easy to describe. Next came the convulsions. I screamed in pain, and Fabien said, "Fear not, Laurent, you are being reborn!"

The convulsions stopped as my eyes closed. Then suddenly, a sea of scarlet red washed over my brain as I began to gasp for air as if I were drowning.

"Breath," Fabien said.

One large gasp for air was enough as I opened my eyes again. There was a clarity that had never existed before. I gazed at Fabien's face and could make out every pore in his skin, even down to the intricate detail of his hair follicles, as he knelt over me, softly cradling and stroking my head with his strong hands. Fabien helped me to stand as if I were a small child about to take its first steps. I felt a bit unsteady, but I quickly regained my strength, walked over to the window, and opened it.

The coolness of the night air no longer chilled me. Fabien walked over to where I stood and gently placed his hand on my shoulder. My eyesight was transformed, and my hearing was significantly enhanced. I noticed sounds I had never detected before, the many creatures they stirred and the branches as they creaked in the wind.

I looked down at my hands, which were now as lifeless and pale-looking as Fabien's. I walked toward the mirror on the wall and saw that I had cast no reflection. The mirror merely displayed the furnishings in the background. It was as if I weren't standing in front of it.

Then an overwhelming hunger forced me to double over in pain. It was so intense it felt as if it would tear me in half.

This hunger wasn't a desire for food; it was a thirst I had never experienced before. It seemed to consume my entire being.

"My God! What is this hunger?" I yelled at Fabien.

"It is the vampire's lust for blood," he replied calmly.

"Well, then, feed me! You made me into this creature, so feed me!"

"Yes, I shall, but first, you must listen to what I say. I have one rule, which for me, justifies our very existence. Some people prey on others; they rape, pillage, and murder. It is those criminals, and only those I feed on, the criminals that society fears. If there is such a thing as evil, surely it is those who prey on innocent, law-abiding, and unsuspecting citizens. I have chosen these evil humans to be my lifeline, and now they will also become yours. We will kill no others. Are we in agreement, Laurent?" he asked.

"Yes, yes! Please, for the love of God, feed me! I cannot take this torture!"

Fabien opened the window and said, "Observe." He climbed onto the windowsill, glided toward the dark sidewalk, and motioned to me to follow. I hesitated out of fear.

"Laurent come to me!" he called. "Remember what I told you about our ability to fly."

I cautiously stepped onto the window ledge, hesitated for a moment and then finally jumped, and began flying just as Fabien had. I thought, *My God! I am airborne!* I felt a slight tickle of excitement in my stomach and laughed in amazement and disbelief as I landed next to where Fabien was standing.

We decided to take a stroll in the park. Under the trees, in total darkness. Yet, now that I was a vampire, I could see things my human eyes would never have detected at night. Walking in the park was something I had always wanted to do with Fabien, but I had never imagined that it would be at night. I thought briefly about never again being able to feel the sun's warmth. I had taken it for granted, but now sunlight could destroy me.

"How was your first experience flying?" he asked with one eyebrow raised.

"It was beyond my wildest imagination!" I said excitedly. "Good, now about your hunger, has it subsided a little?" Fabien asked.

"Yes, a bit. At least for the moment."

"We shall find someone deserving of death soon. By night Paris has many criminals roaming the streets," he said, which reassured me.

"Fabien, there is one thing that you mentioned just before you turned me that I would like you to explain," I said.

He gave me a curious look and said, "Oh, what is that?"

"You mentioned earlier that there is another vampire loose in the world—in fact, the one who turned you over one hundred years ago," I said, but Fabien focused his attention elsewhere.

"Listen!" he said as we heard screams from a distance.

"Let us investigate," Fabien said as his eyes gleamed with excitement.

We used our vampire ability to run faster than any mortal could have done and arrived at the scene of the crime. A man stood there and wielded a sword and had threatened another man. As he turned his attention toward us, the victim screamed, "Help me!"

The would-be assailant raised his sword and said, "There is nothing these two can do to help you. Tonight, you will die, so prepare yourself! Once I finish with you, it shall be their turn!"

"Wrong, it is you who will die tonight!" Fabien shouted, as his eyes transformed into a blood red.

"Run! Save yourself while you still can!" I shouted.

The assailant was distracted by Fabien's threat as the man ran away screaming.

At once, Fabien grabbed the assailant by the neck and lifted him in the air, and proceeded to choke him as he struggled against Fabien's vise-like grip as the man began to choke.

Laurent here is your nourishment," Fabien said.

Instantly, Fabien lowered the man and was at his throat and I at his wrist as we bit the man draining him of his blood.

During this process, I struggled and became conflicted. On the one hand, Fabien and I were about to take this man's life, something I grew up believing was a sin. Then again, this was not a life worth saving. The assailant had attempted to murder someone. We had saved the man's life, who would otherwise have been killed.

As Fabien had said, if we were to limit ourselves to feeding on the blood of criminals, we would be helping rid society of evil.

Fabien dropped the body and retrieved a handkerchief from his waistcoat to wipe his mouth. He handed it to me so I could do the same.

"Quickly, we must dispose of the body," Fabien said as we picked up the corpse and started digging a shallow grave to bury the body. If this man had a history of criminal activity, the authorities would undoubtedly search for a while and then give up and label it as an unsolved mysterious disappearance.

Once the hole was dug, we placed the body in the freshly unearthed dirt. We covered it within seconds using vampire speed and strength. As soon as the makeshift plot was covered with dirt, we wiped it clean from our hands with Fabien's handkerchief.

"Shall we return to your apartment, Laurent?" Fabien asked.

The color in Fabien's face had returned. Gone was the chalk-white, replaced by a rosy complexion. I looked at my hands and saw that some color had come back. It was undoubtedly due to the blood we had just consumed.

We returned to my apartment, entering by the same window we had left through only a short time ago.

"How was your first experience as a vampire, Laurent?" Fabien asked, sounding genuinely concerned.

"All I was thinking about was feeding myself," I confessed. "This is my new reality. I accept it."

Fabien nodded and said, "I struggled with my first experience. I was forced to kill indiscriminately, even families with little children," He turned away from me in shame. After a moment, he composed himself, turned to face me, and said, "Now, allow me to tell you about another vampire. He is the only other to my knowledge; however, there may be others, such as the vampire that made my vampire maker. His name is Stefan, he was not only my maker, but lover as well, to my everlasting regret." I listened intently as he told me how they had met at the Procope, which is why Fabien preferred meeting me at the café Alexandre, careful to avoid the other café altogether for fear of running into Stefan.

Fabien shared with me that he felt he was tricked into becoming a vampire without his consent and that he had met Stefan and was drawn to him by his good looks, wit, and charm. The two had attended cultural events together and finally became physically intimate. Shortly after that, it turned to unending cruelty.

As I heard this, I became enraged with jealousy, making me hate Stefan even more. Fabien described how Stefan delighted in torturing him with these endless killing sprees.

Of the many pillages Fabien told me about, two stood out most in his mind. The first involved Fabien's trusted servant Jacques. Stefan made Fabien witness how he brutally and savagely killed him and that Fabien felt powerless to do anything to stop him. Fabien paused briefly before telling me about the other killing spree that upset him. This time it was an entire family, which included the family's coachman and two small children who heard the parent's cries for mercy to spare the children. Finally, the children discovered that monsters are not just something that existed in nightmares and the wild imaginations of children but that the monsters had sought them out and had shown them that they truly exist. Fabien was powerless under Stefan's control and decided he would never inflict that pain on anyone else. If he were to find another love interest, that person would choose whether to become a vampire or remain human. True to his word, I was given that choice.

After hearing about Fabien's tortured past and the unspeakable acts he was forced to do, my love for Fabien grew. I couldn't contain my sadness listening to how Stefan had tortured him and what he endured all at the hands of that monster, as blood tears ran from my eyes. I reached out to wipe the blood tears that ran down Fabien's cheeks and wiped my own with a fresh handkerchief.

Once we had composed ourselves, I suggested a change of scenery was in order. I had remembered how fond Fabien was of frequenting the café Alexander and suggested we take a stroll over there to lose our thoughts of Stefan in a game or two of chess.

He smiled at me and said, "What a wonderful suggestion. Yes, let's stop all this talk about Stefan. Instead, let's enjoy the solace of our beloved café and each other's company."

I could tell that Fabien had become emotionally drained in describing to me their tortured history together.

I walked over to the window, hearing thunder as I gazed out into the blackened night as lightning lit up the sky. Looking out, I thought I saw someone peering up towards our window. As Fabien walked over to join me, the figure disappeared. As he stood next to me, he kissed my head and asked, "What are you thinking about, Laurent?"

"Strange, I just thought I saw an image of a man staring up at our window," I answered.

"A man? Your imagination must be playing tricks on you; no one is out there. All this talk about Stefan has the two of us on edge," he said as he tried to reassure me. As hard as Fabien tried to soothe my nerves, I couldn't help but feel something dark and ominous was coming. It seemed to consume me. "Come, let's go to the café. I feel as if I shall beat you this evening at chess," Fabien said. I replied with a faint laugh as we left the apartment arriving at the café in a matter of moments.

As soon as we entered it, a feeling of calm and normalcy came over me. I could tell that Fabien felt equally at ease. Little did I know those feelings would soon be ruined with doubt and fear.

We spotted a table towards the back of the café; it was a busy night with many patrons, and we felt fortunate to locate a place to sit. Fabien proceeded to set up the chessboard and all its pieces. Hearing the laughter of the patrons and arguments was not only a pleasant distraction but a comforting sound as we began our chess game.

"It's your move Laurent," Fabien said, looking content.

Soon after locating our table, I noticed someone sitting across the room from us, appearing to have the same pallor as Fabien and I. The man seemed to be transfixed by the two of us, watching our every move.

"Laurent, what has you so distracted?" Fabien asked, sounding annoyed.

I turned away from the man's gaze, which looked like he was looking right through me. I wondered whether that man was a man at all or another of our kind, possibly Stefan.

"My apologies, yes, for a moment, I became distracted; I thought I saw a man who appeared to have our skin coloring," I admitted.

Had I detected an expression of panic on Fabien's face? I pointed in the direction where the man had been seated.

"It appears he has left Fabien; although he seemed to be quite interested in our chess-playing," I said anxiously.

Thinking about this strange man I had seen observing the two of us so closely caused that feeling of doom to return. I tried desperately to hide those feelings from Fabien, which proved pointless. It was as if he could read my thoughts, and despite my efforts to remain calm, I could sense that Fabien was beginning to feel paranoid and fearful, knocking over some of the chess pieces, which showed how unnerved he had become.

"Let us return home, Laurent. I suddenly have lost interest in playing another round of chess," he said, sounding almost defeated.

It pained me to see Fabien this way; he appeared to display feelings of torment, and Stefan was not only observing us but most likely stalking us, if not plotting something against us.

We left the crowded and bustling café, with the mysterious gentleman nowhere to be seen. As soon as I left the café, the weather changed dramatically. The skies were lit with lightning, and thunder echoed in the background as it began to rain. We decided to use our vampire speed rather than stroll home, especially given the uncertainty of the unknown man who appeared to be following us.

Once in the comfort of our apartment, we were greeted with the fireplace ablaze with warmth and color. Francois must have made it shortly before retiring for the evening. We sat next to the fireplace to allow our clothes to dry and observed the flames as they danced and flickered while we heard the wood as it made a crackling sound as it burned.

I became mesmerized by the flames, knowing that something so beautiful could also be tremendously destructive and end our existence. I don't remember how long the silence lasted; it seemed an eternity until Fabien finally spoke.

"This man you claim you saw at the café, do you remember what he looked like?" Fabien asked.

"He was very handsome and had the same skin coloring as you and me, as white as milk, I replied.

"No mortal has the color of our skin. It must have been another of our kind, perhaps even Stefan!" Fabien said.

I cringed at Fabien's suggestion, not wanting to accept it, but deep down inside, we knew who the stalker was; it was Stefan. The tension was palpable. Suddenly, our wonderful time spent together seemed consumed with the looming threat that Stefan posed.

"I have been so careful to avoid him. We must, or he will destroy both you and I should we be spotted together," Fabien said.

"What are you suggesting, Fabien? I refuse to become a prisoner here in our apartments; we must still be able to roam about freely," I said almost in defiance.

"At what price, Laurent?" Fabien asked.

I didn't reply to Fabien's question but instead responded to his question with a question of my own. "Isn't there anything we can do to stop him? Surely with your strength and mine combined, we could overpower him," I angrily replied as Fabien interjected.

"There is nothing you or I can do; Stefan is much older than you or I. His strength is the equivalent of fifty humans, your strength and mine amount to half of that," Fabien said, sounding defeated once again.

I walked over to where Fabien was seated and put my arms around him, holding him as if I were protecting him from anything that would choose to do either of us harm.

Just then, a thought occurred, for Stefan to have become a vampire, he had to have had a maker, another vampire. If there were some way we could locate this creature and perhaps meet with him, we could enlist this creature's help to control Stefan, and indeed this vampire would be older and even more potent than Stefan. However, a few obstacles remained: whether this vampire maker of Stefan's still existed, and where would we locate him?

My thoughts consumed me until Fabien spoke.

"What are you thinking of, Laurent?" Fabien asked.

I shared my thoughts about attempting to locate and meet with Stefan's maker; I pleaded with him to follow my plan. I felt it was our only chance to deal with Stefan.

"Say I agree to this, then how do we contact this vampire? We don't even know if this creature still exists?" Fabien said.

"Fabien, you shared with me that vampires can summon mortals, did you not?" I asked.

"Yes, that is correct," Fabien replied with a questioning look.

"Well, for example, if a vampire can summon a mortal, why wouldn't a vampire be able to summon another vampire?" I asked, feeling a sense of newfound excitement and hope stir inside me.

"There is only one way to determine this; we shall begin this experiment tomorrow evening, as the time is drawing near for us to rest. "Observe," Fabien said and pointed toward the window. The storm had passed hours ago, and the sky had become lighter as the dawn approached. Hours and hours had gone by, yet we had lost all track of time with many lengthy pauses of silence during our discussions of how to contact Stefan's maker. To those of our kind, time goes by so quickly, yet we are not bound by it.

We entered our bedroom, quickly got undressed, and lay on the bed side by side, holding each other's hand as we drifted into an undead slumber.

Once sleep set in, I started to dream about a man with a white beard; he appeared pretty ancient. I had no idea who this man was, only in this dream, another appeared by his side, the same mysterious man that had observed us in the café. This man, who wasn't a man but a vampire, turned to meet my gaze, hissed, and bore his fangs.

I woke up shaken by the vision, careful not to awaken Fabien, and determined more than ever to see my plan through.

I wondered who this man with the white beard was. Perhaps he had come to warn me despite this only being a dream, yet it felt as if it had actually occurred.

The next evening, I decided to give Francois the evening off. No sooner had he left than we began our experiment. We had left the window open, thinking that whoever would appear after being summoned would naturally enter this way. Fabien and I sat on the floor with three black candles arranged in a circular pattern. We held hands as Fabien called out to Stefan's maker, "We gather here this evening to ask the vampire maker of Stefan, Baron of Vitré, to appear before us; if you can hear us, I ask you to come to us."

Outside, the wind had intensified and began to howl. Fabien called out three more times. My heart began to sink. I was starting to doubt this experiment; perhaps only vampires could summon mortals, not others of our kind.

A mighty wind rushed through the window as thunder and lightning lit up and echoed through the black of night, startling us a bit.

Suddenly, a man with a long white beard appeared before us; we soon learned this was no ordinary man. I recognized him as the man from the dream I had had the previous day, and then he spoke, "Why have you summoned me here?" The white-bearded man replied as he bared his two large incisors. We each greeted the vampire by baring our fangs in return.

"Are you the vampire maker of Stefan, Baron of Vitré?" Fabien asked forcefully.

"Who wants to know?" The white-bearded vampire replied.

"It is I, Fabien Levesque. Stefan was my maker," Fabien replied as I held onto his hand. To suggest I felt unease with this experiment and the actual appearance of Stefan's maker would not be inaccurate.

"Why have you summoned me here?" the white-bearded vampire demanded.

"Ancient one, we need your help dealing with Stefan," Fabien said forcefully.

"Why should I want to help you? And who is this other vampire if you are the fledgling of Stefan?" the white-haired ancient one asked.

"My name is Laurent Richelieu. I am Fabien's fledgling, but much more than that, he is also my lover," I said, answering the ancient vampire's question.

"What is your name, ancient one?" Fabien asked commandingly.

The white-haired vampire grimaced upon hearing those words and said, "My name is Thaddeus. I am the maker of Stefan; he was my fledgling until I cast him out.

"I don't understand?" Fabien replied.

"For many mortal years, I had been a close friend of Stefan's family before I became this creature of darkness. I had sworn to Stefan's parents that in the event of their untimely demise, I would look after their child. They knew nothing about my becoming a vampire; Stefan lost both of his parents because of the black plague, Stefan became infected as well, I saved him from mortal death, and he became as I."

"So now we understand how Stefan became a vampire; we do not understand why you cast him out?" Fabien asked the white-haired vampire.

"If you must know, after I turned Stefan, he began making physical advances toward me. Misinterpreting my feelings of love for him, similar to a mentor, or father figure, then the love he had sought from me. I was disgusted by his physical advances and banished him from my presence, never to return!"

It became more evident to Fabien and me how Stefan's rage and jealousy had developed. It was the feeling of rejection and being cast out by Thaddeus, along with Stefan finding another man to turn into his everlasting, immortal fledgling, ending in Fabien's rejection of Stefan as well, which helped ignite an almost inextinguishable fire of rage in his heart.

"So now that I have shared this with you, what more is there left to say?" Thaddeus said as he prepared to leave.

Fabien pleaded with the ancient vampire. "Wait! We need your help, Thaddeus. If you have one trace of compassion left inside of you, please, help us. We love each other, yes. I forbade Stefan's command of never making another vampire. Still, I was miserable with him; you have no idea what he made me do, the torture he put me through, then meeting Laurent, who changed my very existence and has shown me how love truly can be. Please, I beg of you!"

The ancient white-haired vampire shook his head and said, "You will have to contend with Stefan yourselves; I don't agree with your kind of love. I must be off!" as he departed as quickly as he had arrived. Summoning Thaddeus hadn't accomplished much. Other than it provided insight into Stefan's thoughts and what motivated him to act with unrestrained cruelty and hatred for everyone.

I looked at Fabien and said with a heavy heart, "All hope is lost."

"All we need do is avoid Stefan," Fabien replied, sounding defiant.

"And how do we do that? Did he not spot us at the café Alexandre? How did he know we would be there? Was it not the reason you chose to avoid going to the other café, the Procope, for fear of running into him there?" I asked with a bit of agitation in my voice.

"Yes, I had no idea he would come to the Alexandre; however, we must continue doing the things we have enjoyed together," Fabien replied, sounding equally frustrated.

I paused a bit before I replied to Fabien, waiting for my mood to soften. "I guess you are right, Fabien. As long as we remain vigilant and on the lookout for Stefan, then and only then may we continue to enjoy what we once had; otherwise, we are prisoners of our own making," I said.

The following evening we agreed to attend a play entitled *"Agis"* by *Laignelot at the Comédie-Française.* Perhaps we could lose ourselves in the performance and possibly forget about Stefan.

We agreed to use our vampire ability and take to flight rather than hire a coach to get to the theater. We arrived within minutes and quickly made our way inside. Fabien and I looked around the spacious waiting area and expected at any moment to suddenly find Stefan leering at us; however, fortunately for us, he was nowhere to be seen.

As desperately as we attempted to enjoy the evening out, we found it difficult to focus on the performance as we were filled with anxiety and dread. We looked anxiously in one direction and then in the other. I thought, was coming to the theater such a good idea after all?

The performance ended, and we stood up to leave, feeling the ominous threat of Stefan as if he were watching us and plotting his next move until, eventually, he would strike.

We made our way out of the theater and entered the waiting area. Still, Stefan was nowhere to be seen.

"You see, Laurent, there is nothing to worry about; it's not as if Stefan can read our minds. How would he know we were here?" Fabien said. It sounded like he was trying to convince himself as much as I by saying that.

As we walked out of the theater, we decided to be transported home by one of the hired coaches as we entered and gave the driver our address and were off. We sat in the carriage in silence, both of us preoccupied with thoughts about Stefan, each of us feeling as if, at any moment, he would appear and end both of us.

Nearing the location of our apartment, suddenly, there was a jolt and a loud thud, as if something had landed on the roof of our carriage. I reached for Fabien's hand as a look of terror overcame our faces.

Then the long-anticipated and dreaded appearance of Stefan's face, as he bent over from on top of the carriage and displayed his grotesquely twisted face in the carriage's window, bearing his long incisors as he hissed at us with rage.

We cautiously exited the carriage and turned to witness Stefan attacking the coachman as he cried out for help. We made our escape by air, arriving at our apartment in mere seconds, with no trace of Stefan; luckily for us, he had become distracted by taking the life of the coachman, which provided our opportunity to escape. As we entered, I could tell that Fabien was as visibly shaken by this incident as I was.

"He is coming. I feel it to the depths of my soul!" Fabien said as his eyes widened with terror.

"Fabien, if he wanted to attack us, why would he have stayed behind feasting on the coachman?" I asked.

"Stefan is ruthless; to him, it's all a game. He will stop at nothing until he has destroyed you, avenging himself for my disobeying his command never to make another vampire."

"I will protect you, Fabien," I said, trying desperately to comfort him with no success as Fabien walked over to the window. The weather again turned violent; thunder echoed in the distance and became louder as the lightning lit up the sky.

"This cannot be!" Fabien shouted after lightning illuminated the park across from our building. "My God. It's him! It's Stefan, he has followed us here! Quick, you must hide! He must not find you here!"

Within seconds, Stefan was seen hovering outside our window. A menacing feral look on his face which twisted and distorted his features, with the blood of the coachman still trickling down either side of his lips. Before either of us could move or say a word, Stefan came crashing through the window.

"So, you thought you would rid yourself of me, didn't you, Fabien?" Stefan said as he brushed the glass off his jacket. "You know I have been observing you for quite some time, and who might this be? Oh yes, I remember having seen you in the carriage sitting alongside Fabien." Stefan moved closer to me and said, "He looks rather pale." Stefan could tell by my appearance that I was a vampire. "Could it be? Is it possible that you have disobeyed my command? Have you made a vampire fledgling of your own?"

"Why have you come back, Stefan? I thought we were to remain apart!" Fabien said, ignoring his inquiry.

"Well, it appears neither one of us held to our bargain. I knew you would not stay true to your word," Stefan said, sounding sarcastic.

"Laurent and I are happy, Stefan," Fabien said.

"Silence!" Stefan said. "Did you make this young vampire?"

There was a moment of silence; then Fabien answered defiantly, "Yes. He is mine. I turned him, and I love him."

Stefan reacted by picking up a vase and smashed it against the wall. "Because of that, I will destroy him."

"You lay one hand on him, and I shall destroy you, Stefan!" Fabien shouted.

No sooner had Fabien warned Stefan than I jumped on top of Stefan and attempted to wrestle him to the floor. Stefan merely laughed and threw me off as if I were as weightless as an article of clothing. "I will destroy you, fledgling!" he repeated. But as Stefan raised his hand with his razor-sharp nails and was about to end my existence, Fabien rushed in front of me as fast as lightning. Stefan mistakenly clawed his way through Fabien's chest and pulled his heart out as Fabien screamed in agony and suddenly slumped to the floor with a thud.

"Fabien, my god, what have I done? I meant to destroy the vampire fledgling, not you!" Stefan shouted, then looked at me menacingly and said, "Now I shall end your miserable existence as I had originally intended."

I couldn't believe what I had witnessed. Call it survival mode or animal instinct; however, I knew I had to get away from Stefan, or I would suffer the same fate. I vanished instantly, using my vampire speed to exit the window Stefan had entered only moments earlier. Even so, I sensed I was only seconds away from suffering the same fate at Stefan's mighty hands.

CHAPTER 5

A narrow escape

(LAURENT NARRATES)

I escaped Stefan's horror, destruction, and wrath by materializing into a mist. I transported myself to Pere Lachaise cemetery seeking shelter in a family crypt— thinking I would be safe from the clutches of Stefan. The blood-soaked tears which ran down my pallid face were quite a sight. I was in shock; I found it hard to believe that my Fabien was destroyed in front of my eyes.

The vile creature known as Stefan had fulfilled his threat of destroying Fabien if he dared make a vampire fledgling of his own. And now I was alone. The unbearable feeling of that overtook my emotions. I looked around the crypt, barely seeing through the red film of blood streaming out of my eyes like a fountain.

What now? — I asked myself, where am I to go? I knew I would never be safe anywhere in Paris, much less in the rest of Europe. Stefan would hunt me down and destroy me as he had Fabien, ending my wretched existence. Even though my grief was unbearable, the animal instinct of survival soon overcame my pain. I tried to suppress my blood lust as a thought came to me; some of my relatives had left France for the new world as it was known. To a city named New Orleans, named after the town of Orleans in France.

I had heard many other French nationals, as well as Quebecois, had settled there. Perhaps I could start over and try to forge a new beginning for myself and leave Paris and the heartache of losing Fabien to begin anew, remaining anonymous and escaping Stefan. I couldn't stop thinking about Fabien; I felt heartbroken and defeated.

I was unaware of a mist that started to form near one of the stone coffins as the ghost of Fabien appeared. He caught my attention as I spoke his name, "Fabien?" I asked, not believing what I was seeing. The entity looked at me with a loving glance and nodded its head. His features though transparent, had become more visible to my vampire's eyes. I was confused whether this was an illusion or that which I was seeing was the true spirit of my departed soul mate. Then he spoke, and I was convinced he had returned to me.

"Fear not, Laurent; our love is eternal; it is our destiny to be with one another. I shall always be with you, and you shall always be with me; I shall never leave you." I stared, mouth open, as he stepped towards me and extended his hand; I longingly reached out but felt nothing but extreme cold and watched as my hand went right through his.

"You cannot touch nor embrace me, Laurent; however, soon, we shall meet again, and I assure you, this time, we shall be together for all eternity. I must go," the entity said reassuringly; he looked at me with tenderness and love. I cried, "Don't leave me, Fabien; you must not leave me again!"

But it was no use. The spirit had vanished as suddenly as it had appeared.

I felt a second sense of loss, the first naturally being— the deceased individual's body. Now, the second and final blow as my lover reappeared and then vanished, not knowing if I shall ever lay eyes on him again. I wanted so desperately to believe what he had shared with me, that we would be together, but how was that to be? Would his spirit haunt me for all of eternity, or was he alluding to something else? I felt confused and saddened. Yet, the blood hunger overpowered my sadness, and I needed to quench it.

I stepped out of the crypt and sensed I was safe from Stefan, at least temporarily. He couldn't have followed me, I told myself. If he had, I most certainly would have encountered him by now.

In the distance, I heard a dog panting, a mangy-looking creature someone had abandoned. It stopped, saw me, growled, and bared its fangs as if to warn me.

Had I been human, I would have feared for my safety. But a vampire does not worry about such animals. I glared back at the dog and bore my fangs for the dog to see; it made a whimpering sound, and instantly I rushed over and held it as it yelped and struggled to get away. I tore into the dog's neck and began to drink.

I drained every drop of blood from its body as the dog fell silently into my arms. Glancing up at the sky, I saw that the sun was about to rise. I had lost all track of time. I released the dog's corpse to the ground and quickly made my way back inside the mausoleum as I lifted the sizeable concrete slab from a nearby coffin that displayed skeletal remains. I removed the bones, tossed them in the corner of the crypt, and made my way into the coffin. Instantly, I was at rest and dreamt of a lovely place surrounded with buildings with wrought iron balconies, plantation homes with pillars, and magnificent magnolia trees. I felt at peace in this special place and thought it was beckoning me as a lover might. Was it destiny? I thought.

After a week of hiding out in the crypt, I cautiously returned to our apartment. I knew it was time to leave France and begin a new chapter that did not constantly remind me of my previous existence with Fabien.

I decided New Orleans, in French Louisiana, would become my new home. But how long would it take to find a new home? I was uncertain.

I left the cemetery, no longer sensing the threat of Stefan. Indeed after my having spent a week at the crypt, Stefan would have moved on, ending his search for me, at least for the moment. I took to flight, landed in front of our apartment, and quickly entered the front door. There on the threshold, I noticed a letter. I opened it immediately, having seen the return address of New Orleans. It was a letter from my grandfather Pierre, who had immigrated to New Orleans a year after my grandmother's passing.

In the letter, my grandfather wrote that he was gravely ill and would not live much longer; he certainly would have passed before I received the letter. It was his dying wish that I was to inherit his plantation, furnishings, and his loyal servants. His second wife,

Josephine Jacobson, an American, would stay on until my arrival and afterward relocate to Virginia's newfound American colony.

The plantation known as "Le Petit Fleur," named by my late grandfather, would become mine, ending my search for a place to reside in my new city.

My eyes quickly turned their attention to the blood-spattered remains, seeing the exact location of where my lover had been destroyed just a short time ago, as the letter dropped out of my hands.

Stefan had undoubtedly taken the body and disposed of it in some cruel and horrific manner, of that, I was sure. I began the unpleasant task of cleaning up Fabien's blood.

I broke down and cursed Stefan repeatedly while shedding blood tears over my destroyed soul mate. I left absolutely no trace of blood or anything that would raise questions for anyone responsible for packing my belongings. I composed myself and focused my attention on my new existence.

The following evening, I made my way into town to arrange a crate transport, which would be my temporary home across the high seas to the new world. Naturally, all my belongings would come later, after I had met with my deceased grandfather's second wife, Josephine, and secured her departure from my inherited estate. I instructed the shipping company that the crate needed soil. They did not question why, thinking that perhaps I was a bit eccentric for this unusual request, nor did they want to do anything to anger me or jeopardize the arrangement I had paid so handsomely for.

CHAPTER 6

The new world

(LAURENT NARRATES)

The day arrived when I was to make my journey to the New World, and my new estate. I would make my way on board the vessel without being detected, find the crate containing the soil of my homeland, and lie in this container until the ship reached the shores of the Mississippi River.

I didn't doubt I would survive the lengthy and treacherous journey across the sea. I had fed enough on the blood of dogs, cats, and vermin before the sea journey. This blood would sustain my appetite for the long adventure.

Nightfall came as I made my way onto the long vessel. The workmen had just about loaded the crate.

I chose to transform myself into mist, which would cause me to go undetected by the workmen. I spotted the crate at the other end of the ship and ensured none of the workmen were milling about. Sensing that I was alone, I materialized and lifted the heavy lid as if it were light as a feather and secured myself inside. A few hours later, the massive vessel was in motion, and I knew my journey had just begun.

I had many strange visions while I was self-contained in my wooden refuge. Was I starting to grow mad being trapped in this wooden box? Seeing my beloved Fabien's spirit in the cemetery's crypt gave me pause. It wasn't typical for humans or vampires to see ghosts of the dearly departed. Why had Fabien appeared to me? Was he attempting to warn me or comfort me through my grieving process? I was confused by this, and it troubled me.

On more than one occasion, I had reoccurring nightmares of seeing Stefan destroy Fabien. Each time I screamed and awakened to find myself in this temporary home alone. My guilt and anger consumed me, thinking I should have tried to do more to protect Fabien! But how? I was no match for Stefan; being over two hundred years older than myself made him much more powerful than I, much like a full-grown person's strength compared to a child's.

I swore to myself that, eventually, I would exact some revenge against Stefan. Undoubtedly, as I grew older, my strength and vampire abilities would increase. For now, what mattered was arriving in the New World. My plans for revenge against Stefan would need to wait.

The ship made its way across the rough and treacherous sea, bobbing and weaving along the Atlantic Ocean, lasting an entire month, and finally settled into the harbor in the city known as New Orleans. The workmen hoisted the wooden crate and carried it off the ship and onto the pier. The container was to remain on the dock alone, with no questions asked.

I sensed the sun had set, which seemed to be an ability I assumed was part of my vampire powers as I broke open the wood crate as if it were made from kindling wood and emerged.

I was ravenous after the long voyage and spotted a stray dog near the harbor. I seized the opportunity to feed and nourish myself. I made sure no one else was around to witness this.

Instantly, I descended upon the animal, much like a rabid animal, snarling and baring my fangs. The dog recoiled and growled as I scooped it up and bit into its jugular vein, as the dog's blood hit the back of my throat, spraying the inside of my neck. The mangy animal made a slight whimper and, finally, was still as I drained its rich, red life force. Even though I detest animal blood, it served its purpose until I located a human involved in a criminal act that deserved nothing other than death, as I had learned from Fabien.

I took to flight and landed close to the center of town. I could transport myself to other locations by flying; however, that did not extend to over water; otherwise, I would have spared myself the unpleasant and long journey over the Atlantic by ship.

I made my way into town and looked for a room that didn't have a window to shield myself from the sunlight. I would travel to my inherited estate by horse so as not to mysteriously appear out of nowhere and call on my late grandfather's widow the following evening to work out the details of her departure and to meet my newly acquired servants.

I located a room in the center of town known as the French Quarter. The proprietor of a bar was renting it out. It was upstairs, and despite the noise due to the bar patrons who seemed to congregate there regularly, the room provided me the privacy I required.

The establishment was owned by a French-Canadian man in his mid-twenties, Claude Boucher, who had emigrated from Quebec a few years back. Monsieur Boucher and I conversed as the last of the bar patrons prepared to leave. Once the bar was empty, he showed me the room, indicating that the place would be private and, as I had requested, would not have a window.

"Here is the room. As you can see, there is a washbasin for you to freshen up," he said. I looked at him and smiled as I looked around the dingy room, thinking it would serve its purpose as I yawned, which indicated my exhaustion and that I required rest.

"I can see that you are tired, Monsieur. It must have been a very long journey for you; I will excuse myself. If there is anything you require, please do not hesitate to ask," He graciously said and turned to leave.

"Wait. There is one last thing I require Monsieur Boucher, a horse, for purchase. I have business to attend to outside of town tomorrow evening, and I will not be returning.

Will you arrange this for me? I will pay you handsomely for your troubles," I said.

"Yes, of course, Monsieur Richelieu."

True to his word, Monsieur Boucher arranged for the horse to be delivered the following evening. It was a beautiful, muscular black Arabian horse. I was introduced to my horse and told its name was Mercury. I walked over to the horse, stroking it a few times to acquaint myself and develop its trust. It responded with a neighing sound. If by instinct, the two of us bonded as I climbed on top of the magnificent creature. I thanked my host and paid him handsomely for the horse, as I had promised. We said our goodbyes, and in an instant, I was off.

Using my extraordinary night vision, I could steer Mercury in the right direction. We made our way through the trees and wetlands for hours. I knew my horse would not make the journey from New Orleans to Vacherie in one evening; we would need to overnight somewhere, but the question begged, where? After riding for what seemed several hours, I found a house out in the remote bayou. I decided Mercury would need water and rest, and I would need shelter during the scorching daylight hours.

I walked over and knocked on the door. A man who appeared to be in his mid-twenties answered, "Yes, may I help you?" he asked and looked me over suspiciously. I met his gaze with an intensity that drew him in as I began hypnotizing him.

"I require lodging for the night. A darkened room or cellar will suffice, and water for my horse; you will provide me all of this," I said as he held my gaze without as much as a blink of an eye. He naturally agreed. I knew I could rest until sunset and complete my journey the following evening, arriving at the estate later that night.

I made the man's cellar my temporary home. It was dark enough to shield me from the sun's punishing rays. Luckily for me, it was also rodent-infested. I quickly seized one of the scurvy creatures and tore it apart using my sharp teeth, draining the blood of the rat and instantly satisfying my blood lust. As soon as I had nourished myself, I gave Mercury some water, found some hay to feed him, and then settled him for the evening. I walked the owner's property and gazed up at the stars, anxious to begin my new existence.

I rested until nightfall came, boarded my horse, and sped off. I knew it would not be long before I arrived at my newly acquired estate.

I arrived late that evening. Once I had secured Mercury to one of the trees, I made my way around to the front, taking in the splendor of my new home. I noticed the majestic columns of the massive estate and the many oak trees planted on either side of the long walkway which led to the front door.

Despite my late arrival, I noticed a light that flickered by one of the windows and suspected my late grandfather's widow, Josephine, had not yet gone to bed.

I reached for the door knocker and announced my arrival. After what seemed to be several minutes, an attractive woman in her mid-to-forties answered the door.

"Yes, may I help you?" she asked with concern. Undoubtedly she was apprehensive about answering the door so late in the evening, and had not been expecting my visit.

"I am Laurent Richelieu, your late husband's grandson; I believe you were expecting me?" I replied.

She looked me over and broke into a flirtatious grin. "My! Pierre never mentioned what a handsome man you are," She gushed. I found this spectacle embarrassing and rude. And so soon after my grandfather's death. It was indeed in bad taste.

"May I come in?" I asked and ignored the woman's flirtatious advances.

"Why, of course, where are my manners," she said as she led me into the foyer.

This is exquisite, I thought and looked around at every detail in the great house, noting the many crystal chandeliers and the magnificent, polished mahogany grand staircase which led upstairs.

"Please follow me into the drawing room," she said as she continued to flirt and batted her eyelashes each time she spoke to me.

We entered the drawing room with its magnificent fireplace; she sat on a settee and motioned me toward a wingback chair. She picked up a fan and began to use it on herself. *Soon, all of this would be mine*, I thought.

"I don't mean to be rude, Monsieur Richelieu, but let's get right down to business. It's late, and I was just about to turn in for the evening before your sudden arrival," she said. I noticed she had dropped her flirtatious manner, perhaps sensing my disinterest, and was eager to discuss our business arrangement.

I'll admit, despite her being an American, her knowledge of French was quite impressive. I was sure my late grandfather had taught her everything he knew.

"Yes, by all means, Miss?" I asked, not remembering her surname.

"Miss Jacobson," she said, sounding irritated that I had forgotten her last name. "I find it odd that during our entire marriage, your late grandfather very rarely, if ever, mentioned you," She said. I interpreted this as her questioning the legitimacy of my having inherited the estate.

I looked at her as if we were engaged in a strategic chess game.

"I can assure you, Miss Jacobson, my grandfather and I were very close back when he lived in Paris with my grandmother," I stated, almost defiantly.

"I'm sure you were," She replied rather coldly.

"What are you implying, Miss Jacobson? If there is something you would like to share with me, then by all means, do so," I said and looked at her sternly.

"With all due respect Monsieur Richelieu I believe it is I, as your grandfather's widow, who am entitled to this estate, or at the very least, half of it," She said defiantly. I looked her over as if she had gone mad and responded calmly and collectedly.

"Miss Jacobson, I appreciate your honesty; however, let me remind you that I am a blood relative and the rightful heir to this property and all of its belongings according to my late grandfather's last will and testimony. I understood from my late grandfather's letter that you were to be relocating to the commonwealth of Virginia. Or have your plans changed?" I stated. I sensed her mood switch to once again being flirtatious.

"Yes, that was the plan initially. Perhaps you and I can work out some arrangement?" she said, batting her eyelashes and fanning herself simultaneously.

Feeling irritated by this conniving, desperate woman, I got up, walked over to the window, and looked out at the darkness.

I turned to her suddenly and said, "You are not a relative of mine; I have no affinity for you. You are merely the second wife of my late grandfather. You will pack up your belongings and leave first thing in the morning; naturally, I will leave you a small payment to help facilitate your relocation efforts." I instructed commandingly.

"However, before you leave, you will introduce me to all the servants on the property so that there is an orderly transition. Do I make myself clear, Miss Jacobson?" I asked as I leaned in her direction so close I could make out the features of her long eyelashes and the pores of her skin.

"Yes, I understand perfectly, Monsieur Richelieu," she replied and backed down from her challenge, sensing her efforts had failed and that she had no choice but to fulfill her part of the arrangement.

"Now shall we go outside so you can introduce me to all servants," I suggested.

"With pleasure Monsieur Richelieu," she replied, sounding indignant.

I knew my offering to add to the fortune of what my late grandfather had left her would help facilitate her timely departure. In my heart, I felt she had only been an opportunist and had merely cared for my grandfather because of his wealth. There hadn't been any real love between them. My deceased grandfather never mentioned anything about his second wife in any letters he'd written me. Quite frankly, the one thing we had in common was that neither of us knew much about the other; and the thought of her flirting with me so soon after his passing! I realized she didn't care much about playing the role of the grieving widow.

She walked over to pick up one of the candelabras to light the outdoor pathway, and we made our way outside and around to a gigantic bell used to gather up all the servants as she repeatedly rang the bell.

The servants, both men and women streamed in a large group totaling roughly twenty. Miss Josephine announced that the plantation was transitioning and that I was to become their new owner. I introduced myself, and they, in turn, presented themselves to me. Naturally, I spoke to them in French as many had come from the French West Indies in the Caribbean and the French colonies in Africa.

I instructed them to prepare my room and that it required dark velvet curtains. Naturally, I did not share with them that those curtains would sufficiently shield me from the sun's rays during daylight hours and provide me with the required privacy.

I surveyed the twenty-room estate; and decided that there would be enough room for my belongings once they were brought over by ship to add to the furnishings I inherited from my grandfather.

We bid our goodnights to each other and the servants. I shared with Miss Josephine how exhausted I felt, having made the long journey from France to Louisiana a couple of days prior and the two days-long trip from New Orleans to the estate. I offered up my apologies that I would not be able to see her off come morning. She told me she understood and noted my pale complexion and suggested that perhaps I was becoming ill and required rest immediately.

Her mood had certainly changed after I gave her a small bag of coins as I had promised to do. She had become downright agreeable, almost pleasant.

At last, I had seen the last of Miss Josephine. Per our arrangement, she had left the following day, making the days-long journey by carriage to her newfound home in Virginia. She had left me a letter leaving me her forwarding address, which confused me. What was she expecting of me? More money? I thought, why would I need to be in contact with my deceased grandfather's much younger widow? I started questioning her sanity and morals at this point and shook my head in disgust. I picked up the paper, began tearing it up, and tossed it into the fireplace where I felt it belonged.

I waited a month for all the treasured antiques and paintings to arrive. One possession was the most prized, the portrait of Fabien. I instructed my servants to hang it on the wall inside my master bedroom. That way, it would be the last thing I gazed at before my undead slumber and the first thing I gazed upon as I awoke.

I walked around the enormous mansion with one of the servants, examining each artifact, and every painting, inspecting each room, and voicing my approval, much to my servant's relief. I felt at home in my new country and excited to explore this vibrant city with African, Island, and French influences.

I must have appeared as different to them as they seemed to me. I had never seen anyone as dark-skinned as my servants, nor had they witnessed anyone as pale as myself. It's doubtful that any of my servants would suspect they were living with one of the living dead.

I won't call them "slaves" as I loathe the word; I do not feel superior to them in any way. They are my servants, to serve me, but they were treated well and not physically abused. I felt grateful that they were there taking care of my needs, and eventually, I would need to confide in at least one of them and reveal my true self. That day would come sooner than I ever imagined.

It was a hot, humid summer night. The kind of weather that makes the air so heavy you could almost cut it with a knife.

Thinking I was alone in the back of the estate, I suddenly detected movement over by a bush. It was a Jackrabbit meandering around. I rushed over using my vampire speed and immediately seized it in my hands, tearing into its neck with my fangs as the blood ran down my throat. Unbeknownst to me, I was not alone; my trusty servant Barthelme stood nearby smoking and witnessed everything.

Barthelme was a big man who stood taller than me and hailed originally from Angola in Southern Africa. He had bulging biceps, was strong as an ox, and would surely make any woman swoon.

Suddenly, Barthelme cried out, "Master!"

I quickly dropped the dead Jackrabbit and instantly rushed over to him as I stood facing him. His eyes scanned my face anxiously as his mouth remained open in horror at my appearance seeing the blood smeared all over my mouth and chin and from what he had seen.

I sternly told him, "You are to tell no one about what you have witnessed this evening. Your very life may depend on it! Is that clear?"

His speech began to stammer. Ye Yes, Mastah! "Why is your mouth covered in blood? Are you injured? What has happened to this animal?" He inquired.

"Never mind, Barthelme!" I said. "You best not ask questions that you will later regret asking!" I warned. "I repeat, tell no one what you saw. Do you understand?" I commanded menacingly.

"Yes, Mastah," he replied.

I was curious about what Barthelme had witnessed, so I asked him directly, "Tell me, what exactly did you see, Barthelme?"

After a brief pause, he reluctantly answered, "I saw you bite an animal and saw blood smeared on your mouth," as he lowered his head.

I could have ended his life at that exact moment. Still, given my moral dilemma of indiscriminately killing, something Fabien forbade me to do, I let him live. Knowing I would need Barthelme as a trusted servant, I chose to employ a more controlled response.

I demanded Barthelme look deep into my eyes. I repeated the command over and over again. "You saw nothing; you saw nothing!" as I began to hypnotize him into forgetting.

Then asking Barthelme, once again, if he had witnessed anything strange that evening.

"No, nothing I can remember, Mastah!" Barthelme replied and shrugged. After a brief silence, he said, "Mastah Laurent, May I be excused? I still got some chores to finish up."

"Yes, you can leave," I said, disinterested and slightly annoyed.

However, it was too late. The seeds of doubt and mistrust had been planted. I thought, how could I trust Barthelme? I decided I would need to turn him into my immortal servant. He would be my protector and gatekeeper and someone sworn to me with undying loyalty.

The next evening, I decided to summon Barthelme telepathically; he would have no control over his thoughts or actions and would hear my voice call out to him in his mind. I would beckon him to the vast mansion, where I would anxiously await his arrival.

He arrived holding his hat, the sun had just set, and I could see Barthelme's clothes had become stained due to the day's fierce summer sun and heat.

"You wanted to see me, Mastah Laurent," he sheepishly asked.

"Yes, Barthelme, follow me into the drawing-room," I said.

We entered the drawing-room with Barthelme trailing behind me.

"Mastah, what was it you wanted to speak to me about?" he asked.

I paced around the room a bit before giving him my answer. After a brief pause, I said, "Barthelme, I feel the only way I can trust you completely is to have you as my immortal servant and under my control. Rather than destroy you for what you witnessed, it is the only way. I need you, Barthelme."

"I don't understand Mastah, immortal servant?" he asked.

I knew by biting him, he would live much longer than a mere mortal and never grow old or prone to sickness. I would need a servant sworn to secrecy guarding my dark secret. I told him to remove his shirt. I would bite Barthelme on the shoulder so that the two puncture wounds would not be visible to the rest of the servants.

"Take off your shirt Barthelme," I commanded.

He did as I instructed, revealing a muscular, chiseled chest with strong pectoral muscles and an abdomen that was hard as a rock. I leaned over and bit him, he seemed stunned at first, then struggled to escape my powerful embrace, but I was too strong for a mortal, even someone of Barthelme's build.

He tried to speak, but I held my hand over his mouth and finally ceased trying to escape. I drank only a little bit of his blood and bit into my wrist and had him drink only a drop or two of my blood, making Barthelme my eternal human servant. Had I drained him to the point of his mortal death, and had he drunk my blood, he would have become a vampire like me. That was not my plan or intention. Shortly after that, I began hypnotism.

"Barthelme, you are growing tired, so tired you can barely stand up," I said. He slumped slightly in my arms. "Barthelme, I command you to secrecy; you will be my immortal servant, to guard against anyone who may wish to harm me, for I am your eternal Master. Do you understand?" I asked

"Yes, Master," he uttered in a hypnotic slow reply; his face remained expressionless.

"I am one of the living dead, a vampire; I require your services at all times.

During the day, I must sleep; and you must guard and protect me. Have I made myself clear, Barthelme?" I instructed sternly.

"Yes, Master, I swear to you my undying loyalty, your secret I will guard and defend with my life," he stated.

Barthelme kept his promise throughout the years, which brought us into the civil war between the states. The war ended in 1865; a proclamation order ended slavery; nevertheless, Barthelme stayed with me, as he had no choice, and quite suddenly, we approached the early 19th century.

CHAPTER 7

Just the two of us

(LAURENT NARRATES)

Nearly Seventy years had passed, and Barthelme and I witnessed many inventions of the 19th century. Everything from the steam engine trains that could transport a human from New Orleans to New York and electricity and, with that, the light bulb, although I chose to stay with candlelight; call me old fashioned. I allowed for only one modern invention, the telephone, necessary for Barthelme's dealings with the outside world.

There were other inventions, the telegraph, photography, and many more wondrous devices, one more spectacular than the other. Whenever someone asked to take my picture, I graciously declined and told them I was not very photogenic. Fortunately, that sufficed, with no one challenging my refusal. A vampire's image does not appear on film; anyone who would have taken a picture of me would not have believed their eyes and would have only seen what was captured on film in the background.

However, there was one thing that shook me to the core approximately thirty years later, when, in 1897, a book by the name of "Dracula," was written by the Irish author Bram Stoker.

The book tells the fictional story of a Romanian Count, the king of all vampires, who existed amongst ordinary humans. Naturally, my curiosity got the better of me. I read it, and truthfully, it alarmed me as many individuals started believing in the Paranormal. If society was beginning to believe in the existence of ghosts, then why wouldn't they start believing in vampires?

I knew after having seen Fabien's spirit that ghosts do exist. I wondered how many would believe in vampires after reading "Dracula," and if any of these same individuals crossed paths with me, how many would think me to be as odd as the Count portrayed in the novel? I decided to stay extra cautious and not expose myself to the public. Ironic as it may seem, many things that Bram Stoker wrote about in his book were correct. I thought, *was this man a psychic? A shaman, perhaps? How could he know such intimate details about our kind?*

Every description in the book was accurate and included the two puncture wounds left on someone's neck once the vampire has bitten them, the vampire's ability to change into a wolf, bat, or mist, and many other highly accurate descriptions.

I suspect the author had perhaps come into contact with someone of our kind. While the book was described as fiction, there was factual reporting of the infamous Count, who had the invading Turkish troops from the Ottoman Empire impaled on large spears. And legend has it; he bathed himself in blood! Something that intrigued and delighted me all at once.

The years kept melting away, and my loneliness for companionship grew to become intolerable. I knew I needed to get out of my relative seclusion.

Barthelme was a poor excuse for a companion. After putting him under my control nearly a hundred years prior, he hadn't aged physically and looked the same as he appeared the day I turned him into my eternal human servant.

He was an excellent gatekeeper and dealt with anyone looking for me unexpectedly. Barthelme was instructed to tell whoever had stopped by that I was away on business. It did take nearly four or five days to reach New York or Boston, so most did not question my absence whenever someone would come to call.

As suddenly as the nineteenth century arrived, it departed, and I found myself and my trusty servant in the late twentieth century. The year was Nineteen hundred and eighty-three. I had resided in Vacherie, just outside New Orleans, for nearly One hundred and eighty-seven years. Despite the numerous television shows and movies about vampires, which concerned and amused me simultaneously, I needed to get out of my seclusion and partake in some of the city's attractions. Barthelme became my driver and often drove me into town. On occasion, I had thought about the possibility of Stefan tracking me down; I knew I would need more than my vampire skills to defend myself against him, as that alone would not suffice.

I became intrigued with the ancient Martial Arts of the Far East. I decided to locate a Martial Arts Academy to learn the art of hand-to-hand self-defense. I enrolled in a nightly class in the ancient Japanese art of Karate. My speed and agility impressed my instructor, as did my hand and eye coordination. I quickly adapted to accelerated training, fearing Stefan would show up at any moment looking to fulfill his promise of my destruction. I would be ready for him to make good on his threat.

A few months later, I earned a second-degree black belt. I not only enjoyed getting out of the confines of my secluded estate, but training in hand-to-hand combat gave me confidence and made me feel less vulnerable and better able to sustain an attack by Stefan. When I was not training at the academy, my other passion involved attending the many jazz clubs in town, where I would be seated at a dark table near the back.

Each Friday night, Barthelme dropped me off in the center of the city near any one of the many jazz clubs. I could not operate a motorized vehicle and am still trying to understand the automobile's concept. In the present day, they are referred to as "cars" instead of the horse and carriage of my day.

I quickly became very fond of jazz. It seemed captivating, a brilliant mix of instruments, horns, strings, and typically a sultry vocalist to accompany the band. Listening to this music made it seem as if the melody of the instruments and vocalist had transcended deep within my soul. I made it a point to visit all the long-time jazz bars, including "Snug Harbor," "the Bombay Club," and "Preservation Hall."

I did not ask Barthelme to join me as I wanted to be alone, to listen and contemplate my existence, and lose myself in the music entirely. Besides, would he not think it strange to accompany me as if we were on a romantic interlude? Barthelme accepted my preference for male company, but I couldn't picture him and me attending anything out in public together.

The very thought of that made me laugh. Not that Barthelme wasn't engaging; I hired some of the most exceptional tutors in

Louisiana to instruct Barthelme so he could master the English language so that he and I would be able to converse in English. As for my teachings, I decided to study English through "Berlitz," audiotapes and booklets designed to help those like me learn a particular language. Barthelme had secured a modern device called a tape recorder and fortunately one that ran on batteries; I used it to listen to the instruction material, and quickly mastered control of the English language.

Once a week, usually on a Friday, I was driven into town by Barthelme. I marveled at the world around me and wondered what Fabien would have thought of all these modern-day human-made inventions. I could only imagine! Oh, how I missed him! It had been so long since I had any male companionship and embraced another male and felt the taut muscles, not to mention the deep bond that can exist between two men.

As for finding any male companionship, I frown upon casual sexual encounters or "hookups," as it's referred to in the present day, which means meeting a gentlemen caller purely for sex.

Of course, I appreciate physical interaction and even longed for it. However, there was something brutishly animalistic in today's world about meeting a man. Most of the emphasis was on the sexual rather than genuinely trying to connect with another individual. I had frequented some gentlemen's saloons, known as "Gay bars," listening to whatever recording artist was famous. I thought how truly awful! Is this music?

And how awkward was the approach of many gentlemen in these establishments? I was propositioned for sex many times, and I declined their advances each time.

Rather than face endless encounters such as these, I decided to avoid these bars altogether in place of the jazz clubs, which primarily men and women frequented; at least at these establishments, there appeared to be a Decorum.

I was hopeful that at some point in my existence, I would find a companion who, once they learned of my dark secret, would invite me to turn him so that he and I would be together for eternity. I was still determining what to expect and how soon the situation might present itself.

CHAPTER 8

Jack's story

(JACK NARRATES)

When I was growing up in Baton Rouge, Louisiana, in the 1960s, a man couldn't live openly as a gay man. I knew I was different, but I strived desperately, not just to hide but also to change who I was. I tried to dominate my two brothers, Neal and Joe besting them in wrestling and other forms of hand-to-hand combat. My father taught me how to box and told me, "He didn't want his son to become a 'sissy'!"

My father, Frederick was an injury attorney and aspiring politician running on a "family values" campaign platform. He typically railed against the "queers" and them wanting "special rights" such as protection in the workplace and housing. I figured that helped contribute to my self-loathing of myself while my mother Florence largely ignored his rants and was a full-time stay at home mother who focused on being a loving wife and mother to us three boys.

But I always knew the story of my life would be different from his. My earliest recollection of being different was in junior high. I would furiously try not to look too long at my classmates as they undressed after gym class, especially when we all took showers together. I was hell-bent on fighting that desire to watch and diving headfirst into passing for a straight guy.

I joined the football team at my high school, hoping that would change things and toughen me up, making me more of a man. So, I decided to try out, and became a linebacker. I was athletically blessed, with good hand-eye coordination, speed, and a muscular body. I became a football player, but the physical attraction to other guys remained.

You might ask, did I have any experiences with girls? Of course, I had girlfriends, I even had what you might describe as enjoyable sex with them, but what was lacking was the emotional connection. I remember making out with girls in the backseat of my dad's car, imagining that they were any of the hot guys on the football team.

As a good Roman Catholic, I prayed to God every night that the attraction to my sex was only a phase and that I soon blossomed into a complete man with carnal desires for women.

I wasn't fond of stereotypes and wanted to distance myself from all the myths of what a gay man looked and sounded like. Whenever I saw a gay male character on television or in the movies, it negatively portrayed a swishy and effeminate character. Seeing that made me hate myself that much more. I guess you can thank my good old-fashioned southern upbringing for that. Some would say I was a self-loathing gay, and I wouldn't dispute that. I would ask myself, why *has God done this to me? Am I being tested in my faith?*

I convinced myself that no one, including family and close friends, suspected anything, as my voice was deep and masculine, and I didn't display any effeminate behavior. And while I cared about fashion and looking good, I wasn't obsessed with fancy clothes and didn't groom myself in front of a mirror for hours. Despite having done well financially, our family didn't provide me with much money for clothes anyway.

When I graduated from high school, I went out with my straight friends to straight bars, where I received attention from women. I treated heterosexual encounters like a game, but they equally played with my feelings and mainly I became their sexual toy. I thought foolishly that if I slept with many women, my feelings of loneliness and not belonging would go away and that I could bury the pain of hurt and isolation.

I knew I couldn't stay with my family in the confines of Baton Rouge. I wanted my freedom; I wanted to move to a place where I knew no one, and no one knew me, and I would be free to live my own life and follow my desires. I decided to move to the Big Easy, the big and bawdy city of New Orleans, where I could act upon my urges and satisfy my hunger for encounters with men.

I quickly discovered how the city lived up to its name. I slept with whoever I wanted without fear my family would find out. My sexual encounters were with both men and women. For a while, I called myself bisexual, which was more comfortable for my mind, which had been polluted with narrow-minded thinking and religious strictures to accept myself as gay, thanks to my father.

Whenever I found myself in bed with a man, the guilt was so intense that I hated myself. To ease my mind, I held off on any further gay encounters; I decided I needed to "stabilize" my life, which meant sleeping only with women, at least for a while.

I wasn't looking for a relationship, but the relationship found me. I met Lisa at Maison Bourbon, a jazz club and a local and tourist hangout on Bourbon Street, where many liquored-up men and women listened to great jazz.

Lisa was sitting at the bar with a couple of girlfriends. Her laugh was what drew me to her; it was intoxicating. I heard it across the bar. I looked in her direction, and our eyes met and locked; I nodded, and she winked at me. I got up and walked to the table where she and another woman were seated. I attempted some bad humor, introduced myself as Jack, and said I wasn't looking for three's company. She gave me her name. She was attractive enough, big smile, strawberry-blonde hair, and pale blue eyes. She asked me to join them at their table, which I did.

The evening progressed. The girlfriend sensed that Lisa and I were beginning to make a connection, and she politely excused herself and left.

Lisa loved to hear me tell jokes, and yeah, I'll admit they were terrible, but somehow Lisa found me interesting. I felt comfortable around her. For once, I didn't feel like I was being lusted after just for my looks. I thought of Lisa as a friend, even if she might have been my sister, but Lisa was starting to develop serious feelings for me. If truth be told, I did lead her on. I was only thinking of myself, so I thought, what the hell? I tried to bury the gay part deep within myself, however tricky, as I was tempted daily by the men around me.

I pushed away the gay part of me daily, mainly through prayer. I can't tell you exactly how many times I had prayed to God to save me from becoming a queer, more times than you can imagine. My faith was essential to me; I believed, as I learned, that homosexuality was an abomination in the eyes of the Lord. In that context, no one ever told me that Jesus Christ had come not to condemn the world but to save it.

When I was with Lisa, it was like being with my best friend. The only problem was the sex. Poor Lisa, she thought I was impotent! When we were out, my eyes always searched the room, connecting with other men and some women. I could read their thoughts with a long glance or the wink of an eye.

On more than one occasion, I followed up with whoever provided me with their number. There were, in fact, a couple of times Lisa caught me in bed with a woman, with that, the same scenario played out every time; she would get upset, leave crying hysterically, scream and yell and tell me to "go to hell!" and that "I was no good!"

She always came back, begging for forgiveness. Lisa and I were evenly matched as far as self-loathing went. I figured, at the very least, Lisa would be a companion, and at least then, I wouldn't feel so lonely all the time.

I asked her to go steady and told her I would mend my ways and be a good boyfriend. I could finally announce to everyone that I had a regular girlfriend and that she might become my wife someday, hoping that would convince everyone that I was heterosexual. To that, I usually received hysterical laughter from friends. "What, you? The confirmed bachelor?" they would scoff.

Feeling that I had no choice, I asked Lisa to marry me after three months of dating. She was overjoyed and cried with happiness, but I felt as if my heart were breaking. I wanted to cry with her; only my tears would have been out of misery and self-loathing. I felt all the oxygen in the room go out and thought to myself, *what have I done?*

We set a date for a year later. I miraculously remained faithful during that time, as I had promised Lisa.

The date came, and we had the prominent Roman Catholic wedding at St. Louis Cathedral. At my father's insistence, it was a large wedding with over two hundred and fifty people in attendance. I'll never forget that day. It was a scorching, humid Louisiana summer day with dark storm clouds gathering in the sky, perhaps hinting at how rocky our marriage would become.

Lisa looked radiant in a white dress with a cathedral train. For one of the few times in my life I had on a tuxedo. It must have been the heat and humidity, combined with my nervousness that produced two armpit stains the size of small ponds under my arms. I put on my jacket to hide those unsightly stains. My father came over to me and said, "Son, I'm proud of you; congratulations, I thought you'd never marry!" To that, I feigned a smile and caught a glimpse of myself in the mirror, which made my heart sink. I told myself, *you'll probably be dead by the time you reach sixty because that's thirty-seven long, miserable years of living a lie with Lisa.*

Once we were married, our life dragged on; each day and night was the same as every other day, miserable. I was as strong as an ox, so I applied for a job in construction. The pay wasn't great, but more importantly, it helped me to feel like a real man. I mainly landed day jobs. Not going to college prevented me from getting a high-paying office job. I left the house early each morning at five to be on the construction site at six, grateful not to have any interaction with Lisa so early in the morning. She was usually still asleep when I left.

Lisa worked as a sales clerk at a local department store called Maison Blanche. We had little money, which made our marriage even more miserable. At night we would watch mindless television together, mostly family sitcoms and game shows, anything to avoid having to speak to one another. Whenever we interacted, we argued—mostly about money or lack thereof and about sex and lack thereof. I could only escape from her when I was asleep and dreaming; that was an escape into another world, away from Lisa. On occasion, I would have a nightmare, which sometimes involved flailing my arms around and almost hitting Lisa.

"Wake up!" she would yell. "You're having a nightmare!" Most often, she was annoyed that she had been so fiercely awakened.

"Perhaps you should lay off the Jack Daniels you drink every night before you come to bed before it destroys you and your liver, and maybe you wouldn't have bad dreams. Now turn the light off and go back to sleep. I have to get up early tomorrow," she said, settling back into a fetal position with her comforter wrapped snugly around her. The following day at work, guys on the construction site looked at me and said, "Man, you look like shit! Ain't you been gett'in any?"

"That's the least of it," I said.

"I guess I would be having bad dreams too if I was married to your wife," one of the workmen said.

"Knock it off, Rafael!" I said.

"Yeah? What are you gonna do about it, Jack? Sic your wife on me?" Rafael said, laughing.

I thought about what he was saying, and even though I was miserable being married to Lisa, he had no right to talk to me about her like that, especially around a group of guys on the site.

"Naw, I don't need my wife to deal with you!" I pretended to turn around and then suddenly twisted back towards him, my fist clenched, as I threw a punch which landed directly on the side of Rafael's eye. He landed on his ass with a bewildered look on his face. In a day or two he'd have a reminder in the form of a black eye, to respect me and not talk smack about me or my wife.

I have always been a good fighter and had my Dad to thank for that. *At least he had tried to do everything not to raise a sissy.* The guys separated us for a bit, and eventually, we returned to work, forgetting our emotional outburst.

My marriage to Lisa dragged on into days, weeks, months, and years. Except for one or two indiscretions, I had been mostly faithful for nearly an entire decade. Here I was, thirty-three and with nothing to show for it except a lousy construction job, a beat-up old wreck of a truck, and a wife I didn't love, living a lifestyle I had become more and more a stranger to. I couldn't take it any longer. I encouraged Lisa to visit her folks in Shreveport, and she jumped at the suggestion. I could finally take care of some much-needed and delayed business for myself. The only way I was going to hook up with another man was to go to one of the dreaded gay bars, filled with men who were there with their friends, who felt as if they connected. I felt connected to no one.

Looking around the first bar I went to, I made eye contact with this guy over by the pinball machine. I walked over and asked him if I could join him. We traded smiles, and I offered to buy him a beer. He told me his name was Sam and admitted to me as if he were confessing to a priest that he was also married and closeted. Sam had been married for five years. His being closeted was to be our bond beyond the physical attraction. Sam stood about five foot eleven inches tall, had a slight yet muscular build, and a boyishly handsome face, with blond hair and brown eyes. He must have been in his early thirties. We made small talk and had a few laughs as we played pinball. Once we finished, we went over to the back section of the bar, where it was a little quieter, and talked. He told me he liked sports but was also into the finer things. Sam liked art and music and was also into fashion. He described himself as "a renaissance man," which made me suppress a chuckle because it was clear to me that he was completely gay. Then again, who was I to judge him? My smirk disappeared from my face as quickly as it had come. With that, I put my hand on his thigh, rubbed it as he looked at me, and finally leaned over to kiss me.

We agreed to return to his place because his wife was out of town. He had a beautiful apartment in the French quarter. No sooner had we entered; than he suggested that I slip off my shoes and make myself comfortable. He gave me a beautiful smile. I knew the suggestion of slipping off the shoes meant we would be getting down to business—so I kicked off my shoes, and sure enough, we began to make out.

We made our way to the bedroom, a Laura Ashley flowering nightmare. I knew the household linens belonged to his wife, but even so! Sam had mistakenly left the television on, and a news broadcast showing President Reagan challenging another leader to "tear down this wall." I asked Sam if he could switch it off, as I felt the broadcast would interfere with our mood.

I don't know why those flowered sheets raised such hostility in me; I guess it was the idea that Sam's wife claimed that bed for her own, whereas I wanted it to belong entirely to Sam and me, with no female interference. I made it a point to get those flowering sheets as sweaty as possible! Call it a mission of mercy for Sam.

We got undressed. Sam's body was slender and muscular and a swimmer's build; although I don't think any swimming pools were involved, it was more likely regular trips to the gym. When I undressed, I told him to get ready to see fireworks. He laughed and begged me to show him. And I did.

I made my escape as soon as I started to hear Sam snore. I didn't like the awkwardness of small talk after a sexual conquest, and I didn't see myself as the cuddling type. If I wasn't going to do that with my wife, why would I do that with a stranger? I figured he had his wife to do that with.

When I returned home, I turned on the radio, and AC/DC's "Highway to Hell" blared out. I thought there couldn't be a more appropriate song to describe my current situation.

Lisa returned home the following week, exhausted from spending the entire weekend with her parents and two siblings. She was speaking to me, but I could only look past her. I didn't hear a word she said. It was as if I was in a trance.

"Are you paying attention to me, Jack Devereaux?" she asked, sounding annoyed, like a parent addressing a child who wasn't listening. I must admit; I probably suffered from some arrested development or, at the very least, a prolonged frat boy mentality while Lisa took on the role of the adult in our relationship, almost that of a parent.

About a week later, it came to a head. Lisa was making dinner for us, which involved heating dinner in the microwave. It occurred to me that Lisa and I had been married for ten years. I was so miserable! I couldn't take this charade any longer, despite my self-loathing and Catholic guilt. In addition to homosexuality being a sin in my faith, so was divorce. I couldn't help it. I had had enough of the lies, the denial, and the unhappiness. It felt as if I were leading two separate lives, which I was. I looked Lisa squarely in the eyes and said, "We need to talk."

"Jack, I'm a little busy at the moment, as you can see," she said with a frown. I reached for her hand, holding it and looking intensely at her with eyes wide with concern. She finally stopped what she was doing and asked, "About what?"

"Lisa, I'm unhappy, and I know you are too. Let's end this marriage before it kills either one of us!" I said, trying desperately to sound compassionate.

"I don't know what you're talking about, Jack, except that you're distracting me from making dinner for us," she said and pointed to the yet-unprepared frozen food she was holding.

"Lisa put the damn food down and listen to me!"

She looked at me puzzled and said, "I know one thing, Jack. I know you're no longer attracted to me!" her hands began to tremble as she continued fumbling with dinner. "We haven't had sex in over a month," she continued. I cut her off before she could finish. Brutally, I said, "That's right, Lisa, I haven't been attracted to you since our wedding night, and even then, I was thinking of someone else while we made love!" "Who, Jack? The waitress at the diner? Or some other slut you've been screwing around? I know you've had affairs, don't tell me you haven't!" she retorted.

"Lisa, I know you'll find this hard to accept, but it isn't another woman. It isn't any woman at all. I'm not sure I can accept this, yet this is true. Lisa, I'm gay." Lisa stared at me, unable to speak, so I went on. "For a long time, I've been lying to myself, trying to make myself think I was bisexual, but I've had to face the truth. I'm not bisexual; I'm gay."

Lisa dropped a frozen TV dinner on the floor. "What? You've got to be kidding me. You, the big athlete on the football team? The big bad macho construction worker? The same guy I caught several times screwing some slut in our bed? Don't make me laugh, Jack Devereaux! You're not gay."

"Lisa, this is hard to hear when we've been married for ten years, even if they haven't been the greatest ten years. I was in denial; I was lying to myself, so I ended up lying to you. I hated myself so much that I couldn't tell you or accept it myself."

Lisa sat down at the table across from me. I could tell she was beginning to believe what I was saying. "But I don't understand this, Jack. We had times in bed that were good. Okay, maybe not for a long time, but I never got the impression that you rejected my body. And now you're telling me you do. You're interested only in men. I'm finding this hard to grasp, Jack." But I'm done with that; I'm only going to say this one more time, listen. I am a homosexual; I like guys! I denied it for too long; I've fought it all my life! I always have been and always will be until the day I die. No woman on this earth can change that. Even if I wanted to, I couldn't change who I am! And I won't change!" "Dammit! Lisa, I'm thirty-five years old! It's time for me to live my life for myself. I can't take the lying, the deception, and the self-loathing any longer! It isn't fair to me and certainly isn't fair to you either!" I yelled.

"Stop it!" She said, "what about me? You son of a bitch! You mean to tell me I wasted ten years of my life with you? Cooking, cleaning, and loving a man sleeping next to a man who's not even a real man!"

With that, I saw red, and all my pent-up rage and anger became directed at her as I knocked the still-frozen container of food on the floor and yelled back, "shut up, Lisa!" She looked at me with disgust and spat out her words saying, "I hope you rot in hell Jack Devereaux!" She screamed. "Get out! Get out! Get out of my sight." I looked at her angrily and said, "I'll be out in the morning; just give me some time to pack up my stuff!" I suddenly thought how devastating this must be for her, "Lisa, I'm sorry! I'm sorry for hurting you!" I began to cry, "I didn't mean to. Do you remember the first time we met? Your laugh was what attracted me to you, your gentleness. I delighted in making you laugh; I tried Lisa. I tried!" I said, desperately reaching for any emotion beyond just anger. "Yeah, well, you should have thought of that before admitting you're gay. Instead, you've done anything but that, Jack.

Jack Devereaux, I want you to leave tonight! I can't bear to look at you; you disgust me," she said with a cold reply.

Wow! I hadn't thought about being thrown out of my own house; with that, I went into the bedroom, packed a few items into a suitcase, and left. I was leaving most of my possessions and Memories of my former straight life with Lisa behind.

I exited our front yard, trying to think of where I would go, and checked my wallet for cash. Fortunately, I had enough to stay in a cheap motel across town in the seedy part of the city. I had driven past it one day to a construction site. I got in my old wreck of a truck and started the ignition several times with no luck. *Wouldn't it figure?* I thought, so I got out and started walking. The humid night air was miserable; it took me nearly half an hour to reach the motel. I knew a reservation wasn't required.

The Stardust motel never looked as good as it welcomed me that night. I checked in and headed to my room. It was dated and tired-looking in the late nineteen sixties and early nineteen seventies design, but I didn't care. I barely had the strength to remove my clothes, leaving only my underwear on as I climbed into bed. I had a good night's rest and a night of dreamless sleep.

The following day, I went to work, hiding that my marriage had just ended; it wasn't their business to know. I did a full day's work and returned to the motel that night. I was sitting on the bed with just my underwear and socks on. Another head, other than the one on my shoulders, was thinking for me. I was horny and needed some company, desperate to have anyone by my side. The loneliness became unbearable. I decided it was time to get lucky. I hadn't had sex since my encounter with Sam and decided to make up for it.

So, I headed to another dreaded gay bar known as the "Golden Lantern" in the French quarter. If Sam were there, I would ignore him. The awkwardness of having a conversation with a past sexual encounter wasn't in the cards for me, as emotional intimacy with another man was alien to me. Call it too close for comfort. I guess I have my conservative Catholic upbringing to thank for that.

From the moment I walked in, I felt as if all eyes were on me, it didn't help that *"Like a Virgin"* was blaring in the bar. While I wasn't exactly a virgin to same-sex encounters, I was practically a virgin to going out and being seen in gay bars.

I felt as if I were doing something wrong, thinking, *what the hell have I done?* Just as I turned to leave, I stood there and asked myself, *then what, Jack?* I froze in my tracks, lost in thought.

To some who know me or think they know me, they might think I'm arrogant and self-centered, and while I certainly possess some of those traits, there is another side that I don't show too often, if ever—a shy and scared and insecure man at times, especially around other gay guys. Rather than strolling into the place in my usual way, I felt like an altar boy about to be molested by a priest or sheep to the slaughter. This bar had older men more secure in their sexual identity with the usual good-looking younger man hanging on their arms.

Making my way through the crowded club, I finally reached an empty chair at the bar. I asked the bartender for a shot of Jack Daniels, calling it my comfort drink. I saw the other guys checking me out and undressing me with their eyes until one of them walked over to me and said, "Hey there, Cowboy! You look like you're new around here?" *Cowboy?!* I thought to myself, *who the hell is this clown?* "Um, yeah, I don't get out much," I said disinterestedly, hoping he would take the hint and leave while I turned away from his gaze.

"Well now, Drew Phillips here, please to meet ya!" he extended his hand, which he kept extended while I continued to ignore him.

He finally withdrew his hand and said, "You can consider me one of the welcoming committee; we've been eyeing you since you entered the bar."

"Hey, Drew! I'm Jack,"

"Jack, what?" Drew said sarcastically. "Ain't you got a last name, Cowboy? Never mind, I guess you're playing hard to get." He continued, "Well, pleased to meet you, Jack! Can I buy you a drink?" He inquired. I saw him checking my body out as if he were buying a brand-new car. I was disgusted by this.

"Nope, I got one coming," I said as I continued my gaze toward the bar and away from his probing eyes.

"Say, I hope you don't mind me saying this, Jack, but those jeans fit you nicely!" He said as he whistled his approval.

Although he wasn't exactly a troll, modestly handsome enough, age mid to late forties, balding, with a slight beer gut, I thought, *I guess it does catch up with men of a certain age?* He and his come-on repulsed me.

"Hey, Jack! I've got a great idea. Why don't we leave this place and go somewhere you and I can get better acquainted?" He suggested excitedly. I think I held back a trace of vomit in my throat, hearing what he had just proposed as I cleared my voice and said, "Hey, drew, what's your rush, man? I just walked in the door; I haven't even gotten my damn drink yet?" I said, sounding agitated.

"Well, you see, Jack, I have this cute little place in the Bywater, and I've got plenty of booze, and I just scored some pot from one of my buddies here, I promise you we'll have a real good time Jack."

This guy was starting to annoy me. All I needed was a little time to think. Besides, if there were someone in the bar that I wanted to hook up with, it certainly wouldn't be with this character.

"Look! Drew, is it? What are you not understanding?"

As I turned to face him while raising my voice, "why don't you knock it off? I told you I'm waiting for my drink; besides, you're not my type!" I said and turned around to face the bar.

"Hey, Jack, relax!" he retorted sarcastically.

"No, man, you relax!" I replied and shoved him hard as he staggered back and looked bewildered.

"Go to hell!" he said and turned to leave and rejoin his bar friends as I felt all eyes on me. I knew he and his buddies were talking about me.

"Hey loser, go to hell," he yelled from across the bar again, feeling like a big man amongst all his other bar buddies. I stood up, walked over to him and his group in a menacing way, and said, "You know what? You're a pathetic human being! Completely and utterly pathetic!" As I turned to walk out of the bar.

Once out on the street, it hit me. There I was, alone and still feeling horny as hell! Nothing but my growling stomach to remind me I hadn't eaten anything all day! Although, my being horny far outweighed the need for food. So, I decided to try my luck at another gay bar known to be a lot less pretentious. I proceeded to the Rawhide 2010, a couple of blocks from the other bar.

"The Rawhide," as locals called it, was a casual leather bar. Even though I wasn't into the leather scene, I felt like it would be more welcoming and not as prissy as some of the other gay bars in town, with the patrons stinking up the place with their Polo cologne and parading around in their polo shirts with the collar, turned up.

No, these were real men, just soap mixed with sweat and the smell of beer. I call that a manly bar.

As I entered, not one guy looked my way; I immediately felt relief. *I thought this was more like it*, where the guys aren't undressing you with their eyes the minute you walk through the door. There were plenty of hot guys there, but they were all involved in conversations, telling jokes, and laughing. A game of pool had started in the back of the bar, and it struck me as being the gay version of "Cheers," it felt natural, a bit dirty, and I felt entirely at home, probably for the first time ever in a gay bar.

"What can I get ya?" said the ruggedly handsome bartender dressed in leather from head to toe.

"A shot of Jack Daniels. I didn't get to finish my other drink at the last bar I was at."

"Coming up," he said as he poured my drink. "Here you go, man."

I shot him a grin, "cheers!" I said and drank it down in one gulp. "Hit me again!"

He gave me a look, grinned, and said, "You got it, boss." The bar was a casual place filled with ordinary-looking guys in every shape and size.

Suddenly, across the bar, I spotted the perfect male specimen; he looked about twenty-three, with blonde hair, tanned, an honest to goodness California surfer boy! He had one leg propped up on the cigarette vending machine, enjoying a smoke. I took my drink and walked over to him, and said, "Hey" he glanced at me and said, "Hey" as we stood there in an awkward silence. I took a large gulp of Jack Daniels, and decided to come up with something sure to make him laugh.

"I know this might sound like a cliché, but do you come here often?" I said with a grin.

He laughed and said, "Man, that line is as old and tired as some of the queens in this bar!"

We laughed which helped cut the tension.

"Yeah, ain't that the truth!" I replied. "So, what's a nice guy like you doing in a dump like this?"

He just shook his head as his perfectly styled blonde hair flowed from side to side.

"Man, will your clichés ever end?" He said teasingly with a wide grin. "Well, in answer to your question; it isn't to drink!" he suggestively shared.

"Naw?" My eyes narrowed to a squint as I said, "Isn't that a coincidence, me neither!" My reply and my self-assuredness seemed to arouse the hot surfer boy. He had the palest blue eyes I had ever seen, they seemed to dance with the light hitting his eyes.

"Look, I'm just gonna come out and say it; I find you incredibly hot, you're probably the hottest guy in this dump, and I want to take you back to my motel room to do wicked things to you!" I said with a sexy grin.

He looked somewhat surprised and said, "Whoa! Hold on. I don't even know your name. Besides, we just met?"

"Does it matter?" I asked, after a bit of silence, finally giving in. "Okay, I'll play along; my name is Jack Devereaux. Your turn!" I insisted.

"I'm Trey Jones"

"Guess you're not from around here," I asked.

He replied instantly. "No, I'm not. I'm a California boy. Originally from San Diego. I'm visiting my Aunt Grace, who moved out here with her husband a few years ago."

I sized him up before saying, "Well, nice to meet you, Trey!"

"Yeah, nice to meet you too, Jack Devereaux!" he replied.

"So, what's next, my friend?" I said and shot him a wide grin, hoping he'd catch my hint. He smiled that gorgeous California smile and revealed the whitest teeth I had ever seen! "You know what comes next. Let's get out of here!" he replied suggestively.

That's all I needed to hear as we left the bar with the heavy humid Louisiana night air hitting us like a wave crashing onto the shore. We walked together without saying a word, the sexual tension was so high you could cut it with a knife.

Coming upon a dark alley just around the corner from Bourbon Street, we were safely out of the public's sight as I threw him up against the wall as if he were a rag doll.

All the muscles strained against my tight short-sleeved shirt, the veins of my arms protruded as I kissed him passionately, finally ending my pent-up lust since the last rendezvous with Sam.

After what seemed an eternity, we both came up for air and spoke.

"Lead the way, Jack Devereaux!" he said breathlessly.

"Right this way Trey!" I replied.

We laughed, seizing on the moment's silliness, as we realized what I had just said rhymed.

The walk back to my motel was filled with anticipation. We walked on without a sound, only glancing at each other occasionally. Finally, arriving, we entered my room at the motel.

"Nice place you got here, Jack!" He said sarcastically as we laughed.

I picked him up and kissed him, after a couple of minutes I threw him on the bed as if he were light as a feather. We wrestled and squirmed with our clothes on for several minutes as I quickly overpowered him and pinned him down on the bed. He looked up at me innocently and said calmly, almost purring his words, "So what are you going to do to me?" Sensing the size difference between us and my being so much larger, I answered back, "Everything and anything I can!" as I felt the adrenaline rush of intense sexual attraction. I ripped his clothes off in seconds which displayed a small speedo tan line. He had smooth legs and a light dusting of blonde hair on each of his legs, except for two small patches of dirty blonde hair under each armpit. I devoured him; every inch of him smelled of cologne, sweat, and soap.

He responded by moaning, which enticed me even more. I always got off on hearing my sexual partners moan with pleasure.

"Yeah, that's it! That's it!" He said.

After three hours of doing everything imaginable and after having explored each other's bodies, we collapsed into each other's arms.

"Damn, Jack, you're incredibly hot!" he said.

He heaped on the praise. It felt good to feel wanted, if only in a physical way.

I laughed and said in an empty hollow-sounding voice, "Thanks," feeling embarrassed, at which point I could no longer connect with his admiring eyes. He sensed my distance.

"Hey, cat, got your tongue?" he asked playfully. I remained silent.

"Hey, what's on your mind, Jack?" he asked, genuinely concerned.

I shook my head and said, "I'd rather not talk about it, Trey. It's a bit complicated; you wouldn't understand!"

But he kept pressing me as he propped himself on a pillow on the bed. "Yeah? Try me." I looked at him and feigned a smile, and turned away.

"Come on, Jack, you might feel better!" he said.

I'd become increasingly agitated at this point and felt like he was prying. After a brief silence, I said, "Okay, here it is, Trey. I just separated from my wife of ten years, ten long wasted years of my life and hers. I'm a practicing Roman Catholic and self-loathing homosexual. Even though I find you incredibly hot, and we had an amazing time, I want to be left alone! Now, aren't you sorry you asked?" I said and continued to avoid his gaze. After a couple of minutes, I said, "I think it would be best if you were to leave."

He began to frown; I could sense it without even looking at him.

"Why?" He asked, "Talk about making a guy feel cheap!" He said resentfully with a forced laugh. I finally managed to look him in the eyes and said, "Look, I'm sorry, you're a real nice guy. I need some space right now; here's twenty dollars for a cab" I reached for my wallet and handed him the money as he began to protest.

"I don't want your damn money, Jack! I want to stay with you a little longer," he said.

"I don't think that's a good idea, Trey; I think you better leave," I insisted.

"Give me a reason why?" He pleaded.

"Do it! Don't ask me why. I don't owe you a damn reason! Do you hear me? Leave! Before I throw you out!" suddenly, I became violently angry.

"But I don't understand. What did I do? Okay, fine. Have it your way. I'll leave." He said, sounding offended and hurt. "You know what, Jack? Go to hell!" Trey said as he got up, dressed in record time, and left, storming out the door without closing it.

I thought about what Trey had said as I uttered to an empty room, "Yeah, too late, kid. I'm already living in hell!"

Once more, I found myself alone and abandoned; the worst part was it was my doing. A flash of lightning and a loud crackle of thunder came from outside the motel window.

I sat on the bed, feeling like I was the last person on the earth's face. It all seemed too much to bear. I broke down and began to cry. I hated to cry. It made me feel weak and vulnerable; the last thing my Dad would have wanted to see was his son crying like a sissy. I couldn't remember the last time I shed a tear. Still, these emotions hit me like a tidal wave, and I felt powerless to stop the tears from falling. I quickly became a blubbering mess!

Images came flooding into my mind and my high school days on the football team, then meeting Lisa for the first time, all the affairs with other married, self-loathing Bi and Gay men. All my pent-up emotions were coming out at once. As soon as the tears subsided, my sadness was replaced by anger, in the form of my fist going through the cheaply made wall of my motel room.

It made a sound so loud that it woke up one of the neighboring occupants. They yelled, "Knock it off next door, or we'll call the manager!"

I asked myself, *Is this what my life as a gay man was to be like? To live alone and seek out other men only to be filled with self-hatred every time afterward?*

I couldn't stomach the thought, this almost animal-like urge that I hadn't felt with a woman before. I enjoyed the physical contact with men, all except for the afterglow. There wasn't any; it was more a feeling of guilt than anything.

Whenever I hooked up with a guy, I felt as if I'd let my Dad down and his attempts to prevent me from growing up to be gay.

That and the guilt in knowing God must see me as an abomination merely for these urges. All that was left was self-hatred, loathing, and the empty feeling as if I were some sexual deviant. An unclean animal performing sexual acts and living a lifestyle that most of society despised!

I felt a tremendous amount of sadness for Lisa. She must have felt stunned and empty when I came out to her. It certainly didn't help me feel better about myself or how I had left things with her.

I walked into the bathroom and stepped into the shower; the hot water felt good on my skin. I lathered myself from head to toe at least twice, never feeling clean.

I stepped out of the shower, toweled myself off, and glanced at my reflection, seeing the chiseled chest, six-pack abs, and bulging muscles, and thought, *how can someone so good-looking be so utterly messed up in the head?*

I was too tired to dwell on those feelings and crashed into bed. As I lay there staring at the ceiling, I heard the sound of rain hitting the roof of the motel, which to me sounded almost hypnotic, and calmed me as I drifted off to sleep. The thunder awakened me with a jolt, along with someone honking their horn outside the parking lot. I quickly realized how pathetic my life had become, staying in a dump of a motel. I felt guilty and disgusting and that my life meant nothing to me.

To make matters worse, I was without a life partner, and my truck was out of commission. I was in a sorry state. I couldn't stay in my room any longer without going entirely insane.

I glanced at my alarm clock sitting on the nightstand next to my bed; it read midnight; I thought *the witching hour.*

I knew it was late, but I didn't care. I had to go back out and find somewhere or someone to get my mind off my pathetic and lonely existence.

At the very least, the bars stay open until two in the morning, but I decided to skip the gay bars; my Catholic guilt had messed with my head for too long. I returned to my comfort zone, the straight jazz clubs I had frequented in the not-too-distant past.

I thought, *who knows? Maybe I could hook up with the right woman? Perhaps I could bury the gay deep within me one last time? Perhaps they were right after all? Maybe I just hadn't "met the right woman" to be able to "change me" into the man I dreamed of being, a straight guy!* Just before dawn, I paid a visit to a club called "Snug Harbor." Little did I know a chance encounter with a mysterious stranger there would alter my life and destiny forever!

CHAPTER 9

Haiti's queen

(RAPHAELLA NARRATES)

For the record, let me state I am not royalty, or at least I don't think I'm related to anyone of importance, so I'm not technically a Queen. It's just a nickname my parents gave me growing up in Port de Paix on Haiti's island.

My parents would kid me and say, "I think we gave birth to a Queen. You sure she belongs to us?!"

I always thought I came from the wrong family, feeling as if I didn't belong in my surroundings or perhaps was born into the wrong body.

Life in Port de Paix was difficult; in English, it means port of peace, although my childhood was anything but peaceful! My family came to the island of Haiti from Africa, specifically Senegal, in the nineteen sixties to escape extreme poverty for somewhat less. I describe it as substituting one living Hell for another. My father Ayomide (his name means happiness is coming) was an alcoholic; my father never fully lived up to his name's meaning.

We were dirt poor, as most of our village was, and poverty was a way of life for my family. My father worked the sugar cane fields with my mother, Asha; they toiled away ten to twelve hours a day in the hot Caribbean sun when he was sober enough to stand.

I was often left alone in our palm-thatched mud hut when I wasn't in school. Even though my parents had left me alone, or so they thought. Some visitors entertained me, and some frightened me. Of course, I was too young to understand the gift I possessed; I would learn as I got older it was the ability to connect with the "other world."

How shall I say this? You might describe me as a medium; everyone at the time assumed I was conversing with myself. When I spoke with "the other side," the dearly departed, ghosts, spirits, or whatever you want to call these often-conflicted disembodied souls, they would appear before me and tell me to warn someone, avenge their passing, or appear to talk with someone even someone as young as myself. I wasn't frightened most of the time, but there were those tortured souls so overcome with their grief and anger that it was difficult, if not impossible, to look at them. Their contorted faces showed their anger and some dark energy, which was too much to bear at times! Sometimes I would scream at them, "Go away! Go back to where you came from!"

Some entities would taunt me; others would leave out of mutual respect. Some possessed powerful and frightening energy, which included opening doors, windows, and cabinets. When they were upset, they would throw objects across the hut. Any number of cups and dishes would smash against the walls. I quickly cleaned up each mess they had made before my parents came home. Many remained calm, simply not wanting to be forgotten.

Once my parents came home after a long day of tending the fields, they would shake their heads and look at me, saying, "What has the Queen been up to while we were gone?"

I replied, "Just talking,"

My parents wouldn't understand if I told them. They were devout Catholics and were converted by missionaries back in Senegal. I never considered myself to be very religious, more spiritual than anything. It was easier for me to imagine somehow a spirit world or "other side" than it was to envision Heaven or Hell. I thought, if Hell truly exists, then we are living it!

You might ask, had I ever seen an angel? Unfortunately, I never did, despite my Catholic upbringing. As I grew to be a teenager, my fascination with the supernatural intensified, and I felt I needed to explore all the realms of the occult.

My interest expanded into Voodoo; what island teenagers on Haiti hadn't dreamt about raising a dead person's body? I would attend these groups, usually calling on a recently deceased villager or loved one. We tried desperately to make a spirit appear.

We would cast spells using an object called a "pentagram," drawn on a piece of paper, with candles placed carefully at the corners, with a purple one at the top, then a blue, green, red, and white one. An object was placed in the middle, and ash was sprinkled around it; once the candles were lit, we would think about a deceased person. We meditated for five to ten minutes as we all chanted in unison, "I call to the spirits; I call to the dead let me see my dear again. I call to thee to come to me to reunite once more. I wish to see whom I seek and miss so much."

Eventually, we progressed to using a recently deceased body and tried to resurrect it; in essence, we became grave robbers, not looking for valuables other than the body itself. We mostly failed until one incredibly humid summer evening. I managed to reanimate a dead body! A zombie is a, a non-thinking, non-feeling corpse missing its soul. One time, we got it to rise and fell to the ground after a few minutes. The fact that I had brought a corpse back to life was a miracle! I could barely contain my joy, not to mention my smugness with my ever-increasing supernatural abilities.

"Well, look at that! The Queen has resurrected a dead body!" one of the group members said. That was the nickname I was given, "the Queen."

I considered most of the group my friends except for one; she was a sworn enemy; her name was Fabiola.

"Quiet!" I commanded as she and the others shuddered; I knew Fabiola's abilities, as well as the ability of the others which didn't match my skills; I knew I frightened and intimidated her and took great delight in knowing that. I hated her! Fabiola was prettier than me, had many more male callers than I, and worst of all, her parents were esteemed and well respected in local government, not field workers like mine. Having an alcoholic father made it even more unbearable!

There were so many things that irritated me about Fabiola. The other being her French was perfect! Her instructor was someone from Paris! My, what affluence and power can get you! But I knew I had this psychic talent, which made me feel special.

I felt, eventually, I would make something of myself and strengthen my gifts and put them to good use, while poor Fabiola only had her looks, and those would fade with time. She would be stuck on this miserable island for the rest of her life and hopefully marry an alcoholic field worker like my father was; she deserved no better!

One day catastrophe hit our island as if life hadn't been miserable enough. A health epidemic called "AIDS" (acquired autoimmune deficiency syndrome) had arrived.

We had heard news reports from America describing a disease described as "Gay cancer," which hit large metropolitan cities such as New York, Los Angeles, and San Francisco. It was contracted by mainly homosexuals and intravenous drug users.

Our people, or at least the vast majority, were neither. How wrong we were to assume the disease would limit itself to only those two groups of people as the disease started spreading into the heterosexual community.

Our island became infected relatively fast and soon became a pariah. Tourism died, as did a significant portion of islanders.

Shortly after the official announcement in our respected newspaper, "Le Nouvelliste," Haiti's most prominent newspaper publication, the headline across the front page read, "La est arrive en Haiti!" (AIDS has arrived in Haiti!)

I'll never forget the day my father was afflicted with a mysterious fever and purple lesions that had formed on his back, shoulders, and legs. At first, my mother and I thought Father was working too hard and that the purplish blotches that covered his legs were due to extreme sun exposure. My mother demanded to know what was going on and insisted my father go to a local doctor, which for us, was in Port Au Prince, the capital city.

My father begrudgingly agreed.

Our local doctor seemed perplexed and strongly urged my father to seek treatment in a hospital. We visited him a few days after his admission.

The attending doctor, originally from France, came to help our besieged island and diagnosed my father with "AIDS." Which elsewhere had been called "gay cancer" even though my father wasn't gay.

The virus had spread from the US mainland and invaded our island, not caring who was gay or who was not.

My mother was naturally concerned for her husband and ignored some of her symptoms, which slowly began to appear and included swollen lymph glands and a fever.

My mother continued to provide my father with sexual pleasures, which I understood as sexual intercourse. Our doctor suggested my mother receive a test for HIV; she reluctantly agreed and tested positive. My world came crashing down all around.

I felt powerless despite my supernatural abilities. I thought if I was so "gifted," why didn't I see this coming?

I was angry and bitter; I shut myself off from everyone. I couldn't think clearly and could barely breathe to survive. I thought, what am I going to do? How will I care for my parents? With both sick, what will I do if I lose them? Both eventually ended up in L'hopital General in Port Au Prince, lying in beds side by side in the same room. As they lay next to each other, their hands were locked together.

Then came the day the unthinkable happened, my father passed away at two o'clock in the morning, clutching my mother's hand. Her hands showed his nail marks and how they had dug into her flesh during the last few breaths he'd taken before he died. My father professed to be a practicing Catholic; he truly believed he would go to "a better place" I hoped he would, as his life spent here on earth had been Hell. And as with some spouses who pass shortly after losing the other, so did my mother. She lost her battle with AIDS a week after my father died.

I decided at that moment that I needed to leave this wretched island, reimagine a new life for myself, and chart a new course for America. But where exactly? I had heard stories about the city of New Orleans and its inhabitants being of French, Caribbean, and Creole backgrounds. The city was quite historic and dated back to seventeen hundred and ten! I also learned about the Voodoo shops and the many paranormal experiences people experienced there. It intrigued me and drew me in by some unforeseen force. The fact that I had zero money to make this relocation possible made this impossible, at least temporarily. I knew I had to make money and make it fast. I did what most women do on our island when faced with a desperate situation. I resorted to prostitution.

I'm not proud of having sold my body for money. Yet, I was still young, with my body being supple and firm enough to entice a few privileged white men who dared to "take a walk on the wild side." Those rich men were the east coast men from New York, Boston, and Miami who wanted to have sex with a local woman, despite the health risks.

Remembering my late parents and how they died, I insisted on condom usage while engaging in sexual activity. I did not want to end up as they had become only becoming a vague memory to some, or worse, coming back as a ghost to haunt my surroundings.

After my grieving process, I somehow found the strength to go on without my parents and envision a new life. I was still in my late twenties and reasonably attractive.

While I entertained men for sex, I wasn't cheap. I demanded a high price, which they eagerly agreed to pay.

Whenever I encountered even the slightest protest from any men trying to pay more for unprotected sex, I reminded them that AIDS was a fatal disease that had run rampant on our island and that I had lost my parents to the dreaded disease. They reluctantly agreed, as they tugged, pulled, licked, and penetrated me as I kept dreaming of my new life; looking past their lustful gazes, I kept thinking about my escape, my new life. The truth is, it was sheer torture! I hated feeling like a sex slave. Being forced to do unspeakable acts made me hate myself. They considered me more of a sex toy rather than a human being with feelings.

Finally, a year passed, and I had had enough! A particularly obese businessman, with foul-smelling breath and ill-fitting trousers, came into my hotel room in Port Au Prince, forcing himself upon me, wanting a sexual encounter. I knew I had saved quite a lot of money to transition to my new life, as I had been entertaining primarily rich white men and had thought about quitting.

This bloated pig wanted to have unprotected sex with me and insisted on not using condoms, despite my warning him of AIDS. Still, he insisted and wouldn't take no for an answer! I snapped; I couldn't take it any longer. I told him "to go to hell" and pulled out a six-inch knife I'd carried for protection. I threatened to kill him if he didn't leave immediately, and told him I didn't need his stinking money!

Haitian women are known to be tough, and I was no exception. I had never used my trusty knife before, which I had nicknamed "Jacques," but this experience with that pig had hit a new low, and I was quite prepared to use it, which ended my yearlong profession as a high-paid prostitute.

The following day I decided to visit the "Bank de la Republique," Haiti's central bank, where I had opened a savings account only a year prior and accumulated a healthy portion of the money. Later, I would purchase a one-way air ticket to New Orleans at a local travel agency.

The city beckoned me as a lover might. Once there, I knew I would make all my dreams come true and start a new life in this exotic city, which seemed unique in many ways.

As I arrived at the bank, I could hardly contain my excitement. I was in disbelief that I was finally leaving this wretched island, with all its poverty and this disease running rampant, taking my parents with it.

I thought, why didn't their spirits come to me? Why have I been cursed with this "gift" of seeing other entities, not my parents, telling me they had passed to the other side? I felt alone and abandoned but determined to start a new life in America. The land of opportunity, fame, and fortune. I held my head high as I walked into the bank.

A well-dressed woman by the name of Monique assisted me in closing out my bank account. I had saved nearly thirty thousand dollars, giving me enough money to pay for my one-way plane ticket and have more than enough to pay for rent and food until I landed a job somewhere. I had her issue my withdrawn savings in a cashier's check, which I would cash once I arrived in my new city of New Orleans.

The following day I visited the travel agency in town and paid them for a one-way ticket to New Orleans. As luck would have it, one seat remained on board the DC-10 aircraft.

I returned to the hotel room I had used to entertain my customers, packed all my worldly possessions, headed to the airport via a taxi, and boarded the plane. No sooner had I been seated, the engines started to moan and grew louder as the big silver bird took flight shortly after that. As I glanced out the window, muttering a final goodbye to my island under my breath, I shed a single tear thinking of the friends I was leaving behind.

I closed my eyes and tried to rest on the relatively short flight to Miami, which lasted a little over two hours.

I opened my eyes as the airline captain announced some expected turbulence was about to occur and looked over at the empty seat next to me. I couldn't believe my eyes! There she was, my deceased mother! I stared at her and struggled to find the words, any words; she merely smiled and said these words to me,

"Go forth into the world knowing that your father, I, and all of your relatives have passed over to the other side. Help those struggling and feeling anguished, both the living and the dead, as you have a special gift, my child, and you must share it."

Those were her last words; as she slowly vanished, I didn't even have the chance to tell her how much I loved and missed her and my father. Due to the turbulence, I drifted into a deep sleep with the aircraft's rocking motion. I was abruptly awakened by the Captain's announcement that we were preparing to land and that everyone must take their seats and buckle their seat belts.

My flight landed in Miami. I would need to clear customs there to enter the US. I took out all the identification papers and my passport, and the necessary paperwork documenting my recent HIV testing status, which was negative. This procedure was a current requirement as the US authorities carefully screened Haitians as a potential risk of spreading AIDS.

I passed through US customs without any delay. The US customs authorities were welcoming as they searched my bags, possibly for drugs, which they didn't come across. Not even an aspirin!

My connecting flight to New Orleans got delayed due to a storm approaching New Orleans. I wondered if this was a foretelling of my life in my new city. I decided to find the nearest bar as I had two hours to kill before my flight departed.

I sat down at the bar and ordered a Mai Tai; I had never had one before and felt like a tourist on a tropical holiday. I asked the bartender for an extra shot of rum, and he winked at me and assured me the drink would be to my liking. He was right; it was delicious. I decided I needed another, which led to a third.

Finally, it was time to board the connecting flight to New Orleans; I stood in line or, should I say, attempted to stand because of the three Mai Tai's I'd drunk at the bar just a short time ago. I figured they were starting to take effect.

I presented my ticket with a boarding pass attached to my airline ticket, stepped onto the aircraft feeling slightly dizzy from the Mai Tai's, and settled into my seat for the two-hour flight, drifting off to sleep. This time the plane ride was as smooth as glass, having waited for stable weather patterns to return.

We landed at Louis Armstrong International airport in New Orleans as I witnessed the most radiant sun that was about to set; the sky was ablaze with red and purple colors announcing the arrival of twilight. I could hardly believe my eyes. Euphoria swept over me as I disembarked the plane. Once my feet hit the pavement, I knelt down and kissed the ground, and celebrated my arrival to my new home and new beginning.

I quickly retrieved my bags, heading outside where the cabs were gathered as they awaited passengers to take them into the city and beyond. The cab driver pulled up, asked me where to go. I had no idea; I didn't have a reservation for a hotel, not even at a motel.

I asked the driver if he were a native of the city and if he could recommend a place. He asked me what my budget was, I told him low, extremely low. He suggested the Stardust motel; I figured that would do until I found an apartment for rent.

As we made our way into the city center, a group of protestors had gathered and shouted, "Fight AIDS, not people!" "What do we want?!" "AIDS funding!" "When do we want it?" "Now!" "Act up, fight back!" "Fight AIDS!" Another foretelling, I thought. Was I being greeted by a group of protestors after having just emigrating from AIDS-infested Haiti? It seemed all so surreal to me.

The car pulled into the Stardust motel's parking lot as I spotted a good-looking man checking in at the reception desk. A tall man who appeared to have a muscular build. I paid the cab driver and thanked him for his recommendation. He made a pass at me and asked if he could call me. I was shocked! Was this man expecting a sexual favor for merely suggesting somewhere to stay in New Orleans? Somehow I got the impression this guy might be married?

I yelled, "No!" As I gave him a dirty look. He sped off, but not before he shot me the middle finger. I had seen tourists in my native Haiti do this with their hands and quickly learned what that gesture meant. I shook my head and went inside to inquire about a room. As I approached the reception desk, the tall, good-looking man I'd seen a few minutes ago had already left. I got the strangest feeling that I would be seeing him again.

A sixty-something man at the reception desk looked up without speaking to me. I politely asked if he had a room available.

"Yup!" was his response coldly.

"Well then, how much is the room per night, and do you have a weekly rate, just in case I need to stay for a bit?" I asked.

"Thirty-five dollars a night or two hundred and forty-five dollars a week," he answered. I told him I would take the weekly rate.

"You have a funny accent; where ya from?" He said as he squinted his eyes, and looked me over suspiciously.

"I'm from Haiti. I just arrived today," I replied, looking toward the ground. Why had I allowed this overweight man, with perhaps the education of a nine-year-old, to intimidate me?

Finally, looking up at him and said, "Look, I can assure you; I am not infected with AIDS if that's what you're thinking?"

He ignored my reply and said, "Cash or charge?"

"Cash!" I said as I paid him the total amount.

I thought, *some welcoming committee! AIDS protestors, an oversexed cab driver, and a rude motel clerk all in one day. Welcome to New Orleans, Raphaella!*

"Room thirteen, its upstairs!" He said as he threw the key down on the desk.

I shot him a dirty look and, as sarcastically as possible, said, "Thanks!"

I walked to my room and opened the door to lucky number thirteen. The first thing that filled my nostrils was the stale, moldy smell of many years of past sexual encounters over the decades.

Perhaps the Stardust motel lived up to its name in the nineteen sixties, but that was nearly thirty-some-odd years ago, and the place had grown dated and tired. Ugly shag carpeting, a floral bedspread, and a pink-tiled bathroom greeted me.

Before leaving the airport, I bought a city map and studied it. I would walk to my interviews rather than take taxis to acquaint myself with the city and save money at the same time. That way, I would be able to take in the sights of my new city.

The following day I got up early and went down to the reception area to ask the pig at the desk if he had a local newspaper for sale. He pointed to the window and there sat a stack of newspapers that had just been delivered. I paid the man, took the newspaper back to my room and searched the want ads for a job.

I immediately spotted an ad for a short order cook at the "Ruby Slipper" a diner located nearby and decided to call for an interview. I spoke to the manager who seemed nice and we arranged an interview for the following day. I knew the cash I'd brought from Haiti wouldn't last forever and that I would need a job to earn money. I spent the rest of the day walking around the city and even managed to see a marching band in the French Quarter.

The following morning I once again got up early and arrived to my job interview at the restaurant early. Stephen, the restaurant's assistant manager, seemed impressed by this and asked me, "Shall we start the interview?" as he led me to a booth in the back of the restaurant.

He asked me several questions such as, did I have any experience? Would I consider myself a decent cook? How well do I handle stress? And told me the hourly rate was four dollars and eighty cents, in addition the staff pooled their tips with the kitchen staff. That all sounded fine yet I felt distracted, and looked around and noticed the interior of the restaurant, which I could tell in the past had been something else.

Suddenly, I felt a cold blast of air encircle me, and much to my surprise, there stood a gentleman with a handlebar mustache, wearing a bowler hat and a suit with a watch on a chain that hung neatly outside his jacket. He was transparent and merely stood there, observing me.

Stephen sensed I was distracted by something and said, "Do you want the job or not?" sounding slightly irritated.

I quickly accepted and apologized and told Stephen I could start tomorrow; he told me he needed me bright and early at six o'clock as the kitchen staff needed to prep the food and that the restaurant opened at eight for breakfast. We shook hands; he welcomed me "into the family," I told him I was pleased to be working in such a fine establishment and said our goodbyes as I left the restaurant feeling like I was on cloud nine, thinking finally, something was starting to go my way! Perhaps things would turn in my favor?

Having located a job, I needed to locate an apartment as well, which would finally get me out of that dumpy motel!

I know I needed cash and still hadn't cashed nor deposited the cashier's check that was issued in Haiti. I located a nearby bank, opened a checking account with a bank representative, and deposited my cashier's check. I asked the bank teller to give me a thousand dollars in return. Naturally, that amount would be deducted from the total amount of the cashier's check.

After the trip to the bank I returned to the motel I picked up the newspaper and searched the section for apartments for rent. I called the number and spoke to a nice lady that agreed to meet me at an apartment later that afternoon. It was located in the French Quarter on Ursuline near the renowned "Ursuline convent." I would later learn that the convent was rumored to have taken in four or five women suspected of being vampires back in the eighteenth century due to their ghostly pallid complexion and blood smeared across each one's mouth. I had experienced many strange sightings, ghosts, and zombies, but I had never encountered a vampire! I wondered if these creatures really existed. I quickly dismissed the idea.

The studio apartment was located on the second floor above an empty store front. It had charming shutters outside the two large windows facing the street; it was furnished and had a small kitchenette and rented for six hundred dollars a month. I took it without seeing the rest of the flats; call me spontaneous, but I had a good feeling about this place, and the best part was that I couldn't detect any spirits there.

Don't get me wrong; I appreciate my gift and seeing and communicating with the "other side." Still, conversing with spirits is also physically exhausting; it takes a lot of energy to do so.

"When can I move in?" I asked the kind lady named Florence, who had shown me the apartment.

"Tomorrow, if you wish?" She replied with a smile. "I'll just need you to sign a few papers and leave a deposit for your last month's rent as security along with this month's rent."

"That's wonderful. One last question, how long has the store front downstairs been empty?" I asked.

"Oh, quite a while. If you ever think of opening a business I'm sure the landlord would give you a great deal on leasing the space." Florence said with a smile.

"I'll keep that in mind. Thank you." I said as I sat down to fill out the paperwork and give her the cash required to secure the apartment. I could barely wait to return to the Stardust motel to tell the welcoming committee to go to hell and demand my money back for the rest of the week.

As I walked back to the motel, I kept repeating out loud what I would say to the man at the front desk who had been so rude to me upon my arrival.

I marched into the front reception area and said, "I'm in number thirteen; I'll be moving out tomorrow. I want my money back!" I demanded.

He looked at me with a smug expression. "I don't give no refunds; you paid up, and that money is mine." He said with a chuckle, feeling like he had the upper hand.

Turning aggressive, I looked at him and said, "I won't ask you again, pig!" As I reached inside my pocket to pull out my trusty companion "Jacques," which was my six-inch knife, I held it firmly against his throat.

His two eyes, which looked more like two pig eyes, had a look of terror in them as he knew I wasn't joking, and if provoked, I would use this knife to slit his throat. I had a determined look in my eyes as if I meant business and would not back down. I knew in my heart that I was right and that the money I had paid him for the week belonged to me.

"Sure, take it. But I want you out tonight," the man who resembled a pig replied and handed me the money as I spit in his face.

"I wouldn't waste one more hour in this dump; I'll be out within the hour as soon as I pack up my stuff; that soon enough for you?" I retorted.

He nodded, giving himself two more chins to the two he already had.

I made my way up to number thirteen, emptied all the drawers of clothes and belongings into a suitcase, and made my way down the stairs. I could hear the police cars' sirens as they approached, and I decided to exit through the back of the motel.

I thought that pig called the police on me and laughed.

Where was I going to go? I can't move into my new apartment until tomorrow afternoon. I figured one night on a park bench wouldn't be all that bad as I walked to Louis Armstrong Park and found a park bench under a half-burned-out streetlamp. It was sunset; it would be dark soon.

I took out some articles of clothing and bunched them up to form a pillow to rest my head. I didn't need a blanket as it was a mild seventy-four degrees out at six in the evening. It would be dark in less than three hours, and I could rest, hoping for enough sleep to endure my big day tomorrow, starting with my new job as a cook and later moving into my new flat on Ursuline.

I could hardly wait! I sat on the park bench, mesmerized by the park's beauty and nature on display. I heard the birds chirp and watched them chase each other in flight as squirrels hopped about with families out, trying to enjoy the last remains of the daylight hours.

Sunset came, similar to the one I saw upon my arrival in New Orleans only a few days ago. It was as beautiful as before, appearing like some exquisite abstract painting. My mouth was open in amazement. Then suddenly, the sun had set and was replaced with darkness as everyone except me had left. I suddenly felt a slight chill; perhaps I needed that sweater after all?

I reached for it, having bought it upon my arrival in New Orleans, as there was no need for a sweater in Haiti as it never got cold enough to need one. I suddenly spotted a transparent figure of a man as he walked past my park bench, stopped to look at me, and then vanished in front of my eyes.

For the record, I typically see spirits milling about, but they approach me if they need something from me. I wondered whether the entity was having difficulty transitioning to the other side and whether the ghost looked at me for guidance to help assist him. I was sure that I would encounter plenty of other spirits here in New Orleans mainly because of its sordid and often violent past, with slavery and other tragic events that occurred.

I awakened the following day from a dreamless sleep. I checked my watch; a fancy "swatch" I had bought at the Miami airport. The time read seven-fifteen. I had to be at work at eight. I got up, stretched, and located an outdoor restroom where I began to wash from head to toe. One thing I knew about this newly adopted country of mine was that bathing was a necessity; I didn't want to appear or smell like some hired hand from the islands especially given it was my first day on the job.

I was ready in less than fifteen minutes and left the park and reached the corner of Burgundy and Conti, where my new job as a cook was about to start shortly. No sooner had I arrived; than I was introduced to the rest of my co-workers by Stephen. I was immediately made to feel at home and welcomed warmly.

Stephen was a fine-looking man; who stood roughly 1.75 meters tall with African-style braids and a big smile with teeth as white as snow. He told me the restaurant staff felt more like a family than just a group of people working together; I couldn't have agreed more. I longed for some bond or sense of family, especially given that I had no other family.

Stephen gave me a sheet of paper to review containing the daily menu. It could have been more interesting, just the usual food served at a diner. I came up with an idea and called in the manager, "Hey, Stephen! You got a minute for me?" I yelled. Stephen appeared immediately.

"You mind if I add to some of the lunch items?" I asked sheepishly.

"No, I don't mind. That's a great idea! I like someone that thinks outside of the box," he replied.

"Think outside the box?" I asked, looking confused.

He looked at me and chuckled. "It's an American expression; it means to think originally or creatively, and you come up with new ideas," he explained, "Was there something you wanted to whip up?" He asked

The continued puzzled expression on my face told him I was uncertain of his usage of American slang.

"Whip up" means to create, cook up," he explained.

"Yes, I want to add a lunch item to the menu. I cook a mean Jambalaya," I told him.

"Can you think of what you'd like to call it?" he asked, clearly open to the idea.

"We'll call it the Queen's Jambalaya!" I said.

"Better yet, how about Queen Raphaella's Jambalaya?" He said.

"Perfect!" We said simultaneously and laughed.

"I'll tell you what, you make the staff and me some lunch, and we'll be your guinea pigs," he snickered as he walked out of the kitchen.

"You got it, Stephen!" I yelled back. I got busy making all the other items on the menu or "prepping the food," as it's known in the restaurant business.

As soon as I finished, I began making my Jambalaya, which my mother taught me to make.

Once the breakfast crowd left, it was time for the staff, manager, and me to eat. I served up the Jambalaya to each server, six in total, to Stephen, and lastly to myself. Stephen put the closed sign on the front door at eleven, and we all had an early lunch as the restaurant would soon reopen at noon.

I felt nervous, and a bit anxious as the others pitched their forks into their meal. Suddenly, Stephen yelled, "Here's to the Queen's Jambalaya!" and leaned over to me and told me it would be a big hit on the menu. I looked at him with a smile and teardrop in my eye; I had found my new home and family.

About a year into my job, everything turned sour. I started having more visions of spirits walking toward me at work. Stephen had given me some history of the restaurant and told me that it had previously been a bank that dated back a hundred years or more. No wonder I saw ghosts milling around periodically.

Stephen was usually within earshot when I "talked to myself," as he described it. He isn't gifted or "receptive" to the other world, which meant he neither sensed nor witnessed the restless spirits I saw daily.

Finally, one day, Stephen's anger and mistrust boiled over. He began to doubt my sanity and told me the other workers were disturbed whenever I spoke to someone they claimed wasn't there. But I saw them, the many restless ghosts begging for my attention. What was I to do, ignore them?

I saved quite a bit of money in my savings account during that time. I thought the time had come to part with my very dysfunctional family.

My main desire was to open my shop, where I would focus primarily on séances for people to help them connect with their dearly departed loved ones on "the other side." Regarding the Voodoo, I gave that up when I left Haiti, but I figured calling it a Voodoo shop would attract more interest and, with that, more customers.

The following day, I had made up my mind. I was going to quit my job and give Stephen a piece of my mind. I did this before the others arrived so they wouldn't witness it.

I found Stephen going over the menus in the back of the café, as I approached him and said, "Stephen, you're a fool! It would be best if you respect those who have a direct connection to the other world as I do; everything I have encountered here is true. Your mother has visited me here to tell me how much she misses you and how proud of you she is," I said.

Naturally, he didn't believe me and asked me for my mother's name as proof which I supplied him with. "Your mother's name was Emmylou. She was born in nineteen thirty-two in Mobile, Alabama, to two African slaves brought over here before the civil war. She had a scar on her left cheek, an injury from a bully at school when she was just seven. She gave you the nickname "Curious Stevie," as you were always filled with wonder as a child. Now, what else would you like to hear?" I said and grinned.

His stunned expression said it all. Both his eyes and mouth were wide open as if he had seen a ghost. Unfortunately for him, he hadn't and never would. There are skeptics and non-believers, and Stephen qualified as a non-believer. I felt sorry for him.

"I don't believe it! How can that be? You're crazy!" he said, growing increasingly agitated.

"So, you think I'm crazy, do you? After everything I have shared with you? Fine, I quit! Find yourself another cook! Good luck to you," I shouted as I stood up and walked out the door.

Fortunately, I received my check the other day, so I wasn't expecting to return to the restaurant anytime soon.

I made my way back to my apartment; along the way, I stopped at a newsstand, picked up the local newspaper, "The Times-Picayune," and looked at the real estate section. Instantly spotting the ad, which read: "Storefront for sale, contact Tom Renaud," which included his phone number.

The ad had a picture of the Storefront, which looked familiar. As I studied it more closely, I saw the same Storefront below my apartment! It looked perfect, but leasing the space was listed at a staggering one thousand dollars a month! However, I had plenty of money to rent it for now. I remembered what the kind lady, Florence, who had shown me the apartment, said about the landlord being open to lowering the price.

A feeling of complete exhaustion poured over my entire body due to the heat of the day, and the emotional roller coaster that had played out at the café only a short time ago had taken its toll as I dropped the newspaper and fell into a deep sleep.

My mother appeared to me in a dream and offered me her pearls of wisdom, which comforted me. "Raphaella, you have a special gift; your talents are needed by those less fortunate, do not despair! Do not give up your dream of owning your own space. You will prevail; you must never lose faith; do not waste the gift you were born with," She said.

In an instant, she was gone. I awoke and cried out, "Mama, don't go! Don't leave me alone!"

CHAPTER 10

A dual perspective at a chance encounter

(Both Laurent and jack narrate)

(LAURENT NARRATES)

I made my way to the jazz club called Snug Harbor. I planned on an evening of happily listening to soulful music and losing myself in tranquility, at least temporarily.

I have grown fond of this sort of music in the nearly two hundred years I've existed in New Orleans. Somehow, the music magically reaches deep into someone's soul and can cause a range of emotions from happiness to utter sadness. Occasionally, the music has moved me to tears, blood-soaked tears. I had to shield my face from the club's other patrons each time, so they didn't witness such a spectacle.

You might ask, do vampires have souls? I cannot speak for the rest of my kind, but I can assure you I do. Despite having lost my soulmate, Fabien, I have tried desperately to retain some of my human emotions, such as tenderness, compassion, and love. Others of my kind may not care to maintain any human emotions; to them, it's considered a sign of weakness, and many vampires, believe absolute power is everything. Still, I would rather perish than become nothing more than a bloodthirsty creature that merely lusts after blood with no feelings other than rage and the immense powers vampires possess.

Before my exposure to this sort of music, I restricted my music to listening to classical and opera. However, I consciously decided to expand my horizons, to embrace the sounds of my surroundings. To become more open to present-day life, even though living is a word I would not describe as my own.

I was seated by the hostess in the back, as I had requested, at a table for two. I observed the club's patrons escorted to their seats; one particular couple drew my attention. The reasonably attractive woman, who appeared to be in her early thirties, was accompanied by an older gentleman; they must have disagreed about something before entering the club, as both the woman and the man seemed distant.

Other patrons smiled and laughed and seemed quite excited to be at the club, awaiting whatever band was about to perform.

I had come to hear the style of music, I hadn't sought out a particular group or singer, nor would I describe myself as a fan or "groupie."

I watched the continuous flow of people that entered the club and thought how my fellow patrons had no idea of the creature they were seated amongst. If it were not for my teachings from Fabien to not indiscriminately kill and retain some semblance of morals, I would have the power to end each one's life. Lucky for these individuals, that was never my intention.

I'll admit I struggled with that at times; the urges of blood lust can frequently make a vampire lose control. The fact that I had not dined before going out only intensified those cravings.

Having missed nourishing myself before my outing, I couldn't help listening to their heartbeats, occasionally glancing at my fellow patrons. Mostly, they ignored me and turned my attention toward the front door. There I suddenly spotted someone that had originally captured my attention over two hundred and fifty years ago back in Paris. I became motionless, thinking, my mind must be playing tricks on me! How can this be?

A tall man appeared with golden brown hair, perfect skin, and piercing blue eyes. I recognized his face at once. As he passed by my table, I looked at the man, thinking foolishly perhaps he would remember me! I couldn't help but say the name of the one who had consumed my endless nights since his destruction so long ago. "Fabien!" I said as the man turned and looked at me.

"Excuse me?" He asked, looking confused. "Forgive me; I thought you were someone else," I replied as my smile faded.

He cleared his throat, gave me a brief smile, and asked if he could join me at my table. This was precisely what Fabien would have done, being the aggressor and taking charge of the situation.

"Yes, of course; where are my manners," I said as I motioned toward the empty chair. "Won't you join me?"

"Thanks." He said as he sat down next to me. There was a momentary awkward silence between us until he said foolishly, "I know this must sound like a line, but do you come here often?" He asked awkwardly. We both laughed, exchanging flirtatious glances, both our eyes dancing wildly. He had those same azure blue eyes I remembered so well. His smile was bright and cleverly disarming.

"On occasion," I said after a long pause.

"I see. This is my first time," the man quickly added.

"Allow me to introduce myself to you; my name is Laurent Richelieu," as I stuck out my hand; and he took hold of it, he had the oddest look on his face and was visibly disturbed. I knew it was his reaction to the coldness of my hand.

"Sorry, I must have caught a draft or something. Happy to meet you, Laurent; my name's Jack Devereaux."

Shortly after our introductions, the room fell silent as the lights dimmed and the band began to play. The music put my new jazz companion in a trance. I was captivated by this man and watched his every movement. I thought about how Jack embodied the essence of my beloved Fabien!

I caught a glimpse of Jack closing his eyes and swaying to the music; then, he sheepishly gazed at me with a smile that could melt even the coldest heart. I wondered if I still had a heart to melt. I felt we were no longer strangers; I was sure of this. I sensed a connection to Jack and thought it was destiny that he had walked into the same jazz club as I.

I decided to be equally as aggressive and reached under the table to put my hand on his thigh; he did not resist but merely looked at me and flashed a wide pearly smile approvingly.

I felt that same excitement the night I met Fabien so long ago at Park Monceau in Paris. It felt as if I were given a second chance. For over two hundred and fifty years, I retained feelings of love, excitement, and, naturally, a physical attraction.

(JACK NARRATES)

What was it about this refined gentleman that drew me to him? Was it his elegance, his manners, his looks? I have never felt so completely at ease around another man. He made me feel comfortable in my skin for the first time.

He wasn't the usual guy I wound up in bed with on so many occasions, yet there was something mysterious about him I just couldn't put my finger on.

He looked at me tenderly and lovingly as if we'd known each other much longer than just having met this evening. I knew this didn't make sense. My imagination must be getting to me. I thought, don't overthink it, Jack. You don't even know for sure this guy is gay. He did touch my leg, but what did that mean? I was dying to find out. I wanted to know as much about this man as possible.

I thought, would he ask me back to his place? It wasn't just a physical attraction; I wanted to get to know everything about him, and I wanted him to get to know me! I thought, Well, Jack, you're making some progress. It was just a few short hours ago, and you were ready to dive back into the closet, possibly for good, well, not now!

(LAURENT NARRATES)

The band finished their performance as I looked at Jack; he was preoccupied with his thoughts. He had consumed nearly three drinks, presumably to lessen his nervousness and lose some inhibitions. *Oh, how I detested alcohol! It made fools out of most mortals; perhaps in the not-too-distant future, Jack will not need it and require another liquid substance,* I thought.

"Wasn't that magnificent, Jack?" I asked. He didn't reply. "Is everything alright, Jack?" I asked with a concerned look on my face.

"Yeah, I guess so," his speech had become slurred as he slowly became intoxicated. "I just need to know one thing before we continue with all of this," Jack said with a stern look.

"Continue with all of this?" I asked, sounding confused.

"This small talk, your hand on my leg," he said with a grin from ear to ear. I remained silent and looked at him with a blank expression.

"Ok! I'll just come out and say, are you gay?" He asked.

"Gay?" I asked with questioning eyes.

"Sorry! Maybe they don't use that word where you come from. Are you a homosexual?"

"If you mean, do I prefer another gentleman's company over the company of women, then the answer would be yes," I stated.

Jack let out a sigh of relief, "Whew. That was tough," He said and chuckled. I looked at him, somewhat puzzled. As we continued our conversation, most of the other bar patrons had already left.

A young woman, possibly in her twenties, came over and addressed us as "Gents."

"Hey, if you Gents want to hang around here a while longer, you'll have to buy another round of drinks," she said.

I shook my head and promptly paid our tab, "No, thank you, Miss, keep the change," I said as I handed her a twenty-dollar bill and stood up.

"Hey! You didn't have to do that," Jack said in protest, "Hey do you want to"…

And before Jack could finish his sentence, I invited him back to my estate.

"I guess you beat me to it," he said with a grin as he stood up from the table.

I had arranged for Barthelme to pick me up at ten o'clock. I looked at Jack and asked, "Are you alright, Jack?"

"I'm fine; let's go back to your place," he replied as we walked out of the club.

As suspected, my trusty servant Barthelme was waiting directly in front.

"Good evening, Sir," Barthelme greeted me as he got out of the vehicle to open our doors.

"Wow! That's some set of wheels you got there, Laurent!" Jack said.

I assumed the "set of wheels" meant he was impressed with my Rolls Royce.

"So, where are you taking me kind, Sir?" Jack said, trying desperately to sound aristocratic, which amused me.

"My estate is an hour north of here, Jack, in the town known as Vacherie."

"An estate, eh?" He said, seeming to be impressed.

"Where to, Sir?" He asked.

"Home, Barthelme," I replied.

"Right away, Sir," Barthelme said.

"Jack, perhaps you should ride with the window open; the fresh air will improve your condition considerably," I suggested.

"What condition" he muttered under his breath and scoffed at the suggestion.

We sped off into the darkened night. We exchanged very few words. My unexpected date for the evening was a handsome unrefined drunken young man who, at least temporarily, was quite intoxicated. Even if he were able to make conversation with me, what would the topic of our conversation be? Sports playoffs? Or what kind of beer he drank? I already knew what his hard liqueur of choice was.

I thought about this and the realization of Jack being who he was, compared to Fabien, which made me wonder, was I doing the right thing? Perhaps Jack was merely himself, only a striking resemblance to Fabien and nothing more? No, it wasn't a coincidence that we were simultaneously in the same place. Not to mention Jack bearing the exact resemblance to my beloved; no, this was destiny, of that I was sure! I was going to make certain that nothing would separate us again. I would learn much more about Jack once we arrived at the estate.

We pulled into the long driveway past all the magnificent Oak trees that lined the driveway up to my plantation's front entry.

By this time, Jack had regained some sobriety. The cold night air blowing in his face had brought him back to some of his senses.

"Wow!" Jack said as he stepped out of the Rolls.

"Do you approve, Jack?" I asked playfully.

Again, that gorgeous smile washed away any doubts I may have had; perhaps I could groom this "diamond in the rough" so that Jack could become my eternal mate as we laughed and entered the mansion.

I witnessed Jack's mouth open in amazement at the many paintings and antique furnishings, most of which had been brought over from France in the late eighteenth century.

"Jack, let us adjourn to the drawing-room," I instructed.

"Yes, let's!" Jack replied, once more trying to sound aristocratic.

For a moment, I imagined myself as a mortal entering Fabien's drawing room. His entrusted servant offered us an aperitif, never suspecting what that would lead to. As quickly as my thoughts returned to the past, I refocused my attention on the present and Jack.

"Man, oh, Man! You must come from money, Laurent! I've never seen a place like this before; this looks like the White House, or how I would imagine it to look!" He said. How he endeared himself to me almost every time he spoke, sounding simple-minded at times but always straightforward.

"Jack, I'm going to come out and say this as delicately as possible; you've consumed too much alcohol. I think it would be best if you spent the night sleeping it off. I have many guest bedrooms. I'm sure you'll be more than comfortable. You're welcome to stay in any of them you see fit, and on second thought, perhaps we should skip the aperitif. Barthelme will take you home in the morning," I instructed.

"I was hoping you'd invite me to stay over," he said, grinning from ear to ear as he came toward me.

"Jack, I think you're getting the wrong idea. I'm not one to rush into physical contact immediately if that is what you are implying. While I find you most handsome, Jack, I wish to get to know you before we proceed into the next phase, if that's alright with you?" I said rather gently.

I observed his facial expression, which seemed to convey confusion mixed with disappointment. I figured it wasn't often that a man as good-looking as Jack was used to being turned down for his sexual advances.

"Aww, you're just trying to play hard to get," he replied sheepishly and gave me that come hither look as he studied my reaction, which remained stone-faced. I didn't respond to him. After a brief awkward silence, he backed down.

"Yeah, maybe you're right; I hit the sauce pretty hard." He admitted.

"Come now, let's put you to bed, Jack," I suggested.

Once again, Jack became sexually suggestive, saying, "Will you be joining me?" as he giggled like a child.

I looked at him and shook my head. "I will put you into the room next to mine. Should you require anything in the middle of the night, I can readily hear and assist you with anything you require," I said.

We walked up the staircase and down the long hallway until we appeared in front of the guest room.

"Here is your room Jack," I said as I opened the massive mahogany door.

Jack walked inside and noticed how opulent the room was furnished with its large marble fireplace and roaring fire and mahogany canopy bed draped in the finest silk.

The window coverings were made from heavy velvet fabric in a rich burgundy color. Near the fireplace was a Louis the fourteenth chair with an embroidered scene; next to it, a small mahogany end table with a small porcelain figurine of a woman holding a basket.

On the fireplace mantle sat a silver candelabra; there were no lights in the room, as there was no electricity in the entire house. The light from the fireplace danced upon the chandelier's crystals hanging from the ceiling.

I could see Jack's mouth open upon viewing his room for the night.

I broke his thoughts with an offering of kindness. "Is there anything else you require, Jack?"

"No, thank you. All I need is a good night's sleep, and I'll be good as new! He said as we hugged good night.

"Sleep well, and pleasant dreams!" I wished him.

(JACK NARRATES)

I thought, *Man! I had only seen rooms like these in the movies! This guy must be loaded! Sure as hell beats the Stardust Motor inn! But why wasn't this guy into me? And if he is, maybe he's just trying to play hard to get? Naw! This guy is a gentleman. He's from Europe, for Christ's sake! No wonder! I've only met street trash or guys in bars willing to give it up on the first meet-up.*

What would Lisa say about this? Screw her! Why was I even thinking of my ex-wife? The same woman that denounced me as an "abomination of God" well, she would most likely include my new friend Laurent in that category as well. She'd think Laurent must have made a pact with the devil to live like this. What does it matter anyway? Stop thinking about her, Jack; focus on getting a good night's sleep, and let's see what tomorrow brings.

I thought about my new friend Laurent. How dignified he was, what manners and sense of grace he had, a true gentleman. I could tell he was into me, but he didn't want me to think he was promiscuous. Maybe he's only been with a handful of guys, if that, I chuckled.

I looked around the large guest room and asked myself what was missing. At first I couldn't put my finger on it until it finally came to me. There wasn't one mirror in the room or downstairs. I thought *that was strange. Not a single mirror?*

I shrugged it off and began to undress; Laurent had been kind enough to leave me a pair of silk pajamas; I thought; I usually sleep naked, but tonight was different. You're in a beautiful place; sleeping on such expensive sheets naked would be wrong!

I began to put on the silk pajamas. They felt so comfortable and soft on my skin as I climbed into bed and got comfortable.

I noticed the large bedroom window was open, and a slight breeze made its way through and gently caressed my face as I drifted off to sleep and started to dream.

I found myself walking in a dense fog; I appeared to be in some mausoleum with only a coffin visible. I cautiously walked over and carefully lifted the casket only to see myself lying in the coffin, suddenly awakening with a jolt, only to find my elegant silk pajamas had become wet with sweat.

I looked at my watch, which read six o'clock. The sun was about to rise in half an hour. I couldn't stay in bed, not after the nightmare I had. I decided to get up and wander around the grand estate, hoping to explore my new friend's stately home. I wanted to learn more about this mysterious European gentleman. As I opened the door to my guest bedroom, which creaked a bit, Laurent's trusty servant, immediately greeted me.

"Is everything alright, Master Jack?" he asked.

"Yes, thanks for asking Barthelme; I just want to get some fresh air; I didn't sleep very well, now, if you'll excuse me," I said.

"Of course, Master Jack. Please let me know if there is anything I can provide for you?" Barthelme said. Looking at Barthelme's face, I noticed he appeared somewhat anxious.

"Good night Master Jack, or what's left of it," he said.

Barthelme walked back into his room and glanced at me before closing his door.

I decided I needed to see my new friend, Laurent. Hopefully, he was an early riser and was up waiting for me. I carefully opened his large, ornate, heavy mahogany door and immediately noticed the silence. It could be described as dead silence.

Naturally, Laurent's room was even more majestic than I had imagined, far grander than mine. There was a large painting of someone, a portrait, but I couldn't make it out as it was dimly lit with only the candle flames next to Laurent's bed.

I slowly walked over to Laurent's bed. There he lay, motionless I hadn't awakened him. It seemed all the coloring of his face had gone away; he appeared chalk-white! I looked at his chest and couldn't detect any breathing. I took his hand, thinking that might awaken him, but he continued to lay there as if he were in a coma or worse. I lay my head down on his chest to hear his heartbeat. I heard nothing. I thought *every living thing on this planet had a heartbeat. Why doesn't Laurent?* I screamed out in panic, thinking he was dead. The door flung open, and Barthelme suddenly appeared and said, "You shouldn't be in here!" He commanded.

I stood there motionless, felt utterly helpless, and said, "I think he's dead! There's no heartbeat, and he's as pale as a ghost!" I was barely able to speak.

"Get out! Leave! I will drive you back into town Master Jack, but you must leave if you know what's good for you!" Barthelme warned.

"How can I leave when he's in a state like that? Aren't you going to call a doctor or an ambulance? Are you going to let him die like that? What kind of servant are you?" I yelled as I reached for the last remaining bit of sanity left in my brain.

"There are things you do not understand, Master Jack; it is not my position to explain them to you. Leave at once! Master Laurent has instructed me to drive you back to your place. Once the Master has awakened, he will contact you."

"He's dead, don't you understand? I listened to his heartbeat, but he didn't have one. He's not waking up, and here we are, yelling at each other, and still no response? What kind of madness is this?" I said as my voice trembled.

"I will ask you to gather your belongings one more time so we may leave! Master Laurent is fine; it is not what you think! I have been with Master Laurent for a very long time. I know him best! I have experienced what you have seen many times before. Now go pack, and we shall leave immediately!" Barthelme instructed.

I did as I was told, probably for the first time in my life. All I wanted to do was leave and escape Laurent and Barthelme.

Something was going on here that didn't add up. Last night I had too much to drink. I wasn't thinking clearly. Now being "stone-cold sober," my thoughts became clearer. There was a painting in Laurent's bedroom, a large picture with a man in it, whose features I couldn't make out because of the darkened room except for the candlelight beside Laurent's bed.

There were so many questions that needed answering. I thought, why wasn't there any electricity in the house? Why wasn't there a mirror anywhere to be seen? Only a telephone and an old rotary phone at that!

I was dressed instantly and decided to skip showering here and would do so once I got back to the motel.

I wondered if I was still recovering from my drunken state and perhaps had imagined the entire thing. Maybe Laurent was a heavy sleeper with a shallow, faint heartbeat that I couldn't detect.

Barthelme opened my door and closed it, as I gave him the address and drove off. No words were exchanged during our drive back; I was relieved as my head was swimming in confusion filled with so many unanswered questions.

Soon we pulled into the parking lot of the motel.

Barthelme wished me a pleasant day and told me the Master would be in touch with me soon. Laurent and I had exchanged telephone numbers back at the club, but still, it was curious that he had a telephone but no electricity in the house. This man wants to preserve some things of the past, but not all.

I managed to get to work, appeared on the construction site, and started work. I lifted and carried heavy steel bars to their final resting place; I thought about that expression that made me cringe.

I thought about Laurent and wondered if he was okay and whether I would ever see him again.

A few days later, I called Laurent during my lunch break, as I had expected a call from him, which never came. I'd become concerned something terrible had happened to him.

The number repeatedly rang until, finally, Barthelme picked up. "Hello, Richelieu residence, Barthelme speaking"

"Barthelme, it's Jack," I said frantically, "Is everything alright with Laurent?"

A brief silence occurred, which seemed to last an eternity.

"Yes, Master Jack, I had to rush Master Laurent to the hospital. It would appear the Master suffered a seizure, which would explain the lack of a heartbeat; he had gone into cardiac arrest. You are to be commended, Master Jack. Without your help, Master Laurent might be dead. He spent a few days in the hospital but was released the other day. He's doing fine and is back safe and sound. I'm certain you'll hear from him as he will undoubtedly want to thank you personally for saving his life." Barthelme shared.

"Thank God!" I replied.

"Expect to be hearing from the Master very soon. Goodbye, Master Jack, and thank you for all your efforts and concern!" he said and hung up.

I heard a dial tone before I could utter any other words or a goodbye. I made my way back to my motel room as soon as I had finished my shift. I needed a good soak in the bathtub to relieve my aching muscles from my eight-hour day at the construction site and to think things over.

I continued to sit on the bed and thought about how he and I had met; it seemed to be something like out of a movie. I decided those days of me picking up some hot guy or woman in a bar just for sex had ended. I wanted more than just endless casual hookups and needed a relationship.

I wanted so desperately to hear Laurent's voice and, in his own words, reassure me that he was out of harm's way.

I looked at my watch; the time read eight-thirty; I became startled as the phone rang. It felt like I had been sitting on pins and needles since the incident occurred.

"Hello?" I answered.

"Jack?" The voice asked.

"Yes!" I said excitedly and instantly recognized it as Laurent's.

"Jack, this is Laurent. Thank you so much for being in the right place at the right time! I owe you a world of gratitude! I would very much like to see you again as soon as possible. Are you free tomorrow evening, say, eight-thirty, for dinner at my place?" He asked tenderly.

"Yes, of course! I haven't thought of anything, or anyone, since we last saw each other!" I said unabashedly.

"Neither have I, Jack. Well, then, it is settled. Barthelme will pick you up at seven-thirty tomorrow evening.

Bring your appetite, Jack. The food will be plentiful," Laurent instructed.

"Yes, okay, I will. I'm just so relieved that you're okay, Laurent!" I said breathlessly.

"Jack, I cannot thank you enough! I'll look forward to our wonderful evening together," He said.

"Thank you, Laurent; I'll look forward to seeing you as well," I said and blushed.

"I'm counting down the hours, Jack! Until tomorrow evening, sleep well!" He said and hung up.

The next day at work was a complete blur; I felt much like a robot, preoccupied with my thoughts of Laurent and our dinner to come. I finished my shift and rushed back to the motel to shower and get dressed in my Sunday finest. A Sport jacket, dress shirt, dress slacks, and dress shoes. I even ditched my white cotton socks and traded them for fancy nylon dress socks from that designer, Pierre Cardin. I was sure a gentleman of Laurent's standings would notice even the socks a man wore, however insignificant that might be. I wanted to look perfect in every way and look the part of someone like me, fortunate enough to call a man like Laurent my boyfriend.

The thoughts I was having seemed so strange. I had never been comfortable around other gay men; I looked at them as purely physical conquests. However, Laurent was different. Was I hoping for a future together? Could I even imagine one with another man? My Catholic upbringing said no. Instead, I decided to go with my gut instinct for once and not base my decision on my faith. Barthelme arrived precisely as agreed at seven-thirty. He had opened my door and waited until I entered the vehicle and closed it. I enjoyed the showiness of it all. I wanted to better myself and become more refined, like Laurent. I was determined to develop manners and challenge myself to be anything but the lower-middle-class guy I grew up and identified with all my life. Laurent made me want to be more like him. I enjoyed this role-playing. I figured, if nothing else, at least I could pretend.

(LAURENT NARRATES)

As Barthelme arrived with Jack, I felt I was awaiting some important government representative. How strange that I should be feeling this way! A two-hundred-and-fifty-year-old vampire anxiously awaiting someone?

I made sure everything was perfect. Barthelme had been preparing the estate for Jack's arrival all day, everything from polishing the silver to cleaning the crystal, and created what was sure to be an exquisite feast for Jack.

I could hear the car as it approached as I walked toward the window to gaze out briefly. I didn't want Jack to catch me as I peered out the window. The front door opened, and with that stood the most handsome man, even more than he had appeared the night we met at the Jazz bar.

Jack had cleaned himself up rather nicely! The start of a day-old beard that Jack had worn at our first encounter was gone. He had gotten his hair cut and styled and was dressed appropriately for dinner. He had made quite an effort. I couldn't have been happier than I was at that moment, and my smile conveyed that.

"Jack, how handsome you look!" I said, voicing my approval.

"Thank you, Laurent, as do you. It's a pleasure to see you and to be back here under much more pleasant circumstances! I'm so glad that you're okay and feeling better. I guess I saved your life!" he said and laughed.

For a moment, I became confused by what he meant. My expression gave that away. Then I quickly remembered how Jack had found me in my undead slumber where no sign of "life" was present, which included the lack of a heartbeat. The color of my skin would have also resembled a corpse. Jack truly felt as if he had intervened and rescued me from a near-certain death. Not yet knowing my secret, I offered up my thanks.

"Yes, Jack, you are a lifesaver!" I said. "Shall we adjourn to the drawing before dinner?" I suggested.

"Yes, that would be lovely!" Jack replied, which I felt was very uncommon for him to use these words. I thought, was Jack putting on airs, or was he genuinely making a conscious effort to become the gentleman I knew was buried deep inside?

We sat on the sofa near the roaring fireplace, gazing into each other's eyes.

I had two windows open as a refreshing summer night's breeze blew in, which smelled of jasmine and honeysuckle; the aroma was overpowering and hypnotic.

"Ah! Just smell that, Jack! Isn't that heavenly?" I asked as I closed my eyes.

"Yes, Laurent, it's heavenly." He replied.

At that point, I looked at Jack and found him laughing a bit.

"Are you amused by something, Jack?" I asked.

He looked at me as he stopped laughing and said, "I'm sorry, Laurent, but this is so out of my element. I'm just trying to impress you; I'm putting on airs."

I thought, *Aha! As I had suspected.* I looked at him, shook my head, and said, "Jack, you are quite an enigma."

"Enigma?" he asked, looking confused.

"It means you are something special. It's as if you are the chosen one."

"Chosen one?" He asked, looking even more confused.

Before we could continue our discussion, Barthelme called us into the dining room and announced that dinner was about to be served.

Our festive evening was about to start.

We walked into the dining room, seeing the candelabras lit. The dining table, which sat twenty, was decorated with Wedgewood china and crystal glasses, and silver utensils added to the elegantly decorated table. A lovely bouquet of freshly cut flowers filled the crystal flower vase. It had been a long time since I had entertained anyone. Mainly, the table sat empty.

"Jack, please sit next to me; I will sit at the table's head," I instructed.

Shortly after being seated, the wine began to be poured. Barthelme came over to offer Jack a glass. "Yes, please!" Jack said.

Barthelme came over to me out of courtesy, as he knew I did not drink alcohol, knowing blood was the only thing to sustain my existence. I indicated to Barthelme that I would not partake.

"You don't drink, Laurent? Jack asked.

"No! I can't handle the stuff, Jack, if you know what I mean?" I said and winked.

"I understand," he replied.

Barthelme announced the first course, a Chicken consume with herb-baked crotons and French bread and butter.

I thought about how long it had been since I had eaten any mortal food. The thought of it nearly sickened me.

Jack noticed that I was drinking but not eating and asked, "Aren't you eating, Laurent?" Barthelme had poured me some blood earlier, which he served me in a silver goblet, hoping Jack wouldn't see precisely what I was drinking.

"No, Jack, I hope you don't mind, but I will not be dining this evening. I had a late lunch this afternoon; I'll enjoy my tomato juice. I didn't want my lack of appetite to interfere with our wonderful evening together," I said apologetically.

"That's okay; it's just nice to be here and have the pleasure of your company Laurent," he said as Barthelme offered him another slice of homemade French bread.

I looked at him longingly and smiled as I picked up my wine goblet containing blood and took a sip, which washed down my throat and felt good.

Barthelme returned and cleared Jack's bowl and bread plate. He served Jack his main course, petit filet mignon with roasted red potatoes and white asparagus drenched in a Béarnaise sauce.

"Wow! It looks delicious!" Jack said excitedly. I merely sat there and observed my new love interest.

I desperately wanted to believe that Fabien, my soulmate and maker, had returned to me as Jack. As if by some miracle! I wasn't about to let anything or anyone interfere in this process.

I would wine and dine and win over Jack's heart. When I felt the time was right, I would reveal my secret to him and let him decide if he would like to accept the dark gift I would offer him. It would be Jack's decision whether to accept or not.

Once we finished dinner, we adjourned to the drawing room to let Jack's dinner settle. Barthelme replenished my goblet with more blood and poured Jack more wine.

"Let's leave the French doors open to the garden; it's such a lovely evening out, Barthelme; there's no need to close them," I instructed.

"As you wish, Master Laurent. Will there be anything else?" Barthelme asked in a hushed voice.

"No, Barthelme, thank you, that will be all," I replied.

"Excellent, Sir!" with that, Barthelme retired to his room.

(JACK NARRATES)

I had to take it all in and thought, this was like something out of a movie. This refined European gentleman, is he that into you? It didn't make sense. We're so different! As if we're from two other worlds! What does he see in me? This mysterious, cultured man could have any man he chose to have; why me? The pressure I felt to maintain this well-mannered individual's interest seemed too much; it wasn't me! I just wanted to grab a beer with some guy, screw his brains out, and leave. No! That was the old me, the lonely, empty, pathetic soul I used to be before I met this fantastic man. I needed him, and something told me he needed me; for whatever reason, perhaps I would find out soon enough.

"Jack," Laurent said. His words suddenly pulled me out of my thoughts. "Is everything alright?" he asked.

"Yes! I'm sorry. I was thinking about how grateful I feel to be with you tonight!" I said.

Laurent gazed at me affectionately and leaned over and kissed me. It was tender and romantic. I noticed his lips didn't feel cold to the touch, which they usually were.

"Jack, you have no idea how happy I am that you are here with me!" Laurent said as he tenderly touched my face.

"What's the matter, Jack?" Laurent asked me.

"You look much healthier, Laurent. I meant to tell you that over dinner. When I arrived, you looked pale, and your skin color changed throughout our dinner. Now at least you don't have the skin color of a corpse." He said, meaning that as a compliment.

"Perhaps you should spend a little more time in the sun?"

I noticed the smile left his face as he replied, "No, I have a rare skin disorder, so I try and avoid any contact with the sun, which could lead to an unsightly burn. That you would not want to see, Jack."

Abruptly he stood up from where we were both seated and walked over to the French doors. In the distance, dogs began to howl.

"Why do you think those dogs are howling, Laurent? Does that happen here often?" I asked. He turned and looked at me with a sinister grin and replied eerily, "Perhaps they sense danger Jack, or perhaps they are just hungry?"

His response made me feel uncomfortable. I wasn't used to feeling intimidated by other men. I was usually so sure of myself that I could physically defend myself against any man. But Laurent was different. At times, he had such self-confidence that he almost came across as invincible.

I thought Laurent had made me rethink everything I've ever known. He's even had me doubt myself for the first time in my life! Who is this man? Why do I feel so helpless and weak whenever I'm around him? It's as if I'm not myself or supposed to be someone else. Listen to yourself, Jack; you're starting to sound crazy! I needed to excuse myself for the night and think things through, so I quickly came up with an excuse.

"Laurent, if you don't mind, I'd like to go to bed; I suddenly feel exhausted," I said.

"Of course, Jack, I understand. You worked all day on the construction site." He replied.

"Yes, it's hard work," I said and yawned. "Thank you for the wonderful dinner Laurent; it was spectacular," as I stood up to leave.

"Jack, I hope you don't mind, but I'll stay up a bit. I'm rather nocturnal, and perhaps you are more of a morning person. If you would like, you're welcome to stay in the same guest bedroom as your last visit. It is the room closest to mine," he said assuredly.

"Yes, that's fine. Good night Laurent." I said and feigned a smile.

"Good night Jack, pleasant dreams. One other thing, I won't be around when you awaken; I have some business to attend to in Atlanta," he said.

"When will I see you again?" I asked sheepishly.

"Soon, Jack, very soon," he said warmly with a tender smile.

I made my way up the long stairway and walked down the semi-darkened hallway, a wide passage illuminated with a lit candelabra placed every few feet. As I walked along, I passed statues and oil paintings that looked old and very expensive. I've never been much of an art lover, so I couldn't tell who the artists were, but no doubt they were European.

I entered my room and flung myself on the bed. I suddenly felt exhausted. I knew deep sleep would set in soon.

I began to undress, slipped on my silk pajamas from my previous stayover, and smelled the fabric; they appeared freshly laundered.

I could still hear the dogs as they continued to howl outside as I climbed into the canopy bed. This scenario reminded me of a horror movie I had watched once, but I couldn't remember the name for the life of me.

A cool breeze blew over my entire body from the open window in the bedroom; it felt good, caressing my body as a lover might.

I managed to fall asleep quite suddenly; and hadn't reached a deep sleep as I began to stir in bed and wrapped myself in the silken sheets and goose down comforter, laying in a fetal position in the direction of the window.

I opened my eyes and saw what appeared to be the outline of a man as he stood nearby observing me. I thought I must be hallucinating, or maybe I was asleep, which was all part of a dream. This vision can't be real? I'm on the second story of Laurent's mansion; how could anyone be in my room?

I continued to stare at the darkened figure hidden in the shadows. What was I seeing? It appeared to be two red eyes glaring at me. They looked like two rubies on fire as I yelled out, "Laurent!" There was no reply. Perhaps he'd gone outside for a stroll and couldn't hear me.

"Who are you?" I demanded, but the shadowy figure remained motionless and didn't reply.

I climbed out of bed and slowly started to approach the figure. Before I could get close enough to see its face, the figure vanished into a mist and made its way out the open window. I pinched myself to ensure I wasn't still asleep and having a nightmare. Much to my amazement, I felt the pain from my self-inflicted pinch, confirming this wasn't a dream but a living nightmare! How could someone possibly get into my room and something with two red eyes?

Perhaps what I saw was a ghost. That's what it must have been; I told myself as I cried out again, only much louder this time!

"Laurent!" I screamed at the top of my lungs. Instantly, the door to my bedroom sprang open as Laurent appeared.

"Jack, what's wrong? You must have been having a nightmare!" he said as he desperately tried to comfort me. I thought, perhaps

I had dreamt. No! I hadn't; I was fully awake! As I began to shake with fear.

"Laurent, I saw someone just now glaring at me with two red eyes; it just stood there staring at me!" I said, nearly hysterical.

"What do you think it was, Jack?" Laurent asked with a look of doubt.

"I don't know, a ghost? Or something, it had two red eyes that glared at me," I repeated. I immediately felt even suggesting such a thing.

"Two red eyes glaring at you? A ghost?" Laurent replied and began to laugh.

"I know what I saw, Laurent; I didn't imagine it," I retorted.

"Jack, you admitted how tired you were. When a person is in a state of exhaustion, the mind can play terrible tricks on the eyes," Laurent said and tried to reassure me.

"This happened, Laurent!" I said and raised my voice.

"Perhaps it was a nightmare? You were dreaming." Laurent replied.

"Maybe you're right, Laurent. Perhaps it was just a nightmare. It's either that or I'm losing my mind!" I said.

"Jack, I have to get back to bed. I have to be up in a few hours to leave for my business trip," Laurent said apologetically.

We said our goodnights as Laurent left my room.

CHAPTER 11

A slow descent into hell

(JACK NARRATES)

I glanced at my watch; the time read four o'clock. I thought, every time I spent the night at Laurent's, I never ended up having sex with him; instead, I have the strangest nightmares, that and staining his soft pajamas twice now. I took them off and decided to sleep in the nude, not wanting to feel the sweaty material sticking to my skin as I fell into a deep sleep and began to dream.

I found myself wandering down a darkened hallway and passed by horrific paintings depicting scenes of bloodletting and burning buildings, portraits of ravenous dogs and wolves that snarled; as I passed each picture, they seemed to come to life.

The blood spilled down from the pictures onto the wood floor, and the hungry dogs and wolves growled and lunged at me, yet somehow I managed to continue my journey. I walked down the darkened hallway, where I noticed the time on each clock wasn't running; they appeared to have stopped.

I finally reached the end of the hall, seeing a portrait shaded partially by the hallway's darkness.

Finding a nearby candle, I held it up to the portrait, but before I could make out the face in the picture, I awoke yelling, "Let me see!"

This time it was Barthelme who came to my rescue as he knocked on my door. "Master Jack, may I enter?" he asked with concern.

"Yes," I shouted.

"Are you alright, Master Jack?" Barthelme looked puzzled.

"Yes, just another one of my nightmares; I guess this place inspires them," I said as I feigned a smile.

Barthelme being the cultured servant he was, ignored my remark and began to explain that the Master had already left for Atlanta and asked me if there was something he could bring me. I asked for a shot of something, anything containing alcohol.

"Right away, Master Jack," Barthelme answered.

Why did he refer to me as "Master Jack"? I didn't live here, nor was I his Master? Why did he call Laurent "Master Laurent," as was the custom back in the slave days? I might be from the South, but the thought of a black person calling me "Master" made me uncomfortable.

After what seemed an eternity, Barthelme returned with a glass of bourbon. I took it from him and took one big gulp, feeling it burn my throat as it made its way down into my stomach, hoping it would calm my nerves. He stared at me for a brief moment. A deafening silence had developed between us.

After a long pause, Barthelme asked, "Will there be anything else, Master Jack?"

"No, Barthelme, thank you!" I said, feeling embarrassed as if I were a child and had been given a glass of warm milk by my parent.

I decided that I needed a break from my budding relationship with Laurent. We had gotten together twice, and nothing physical happened except a kiss and all of these strange occurrences and strange nightmares. I still wasn't convinced the figure with the red eyes was just a dream, but what was it? I was starting to wonder what kind of game Laurent was playing or simply the fact that his house was haunted.

A few hours later, in the early morning hours, Barthelme drove me into town.

"I hope the Master and I see you again soon, Master Jack," he said.

"Thanks," I offered up awkwardly as I shrugged my shoulders. I needed time to think, to sort things out. Since meeting Laurent, I hadn't thought of anyone else; he was all-consuming; it was one of the most amazing things that happened to me. Yet, at the same time, it strangely was one of the most disturbing things to happen to me. Perhaps my imagination was more vivid than I thought.

I tried reassuring myself and told myself, how could there have been someone in my room, and what could explain the red, glaring eyes? Monsters don't exist except in fiction. I must have dreamt the whole thing!

Laurent thought I was a fool for mentioning what I had seen. However, there was one thing that puzzled me.

When I described my experience, the expression on his face almost appeared to be an acknowledgment. Did he believe my story?

As I got out, the rolls pulled into the parking lot, and I waved goodbye to Barthelme.

As I climbed the motel stairs, I felt exhaustion hit every inch of my body. I needed to rest, having had a sleepless night at Laurent's. I undressed and kept only my underwear and socks on. As soon as I lay down on the bed, I fell into a deep sleep.

I slept a few hours and awoke from hearing my growling stomach. It was time I found a place for a late breakfast or early dinner. I glanced at my watch. "Holy shit!" I said as the time read eleven-thirty.

I quickly showered, got dressed, and went to the "Ruby Slipper," a diner-type restaurant serving all-day breakfasts for those who tend to sleep in.

Walking along, I passed a newsstand and decided to pick up a paper. I glanced at it quickly to the front page's left was a headline about San Francisco experiencing a devastating earthquake during the World Series. The other article was about a local girl having been attacked and nearly left for dead. It would provide me with exciting reading material while I enjoyed my breakfast.

I was practically starving as I arrived at the Ruby Slipper at twelve-thirty, as I made my way in and was seated. I ordered enough food for an army, including two eggs, bacon, toast, home fries, and coffee.

As I read the story, I felt the hairs on my neck standing up. It sent shivers up and down my spine. "Mary Margaux, age thirty-two, found half alive with two puncture wounds in her neck."

The article described the victim being admitted to Ochsner medical center for treatment. She described the assailant as having two red eyes, a hypnotic glare, and a European accent.

It sounded like fiction. Like something from a scene out of "Dracula," especially the part about the red eyes and two puncture wounds and draining the victim of her blood? I was shaken and thought I had the same vision while staying in Laurent's guest room. Was that a dream, or had the attacker somehow managed to get into Laurent's mansion where I was staying? Perhaps it was the same attacker?

I thought, listen to yourself, Jack, that's crazy thinking! Your imagination is running on; over time, vampires don't exist.

But what would explain the same red eyes I saw just the other night at Laurent's, as the victim had reported seeing from her attacker?

I decided I needed to visit the young woman in the hospital and play detective to ask her some questions. Maybe she could provide some answers I was seeking, which didn't appear in the newspaper article. I was hoping whoever was standing guard outside her room would let me in, and if not, I'd hopefully come up with a reason why I was coming to see her.

After finishing my meal, I stopped by a nearby convenience store, bought a small notepad and a pen, and walked to the hospital. The head nurse greeted me at the nurse's station, a plain sort of uptight woman who wasn't at all pleasant as she directed me to room three hundred and two.

I made my way to the elevator and arrived on the third floor. I exited the elevator and walked down the hallway until I reached the entry to Mary's room. As I had suspected, a policeman was seated outside her room; little good did it do as he appeared to be asleep.

Some protection, I thought! I fought hard not to laugh out loud.

I cleared my throat loudly, hoping to wake him, "Ahem," as the policeman promptly woke up and stood, appearing startled.

"Hello, officer. I'm Mary's cousin. I heard about what happened to her and wondered if I might visit with her for a few minutes," I asked.

He looked me over. "You said you're related to the young lady?" He asked in a strong southern drawl.

"Yes, Officer, I've come all this way from Baton Rouge after hearing about what happened to dear Mary; we almost lost her!

We're all so relieved to hear she survived!" I said, trying my best to sound convincing and not blow my cover.

He looked me over suspiciously, then said, "Alright, I'll give you five minutes."

"Yes, of course, thank you, Officer," I said as I reached for the door handle.

I opened the door and discovered Mary asleep. I quietly crept over to her bed and put my hand over her mouth before she could wake and scream for help. She instinctively reached for my hand, her eyes wide with terror.

"Hush! I'm not going to harm you; I just wanted to ask you a few questions." I said, trying to reassure her. "You won't scream, will you?" I asked her.

Mary nodded, agreeing not to make a sound, and looked at me with her pale green eyes, which began to soften a bit, appearing less wild as I removed my hand from her mouth. She asked if I was a reporter, thinking to myself, thank you, Mary, for providing me with a cover.

"Yes, good guess. I'm a reporter," I said and told her my name was Sam and that I worked for the Advocate newspaper in Baton Rouge, and that her attack had made a newsworthy read in the entire state of Louisiana as far away as Baton Rouge.

She blushed at hearing the news. "What can I answer for you, Mister?" She asked.

"Mr. Thompson," I said, quickly thinking of my high school football coach's name back in Baton Rouge. Listen, the policeman outside your door keeping watch has given me a limit of five minutes. We've already used up two. Let's begin," I said. She nodded once more.

"Do you have any idea what your attacker looked like?" I asked.

She seemed to struggle with her response as she turned away from me and started to cry. "He had dark hair, a slender pointy nose, and two red eyes. He had some accent; he didn't sound like he came from around here," Mary said and struggled to continue telling her story. After a brief pause, she said, "He approached me by the Café DuMond and asked me if he could bum a cigarette off me. I told him I didn't smoke. Then he asked if I lived here locally", she reported.

I took Mary Margaux to be a prude and not a loose girl. She told me he was looking for someone local to show him around town and the sights as he was new in town.

"He made it clear that he was not interested in women in a romantic way," she said with a smile and stopped crying.

I became even more intrigued as Mary continued telling me her story. They had walked down towards the waterfront when suddenly he went for her neck. She realized the attacker lied and was interested in women; otherwise, why would he go for her neck? Mary told him to stop; he said it wasn't what it appeared to be, that he had a hunger and attempted to bite her. That's the last thing she could remember before she passed out.

I made some notes on the pad I'd purchased at the convenience store and hoped it would appear professional.

At that moment, the door opened, and I quickly hid my notepad in my newspaper as the policeman told me my five minutes were up.

I thanked Mary for the information, concealing my notebook inside the newspaper so the policeman would still think I was Mary's cousin.

"Thank you, Cousin Mary!" I said as I quickly left the room and went down the hallway and into an elevator just about to close.

I heard the cop's footsteps come running behind.

Mary must have told him I was a reporter when I had introduced myself to him as her cousin from Baton Rouge. Moments later, I reached the street, ran as quickly as possible, and hid down an alleyway. The policeman came from the hospital's main entrance and stood there looking for me.

I waited until I saw the cop leave, undoubtedly heading back to the hospital to stand guard over Mary.

I heard my heartbeat beating wildly, knowing I could have been taken in for questioning, masquerading as her cousin and a reporter.

Despite that, it was well worth the effort. Mary had provided me with enough information regarding the attacker's features, particularly his red eyes!

After returning to the motel, I kicked off my shoes and opened a beer I had picked up at a nearby convenience store. The beer felt good as it hit the back of my throat; as I looked over my notes and read how Mary had described her attacker.

I sat on the bed and thought about what she had shared with me. An attacker telling her he had a hunger and then attacked her neck? A hunger for what? Blood? Then the red eyes she described. Dark hair, a sharp pointy nose, a strange accent, and ruby red eyes sounded like a character from a horror movie. I thought, Was it Dracula himself that had returned from the grave? But didn't that fictional character live in Transylvania? Then moving to England, but that was fiction! Vampires don't exist! Or do they? As I felt the hairs on the back of my neck rise.

Honestly, who wouldn't want to live forever and not grow old and die? Who wouldn't want to stay up all night and sleep the day away? I would sign up for that, or would I?

I decided another way to clear my head of all this talk about vampires was to go out to a club. I had saved up a little money and quit my construction job; having no time constraints, I could go out on a "school night." Perhaps I'll find another more respectable and refined job as Laurent would want. He disapproved of my doing manual labor anyway and had expressed that thought to me over one of the many dinners we had together where he never joined me in eating. I thought about how odd that seemed!

I left the motel and walked over to The Rawhide; I could hook up with someone to forget about all the strangeness around me.

Laurent never made any moves on me which also seemed odd. I thought, He doesn't eat and isn't into sex, so precisely what is he into? I was pleased that I had made some progress with being more comfortable being gay; I'll admit, I had Laurent to thank for that. At the very least, I owed him that.

He made me feel that being gay wasn't just about having sex, but there were other things, such as wanting companionship and a closeness similar to friendship. It saddened me to think about him. I barely noticed the dark figure that appeared beside a tree in the park across from the bar. I thought someone was following me or, more accurately, stalking me. My thoughts quickly returned to Laurent.

If he's so perfect, Jack, what the hell are you doing going out on him and behind his back, and why you aren't with him instead? He must be back from his business trip to Atlanta by now. You should call him. But wait, he never gave me his phone number? Instead, I had given him the phone number to the Stardust motel. How would I reach him? He doesn't even have electricity at his mansion. He told me he wanted to preserve the estate in its historical context or bullshit like that; how on earth would I be in touch with him? I thought despairingly.

I entered the bar feeling guilty about going to a club without Laurent. Why did I feel as if I was cheating on him? Maybe it was the only real connection I felt to another man for the first time in my miserable life.

I walked over to the bar and decided to order anything but a Jack Daniels, my old staple. I wanted to break that pattern and instead ordered a gin and tonic in Laurent's honor. Then again, I should have ordered a glass of tomato juice or whatever the red substance Laurent was drinking.

The bartender recognized me as a regular from the past. When he heard my drink order, he looked at me as if I had grown an extra head.

"Hey man, did you join a country club for queers or something?" He asked.

Now the old me would have taken offense at his comment and told him to "go to hell," but this was the new Jack. I laughed it off and told him, "Yeah, I'm moving on up in the world, like The Jefferson's, you know that old TV show? Even they got tired of being poor," and began to laugh.

He gave me a look, shook his head, and said, "One gin and tonic coming up," which turned some heads. This place was a manly beer-drinking bar.

My tough exterior didn't quite match the insecurity I felt inside. I thought I'll show all of them! From now on, it's the new Jack Devereaux! But then again, why am I out at a Gay bar and a leather bar at that? Why aren't I with Laurent instead?

Before I could think about anything else, this strikingly handsome man with dark hair and deep-set eyes caught my eye as he entered the bar and walked over to where I was standing.

"I couldn't help but notice you as I entered the bar," he said.

He stood slightly taller than me, with broad shoulders, dark hair, and a distinctive nose. He had an accent I had difficulty placing. I noticed his skin was as white as milk; the only thing missing were the red eyes, as in Mary's description.

I asked him where he was from.

"I'm from Europe," he said with a grin.

I looked at him closely; perhaps he thought I was some redneck from Louisiana. I sarcastically said, "Well, that's a bit vague. I know Europe is a continent, not a country. Which country in Europe are you from?" my geographical knowledge seemed to impress him.

"I'm from the land of the Eiffel tower and champagne," he said, looking me over.

"Let me guess, France!" I answered.

"Very good! So, you're familiar with France?" He asked.

"I have a French friend; perhaps the two of you can meet sometime, provided we get to know each other better first?" I said with a grin and began to flirt with the mysterious Frenchman.

If Laurent were insistent on playing hard to get, my new friend would give him a little competition.

"Forgive my rudeness. Allow me to introduce myself; my name is Stefan, and you are?" He asked with one raised eyebrow.

"My name's Jack Devereaux," I answered.

"Ah, so you are French as well? As he spoke, I noticed the slightest trace of what appeared to be blood on his shirt collar, which distracted me.

"Well, I guess you could say that. Actually, I'm Cajun, born and raised in Louisiana; although do I have some French blood. Speaking of blood, I hope you don't mind me mentioning this; you have a tiny stain on your shirt collar," I said, and immediately felt awkward for having mentioned it.

Suddenly our conversation came to an abrupt stop. My new friend, and hopefully, my hook-up for the night, had suddenly become uncomfortable with the mention of blood as he turned away from me.

"I'm sorry! Did I say something to upset you?" I asked.

His reply with a hearty laugh left me once again at ease. He told me to forget about it, admitting that he must have cut himself while shaving and felt embarrassed for having gone out in public with a stained shirt.

"Let me buy you a drink Jack," he offered.

"Sure, what the hell? I've only had one, and somehow I feel like it's going to be a long night," I said and winked. He responded by giving me a sinister grin, a look that gave me the creeps yet oddly enticed me.

"What's your pleasure, Jack?" He asked.

"Jack Daniels," I said, thinking how soon the old ways return, so much for my short-lived attempt at drinking gin and tonics and becoming more refined for Laurent.

Unlike my other Frenchman, Laurent, I sensed this man to be more of a dominant type. He struck me as someone who realized his power and was used to getting everything and anything he wanted. I was intrigued by this show of force and, truthfully, highly physically attracted to him.

I had always been the dominant one in the not-too-distant past, but I decided to go with the flow and allow someone else the pleasure. After all, wasn't that what being gay meant, not to be limited to only one position? Despite both Stefan and Laurent being from France, they couldn't be more different from each other.

As Stefan walked back from the bar with our drinks, I couldn't help but notice how tight his jeans fit him and how muscular his thighs were. His swagger and how he moved had me temporarily mesmerized and imagining all sorts of sexual acts.

Stefan offering to buy me a drink was a good sign; it meant he was interested, and getting laid had become even more of a possibility. As he handed me the glass, I asked him what he was drinking, "a Bloody Mary," he replied.

"Isn't it a little late in the day to be drinking one of those?" I asked him.

"It's never too late to have a Bloody Mary!" he sarcastically said with a hearty laugh. I began to laugh as well. All this talk about

Bloody Mary had me think about the poor girl who had been attacked. I decided I would mention it and gauge his reaction.

"Did you hear about the attack down by the waterfront the other day?" I asked carefully, watching for any reaction as I drank my Jack Daniels.

"Yes, I did, although I didn't finish reading the article. Poor girl; who would do such a thing?" He said calmly.

The more I thought about the attacker's description, the more suspicious I had grown about this guy. Either he was a good actor, or it wasn't him. I needed to dig a little deeper and describe the attacker to Stefan. I told him the attacker had dark hair, a distinctive nose, and the attacker had a European accent.

He looked at me and said, "The description fits me perfectly, but where are my red eyes? Are you honestly implying that I'm the attacker? If I were the attacker, why wouldn't I be out looking for another victim instead of in this bar talking to you?" I stared at him blankly.

"Such a shame about the victim; what was her name?" He asked.

"Mary," I answered.

"Such a shame Mary didn't survive, isn't it?" He said, sounding almost victorious when talking about her supposed death.

"If you had continued reading the article, you would have known that she survived," I said, noticing how quickly his mood changed; a sudden look of concern struck me as suspicious.

I thought, was this man the attacker? What could explain the red eyes seen by Mary as described in the article?

"Jack, do you want to spend all night talking about some random woman that was attacked, however tragic, or do you want to get to know each other better?" he said and winked.

"I don't know; you tell me," I replied and held his gaze.

He looked at me and said, "Rarely, if ever, have I ever been challenged, Jack. Can we go back to being physically drawn to one another" he said as I took a drink from my Jack Daniels and noticed he never once took a sip from his cocktail.

I briefly thought about overpowering him and handing him over to the police if he was the attacker. They would offer up some reward money, plus I would be doing Mary and other potential female victims a favor by getting this guy off the street. What puzzled me was that he genuinely came across as being interested in men, or more to the point, interested in me. So why would he have attacked a female? It just didn't piece together.

Instantly I heard one of my favorite songs begin to play, "Forever Young"; the DJ must have been reading my mind.

Attempting to break the tension between us, I asked him, "Hey, do you want to dance?"

"Sure, "let's go for it!" as you Americans say!" as we hit the dance floor and freestyled to the music, our dancing seemed to continue nonstop, partly because the DJ played the extended version of the song.

As we moved around each other, Stefan gave me these intense looks as the music continued to play. I listened to the lyrics, "do you want to live forever, forever, and ever!" That sent a shiver up my spine and made the hairs on the back of my neck stand up. I wondered if this were a coincidence, the song the DJ decided to play for my dance with Stefan. I thought, how crazy this all seemed! I began swooning to the music, which enticed Stefan, who was quite a distance away from me and suddenly by my side, locking himself around me. I tried to get him off me and maintain some distance. It was no use; he was too strong, unnaturally so you might say!

Stefan wrapped his mighty arms around me as if attempting to give me a bear hug. I felt powerless to resist him. I'm sure this spectacle looked odd to the other bar patrons. As I looked deep into his eyes, they seemed to say, I have you exactly where I want you, and you don't have any control over anything!

Did I detect a hint of red in his gorgeous blue eyes? I wondered if I had imagined that or if it was a part of the club lights that shone on the dance floor from the ceiling above.

I'll admit I felt physically intimidated by another man for the first time in my life. I wrote it off as just a case of nerves, and my imagination ran wild. All this talk about Mary and her attacker. I tried desperately to put all those thoughts out of my mind and instead focus on this incredibly sexy man who seemed interested in me physically.

Stefan leaned over and whispered in my ear suggestively, "I think we should go back to your place, Jack."

I felt conflicted; on the one hand, it had been a long time since I had any physical contact with anyone, and I would welcome releasing some pent-up sexual energy. On the other hand, I felt intimidated by Stefan. I reluctantly agreed.

"Sure. I'm staying at a motel not far from here; we could walk there. It's called the Stardust Motel. Is that okay with you?" I asked.

"Anywhere is fine, Jack, as long as you and I are alone," he replied and suddenly released me from his powerful embrace as we exited the dance floor.

I thought, how many men had I dominated physically over the years? Had they felt the same way about me? The irony had me chuckle a bit.

We left the bar as the steamy humid summer night's air hung heavy and thick.

We walked under multiple gas lamps as we passed building after building with wrought-iron balconies; I had never really appreciated the city's charm and beauty until this evening. I wondered how I had taken it all for granted.

We finally reached the motel; I admit, I was embarrassed for taking Stefan to such a dump. I felt his eyes watching me closely as we made our way to my room.

As soon as I unlocked and opened the door, Stefan paused outside and asked me whether he was invited in. I thought that was a strange question and said, "Yes, of course, Stefan, it's why I invited you back here," I said.

"I was brought up with manners, Jack; forgive me, I'm a bit old-fashioned," he replied.

I wondered what would come next as I took a seat on the bed as Stefan walked over and leaned over me; I thought, did I hear him growling a bit? As I began to shiver. "You're shivering, Jack? You know, you remind me of someone I knew a long, long time ago, someone very special to me; I realized that the moment I laid eyes on you as I entered the bar. You and he could have been twins."

"What happened to him, Stefan?" I asked with a bit of apprehension as he turned away from me.

"He died; he was taken from me, Jack. We never got to live together for very long. I regret that," He said, as I noticed his mood change to sadness.

I could sense he was softening up; perhaps our conversation about his deceased love interest would ruin the idea of sex.

"Perhaps I should go, Jack. You seem a bit disinterested in me sexually," he said and appeared to be looking right through me.

"No, that couldn't be further from the truth, Stefan. I find you very interesting and a bit mysterious. I want to learn more about you. I would love to see you again?" I said, holding my breath slightly, waiting for his reply.

"Perhaps. You intrigue me Jack; you are so much like him," He said, not being able to shake his somber mood.

"What was his name, Stefan?" I asked, and immediately felt awkward about having asked such a sensitive question.

"His name was Fabien; we lived together for a brief period. We were thrilled in the beginning the world was our oyster! We had wealth and power, yet that was not enough!" He said as he suddenly became angry.

"Fabien told me he couldn't be with me. He wanted to leave and didn't love me, which nearly destroyed me. I never told him how much his leaving affected me; instead, I agreed to let him go. Foolishly he left me for another, and that was his mistake," his mood changed from anger to sadness. He turned away from my gaze and wiped his eyes. When he faced me, I noticed smeared blood near his eyes.

"Stefan! Are you ok? You're bleeding!" I said, sounding alarmed.

"I'm fine, Jack; I merely cut myself shaving this morning; that was the spot of blood you saw on my shirt collar earlier. I'm afraid I have reopened the cut, which appears to have blood running down my face. I apologize, Jack. I should go; I think the mood for sex has been ruined. Yes, I would like to see you again if you're interested. But for now, I must go," he explained, sounding distant.

"But how will I reach you? Where can I find you?" I asked, pleading.

"I know your location, Jack; if you're not here, I will leave a message with the front desk on how you can reach me; are we in agreement?" he asked in a way that I couldn't refuse.

"Better yet, why don't we say next week, Saturday evening? I can pick you up here, and we'll go to dinner and a movie?" He asked.

"Sure, that sounds great! I said excitedly.

"Wonderful, I'll be here shortly after sunset."

"Yes, Stefan, I'm looking forward to our date together."

He leaned toward me to kiss me, careful not to smear the blood on the side of his face on mine; it was a tender kiss; his lips, however, felt like ice, which reminded me of Laurent's lips.

Stefan displayed many sides of his personality. In an instant, he could switch from being the brute that had put me in a bear hug while dancing at the club to someone who still seemed to be mourning his dead lover. There was so much about Stefan I was dying to find out, not to mention having another guy interested in me when Laurent couldn't make himself available to me. I suddenly didn't feel so guilty going out on Laurent.

"Until Saturday, Jack," he said.

"Yes, until Saturday, Stefan," I replied.

He got up and walked toward the door, stopping and turning in my direction and smiling at me as he left.

He left the door open as I stood up from the bed and walked over to close it. I threw myself on the bed and thought, *lately, every guy I meet stops short of any physical contact unloads their past on me, and suddenly, the mood is gone! Damn it! Maybe it's me? Perhaps I'm losing my touch?*

I removed my shirt and stood in the bathroom mirror, examining my chiseled chest and arms from all my years at the construction site. As I looked more closely, I noticed hand imprints on my sides, which began to bruise! Thinking, man, this Stefan is powerful! That must have been where he held me in that vise-like grip back at the bar while we were dancing.

I began to think about Laurent, the other mysterious Frenchman, as I anxiously awaited his return from whatever business trip he'd traveled to. I started to feel conflicted about being torn between two lovers.

Laurent had a certain air of sophistication, which was the opposite of my new love interest Stefan, despite them both being from France. Even over there, you have your upper-crust white and blue collars. Laurent was white-collar, with his estate, a servant, a Rolls Royce, and his love of the arts.

While Stefan went to gay bars, wasn't clean-shaven, and his hair wasn't perfect. The thought of seeing Laurent out at a gay club made me laugh. He wouldn't be caught dead in a place like that.

Thinking about these two men and how different they were, made me laugh. How is it that a plain Louisiana Cajun boy should be dating not one but two guys from France? I thought about the irony of all of that.

I decided I needed to shower after having danced with Stefan in the smoky bar and quickly undressed as I entered the bathroom, thinking, I've already been in this dump a month! One month since, I left my wife and straight life behind, leaving everything that had become familiar to me. Having met Laurent changed my world. I felt like a different person when I was with Laurent; I knew he would show me things I had never experienced before, educate and refine me, and perhaps change me into something more like himself.

But compared to Stefan, who seemed interested in me sexually, something about him made me feel uneasy. He was a complete mystery to me, whether his strength and manliness drew me to him or that I felt threatened by that. I was lost in my thoughts as I stepped into the shower. The hot water hit my face, running down my shoulders and towards my aching sides.

The water felt good, almost healing. I listened as the water hit the tiled floor, splashing and making an almost hypnotic, soothing sound.

I got out, toweled myself off, and slipped into bed. In minutes, I was fast asleep.

I started to dream and pictured myself in a castle, dressed in period clothing. I couldn't tell what period precisely as I walked down a long hallway lit only with candelabras when suddenly the image of a man appeared in the fog at the end of the hall. Everything about this man seemed normal except two gleaming, piercing, red eyes, which looked directly through me to my soul.

I moved nearer to the man's image and suddenly saw his face; it was Laurent. His eyes were ablaze and hypnotic. Suddenly another embodiment of a man appeared with the same red eyes.

The two stared at me when suddenly an unearthly guttural growl from both of them followed by hissing sounds; it appeared as if they were claiming their prize, which was me!

Unexpectedly each one was upon me when suddenly, waves of red came crashing down around all three of us. It seemed to be streaming through the walls, but what were these waves of red? Was it blood?

I tried to swim in the pool of red, trying my best not to have it pull me under and drown me. I resisted and tried desperately to keep my head above water, but it was no use; it was too powerful. I felt like I had lost all of my strength as the red sea finally managed to take me under.

Once below, both swam towards me, opening each one's mouth. Both appeared to be drinking the liquid as they swam nearer and nearer. I tried desperately to swim away from my two suitors, but they surrounded me, one on either side. I looked at each in the red haze of the liquid and screamed out, "No!" I awakened with a jolt and found myself drenched in a cold sweat; I felt comforted to find myself in my bed at the motel. This old dump never looked so good to me.

I began to shake, and my breathing became heavy; I couldn't tell the difference between dreams and reality for a while. I couldn't remember the last time I felt so frightened and unsure. What did the dream mean? Why were Laurent and Stefan trying to hurt me? They almost appeared locked in a battle attempting to claim their prize, me.

I better not bring this up to either of them; I don't want to risk sounding crazy and losing them; they would surely question my mental state if I dared to share this nightmare with them.

Finally, I had two good-looking, attractive, yet mysterious men interested in me after all these years, Jack Devereaux, the ex-football star and blue-collared boy from Baton Rouge, who just so happens to be a closeted gay guy.

I wondered how Laurent and Stefan felt about their sexuality and whether they should meet each other.

I thought, what the hell! Deciding at that moment that they should meet. I'm sure they would have a lot in common, both from France, who knows? Perhaps even from the same town? Maybe we could all become best friends. What was there to lose?

CHAPTER 12

The dinner invitation

Jack returned to bed, wondering whether the bad dreams would return or if he would enjoy a restful, uninterrupted sleep. Luckily the nightmares hadn't returned, and Jack enjoyed a long, overdue seven-hour rest.

The following day Jack checked with the front desk manager to see if he had received any calls; as luck would have it, there was one. It was from Barthelme, asking Jack to return his call with a number in the message.

Jack sprinted back to his room and called Barthelme, anxious to find out whether Laurent had returned; he picked up after the third ring. "Richelieu residence Barthelme speaking."

"Hello, Barthelme, it's Jack. Has Laurent returned from his business trip?" Jack asked.

"Yes, he has; the master would like to see if you can join him for dinner this Saturday night?" Barthelme asked.

"Gosh, I already made plans," Jack said apologetically.

"I'm certain the master will be very disappointed," Barthelme said.

"I know this may seem rude, but do you think Laurent would mind if I brought a friend along? As luck would have it, my friend is also from France; maybe they'll become friends? I would hate to turn down Laurent's dinner invitation and disappoint him," Jack said, sounding apologetic.

There was an awkward pause, then finally, Barthelme answered, "I'm certain Master Laurent would not mind you bringing a friend along."

Jack felt awkward about asking to bring a friend, especially knowing Laurent wanted to have Jack all to himself. But the fact that both men were from the same country could be an icebreaker, and perhaps Laurent would enjoy Stefan's company as much as Jack.

At long last, Saturday arrived, and Jack took inventory of his clothes, mainly denim jeans, flannel shirts, and maybe a polo shirt or two, plus the sports jacket and trousers he'd worn the last time he was invited for dinner at Laurent's. He couldn't wear the same outfit twice or any other clothes; they were too casual. No, this would require a trip to the fancy Men's boutique on St Charles called "George Bass." Later that day, he entered the store and asked the salesperson to help put together a suitable outfit for a, as Jack told the salesperson, a fancy dinner party. He tried on several and finally decided on a classic navy blue blazer with gold buttons, a white designer dress shirt, pleated pants, another pair of nylon dress socks, and a pair of dress shoes; he was certain Laurent would approve.

Jack had put some money aside to buy his now ex-wife, Lisa, something. Instead, Jack would use that money to purchase clothes and shoes for his dinner with Laurent and Stefan.

Back at the motel, after having showered, he dressed in the outfit he'd purchased at the fancy store earlier that day and looked himself over in the mirror. Saying to himself, "Jack Ol' Boy, how could these two men not be into you? You look like a male model!" As the sun began to set, Jack looked out the window and saw that Stefan still had not arrived. There was never a definite time agreed upon, only once the sun had set. Jack wondered when Stefan would come. He walked into the bathroom to spray a little more cologne on and returned to look out the window and spotted Stefan walking up the stairs as daytime had turned to night.

From the little he had seen from the window, Stefan had cleaned himself up rather nicely as well; he had shaved off the five o'clock shadow he had the last time they saw each other at the bar and was dressed as nicely as Jack. Both would appear respectable enough to join Laurent at his estate for dinner.

Naturally, Jack couldn't resist thinking about the possibility of sex. Who knows? Maybe Laurent would find Stefan equally attractive enough so that it might end up in a three-way? The thought of that caused Jack to laugh and *thought Good luck! Laurent is way too refined for that kind of activity!*

A knock at the door as Jack opened the door and greeted his date, "Hello, fine Sir, how handsome you look!" as he leaned his face toward Stefan to kiss him, Stefan returned the favor, and once again, that biting cold that he felt from Stefan's lips.

Jack composed himself and said, "So, change of plans, Stefan, I have a dinner invitation from a friend I couldn't turn down. I asked if it would be alright if I brought you along with me. Naturally, they said yes. By the way, my friend is also from France, so you two should get along just fine," Jack said excitedly.

"From France?" Stefan asked. Jack noticed that Stefan seemed intrigued by this bit of news. After a brief pause, Stefan said, "Well, if he's from France, how can I resist? Besides, that will spare me having to take you out for dinner and a movie, as we talked about," Stefan said kiddingly.

"Great! His driver should be here any minute to pick us up," Jack replied.

"His driver? Well! He sounds like a fine Frenchman of means; I'm very much looking forward to meeting him," Stefan said.

Jack thought he detected a hint of sarcasm but wasn't sure. No sooner had those remarks been said, Barthelme arrived as planned. It seemed he always appeared right at the moment as if he had some homing device. It was truly uncanny.

Stefan and Jack left the motel room and walked down the stairs.

"Barthelme! I would like you to meet my good friend Stefan."

"A pleasure," replied Barthelme as he held the door open for both men, closed each passenger door, and stepped into the Rolls Royce.

"The pleasure is all mine, Barthelme," answered Stefan.

Jack could tell by the look on Stefan's face that he was impressed.

Both men sat in the back seat, gazing out the window, chatting about various subjects, and giggling with a bit of handholding, which drew Barthelme's attention, knowing that his Master had romantic feelings for Jack.

Barthelme looked in the mirror, expecting to see both men and only seeing Jack's reflection. Barthelme looked horrified, as if he had seen a ghost, unbeknownst to Jack or Stefan.

Barthelme knew enough about the undead to realize they did not cast a reflection and became alarmed that another vampire was coming to his Master's estate.

Upon his arrival, Stefan commented on how lovely the estate looked and that he was looking forward to meeting this mysterious fellow Frenchmen Jack had spoken so highly about, which was a lie. Jack had shared very little with Stefan regarding Laurent.

Barthelme asked Stefan his last name, to which Stefan replied, "Baron Vitré."

As Barthelme opened the large front door, he saw his Master as he descended the grand staircase and proceeded to announce the uninvited guest, "Master Laurent, may I introduce to you Stefan Baron Vitré?"

Laurent was near the bottom of the staircase when he abruptly stopped and stared at the uninvited guest. He instantly recognized Jack's friend as the same creature who had destroyed his beloved Fabien over two hundred fifty years ago in Paris.

Laurent looked sternly at Stefan and remained silent. He avoided Jack's gaze altogether. There was a momentary silence between all present. Stefan returned Laurent's stare equally as intense. Until the host finally spoke, breaking the uncomfortable silence. "A pleasure to meet you, Monsieur," Laurent said coldly, not addressing Stefan by his last name, which Barthelme had just announced.

"Baron Vitré, Monsieur Baron Vitré, if you will, kind Sir," Stefan replied and corrected Laurent.

"May we enter?" Stefan asked.

"Where are my manners? Yes." Laurent flatly replied.

Jack thought, am I seeing a bit of jealousy, or is it something else?

"Shall we adjourn to the drawing room?" Laurent asked.

"Yes, that would be nice, Laurent," Jack replied on behalf of himself and Stefan.

Once inside the drawing room, a roaring fire greeted everyone, which seemed to cozy up the frosty atmosphere between the two Frenchmen.

"What an exquisite estate you have, Monsieur. My apologies; I did not get your last name. Stefan said as he attempted to break the iciness between them with seemingly no success.

"Richelieu." He said. "If you'll both kindly have a seat, I must address something with my servant Barthelme. Please excuse me," Laurent said as he exited the drawing room and hastily headed into the kitchen, leaving Stefan and Jack alone.

During Laurent's absence, Stefan began to nuzzle Jack's neck. "Stop, Stefan! Behave yourself; I'm sure Laurent would disapprove," Jack said and chuckled.

Another scene was playing out in the kitchen. Barthelme had been preparing a delicious dinner consisting of duck with a cranberry orange glaze, whipped potatoes, sautéed cabbage, and onions. The aroma of the food hit Laurent's nostrils as soon as he entered the kitchen, as he held back his nausea. He immediately confronted Barthelme as he menacingly approached his servant.

"What is he doing here, Barthelme? Laurent demanded in a hushed whisper.

"What do you mean, Master?" Barthelme replied innocently.

"How dare you bring this miserable creature into my home, the same monster who destroyed my beloved," Laurent snarled in a hushed tone.

"I don't know what you're talking about!" Barthelme replied.

"You mean to tell me you had no idea who Jack brought along as his guest?" Laurent asked as his anger subsided.

"Master Laurent, I had no idea who he was; the only thing I saw in my mirror as the two of them sat in the back of the car was Master Jack's reflection and not his friend Stefan's.

"I guess I cannot blame you, Barthelme; you never met Stefan before this evening; after all, Jack invited this miserable creature to join us for dinner, Laurent said and regained his composure.

Suddenly, the kitchen door opened, and Jack and Stefan appeared as each of them stood at the entry to the kitchen.

"Is everything alright in here, Laurent? You've been gone quite a while?" Jack asked, sounding concerned.

"Yes. I thought I smelled something burning and decided to check in with Barthelme; everything seemed to be under control.

Please, gentlemen, let's return to the dining room; I'm certain Barthelme will be able to salvage our dinner," Laurent said and led them back to the table.

Jack returned to his seat while Stefan remained at the kitchen's entry.

"May I borrow a moment of your time to speak with you in private, Monsieur Richelieu?" Stefan asked.

"If you insist, Monsieur Vitré, Barthelme, leave the room, do not return until I summon you," Laurent commanded as Barthelme quickly exited the kitchen.

"Well, you wanted to speak to me in private, so speak," Laurent sarcastically said.

"You may call me Stefan; may I call you Laurent?"

Laurent didn't respond and ignored his question.

"Well, you and I have someone in common, your friend Jack, or his name Fabien?" Stefan said as he chuckled.

"Let's stop this charade, Stefan! Surely you remember me?

Or shall I say, I will never forget you or what you did to my beloved! How dare you enter my home uninvited," Laurent said, filled with rage, as he slapped the other vampire across the face.

Despite that, the other vampire remained calm and said, "For your sake, I will ignore that emotional outburst; however, you are incorrect, Laurent. Jack invited me as his guest; still, I had no idea where and who I was to have dinner with. In a thousand years, I would never have suspected that you and I would once again see each other, much less be invited to dine at your estate. Yes, I do remember you. It was you; after all, I was coming to destroy," Stefan replied, sounding smug.

"I want you to leave here immediately. You are not welcome here," Laurent snarled, his face twisted with rage as he bore his fangs at Stefan.

"I'm afraid I can't do that. It would be rude of me to leave suddenly when the night has just begun. Isn't it Jack's decision whether I should stay or go? Wasn't it he that extended the invitation to me? Shall we ask him if he would like me to leave after you invited me to enter?" Stefan stated mockingly, feeling as if he had the upper hand.

"You know that's impossible. Jack knows nothing about what we are or our past together!" Laurent retorted.

"Well then, it is settled. I shall stay. On a good note, I won't be eating, as I have the same dietary needs as you. So please tell your servant that I shall not need a place setting. I shall nourish myself later, as I suspect you will. Now, shall we join Jack at the dining table, Laurent?" Stefan said as he held the door open for Laurent as they returned to the dining table.

"I was beginning to wonder what happened," Jack said with concern.

"Yes, Stefan and I recalled how our paths had crossed years ago in our home country; neither one of us made that connection initially, Jack," Laurent said as he struggled to sound convincing." "We had so much catching up to do." Stefan said with a grin.

This sounded odd to Jack, and he wondered why they would have needed to speak to each other privately about that.

Barthelme arrived and announced dinner was being served; Stefan and Laurent took their respective seats as a deafening silence descended upon the dining room.

Jack was the first to be served. Barthelme had been instructed to offer him a generous portion, and Laurent and Stefan were to be given very little. Laurent had asked his servant to prepare food for both vampires to avoid raising any suspicion from Jack.

"So, how do you two know each other? Or is there some mystery behind that?" Jack asked and started to eat. Jack noticed Laurent and Stefan moving their food around, never once eating any of the delicious dinners Barthelme had so painstakingly prepared.

"We met briefly in Paris, wasn't it, Laurent?" Stefan sarcastically asked.

"Yes, it was quite brief," Laurent coldly answered and looked at Stefan disapprovingly.

"Man! This duck is incredible! Why aren't you guys eating?" Jack asked, oblivious to the underlying tension rising between the two vampires.

Both vampires ignored Jack's remark and appeared to be staring the other one down.

"Hey, guys," Jack said and tried to get the attention of Laurent and Stefan. Each appeared consumed by the other until Laurent finally broke the silence and said, "I'm afraid I don't have much of an appetite for duck. Barthelme seems to always forget that. However, there will be much more for you to enjoy, Jack."

"I dined late this afternoon; I'm afraid I'm not that hungry, Jack. However, I am rather thirsty," Stefan said mockingly, and displayed a sinister grin, looked over at Laurent, and gave him a wink.

It appeared that Laurent had decided to drink rather than eat and held a glass with a very thick red substance, which he seemed to relish with every sip.

"Monsieur Richelieu, may I sample a glass of whatever you're drinking? I'm certain it will be delicious," Stefan said.

"Barthelme, pour Monsieur Vitré a glass from my finest collection," Laurent instructed.

"Right away, Master Laurent," Barthelme replied, knowing the code words "finest collection" meant dog's blood, as he poured Stefan the same from the carafe Laurent was drinking.

"Merci Monsieur Richelieu," Stefan said.

"Hey, the two of you are making me jealous; I want to sample some of that!" Jack said, unaware of the substance Laurent and Stefan were drinking.

"I don't think you're quite ready for that, Jack; it's very potent, perhaps in due time," Laurent replied uncomfortably and looked at Jack rather intensely, then switched his gaze to Stefan.

"Jack, how did you meet Stefan?" Laurent asked, seeming disinterested in the answer.

"We met at a club called the Rawhide!" Jack answered. His speech had begun sounding slightly slurred. Jack appeared amused by his response as he laughed. It was apparent to both vampires that Jack was becoming intoxicated from the wine, which Laurent knew to be Jack's standard practice.

"The Rawhide?" Laurent asked, and raised his eyebrow that appeared to show his disapproval.

"Yeah, Laurent, it's a club where men go to meet each other; I've asked you a few times to join me, but you always turned me down. I decided to go out on my own to clear my head and have a bit of fun, and that's where I met Stefan," Jack replied defiantly, his courage aided by his alcohol consumption.

"I see; I had no idea you were looking to meet other men, Jack?" Laurent replied, sounding insulted.

"Look, you were out of town on business or something like that; what was I supposed to do until you got back; sit around and wait for you?" Jack retorted forcefully.

"I was under the impression that we were dating; apparently, I was wrong," Laurent said, his tone reflecting the hurt of Jack's admittance of having gone out on him.

"Listen, it's all very innocent. Stefan bought me a drink; we danced a little, and we laughed. He told me I reminded him of someone he knew long ago." Jack admitted.

"I see," Laurent said coldly.

"If you're wondering if we made out, we didn't," Jack replied, appearing to confess to Laurent, possibly out of guilt.

The mood inside the dining room had taken on a dramatic and cold atmosphere. Laurent's facial expression displayed nothing but loathing for Stefan and contempt for Jack.

"Excuse me, but am I to assume that the two of you are seeing each other romantically?" Stefan asked.

"Yes," Laurent replied.

"No," Jack replied.

Stefan laughed and said, "Well, which is it? Yes or no?" As Laurent struggled to control his seething anger. At the same time, Jack appeared to have consumed more and more of his wine, oblivious to Laurent's reaction. Laurent knew he had to take control of the situation.

"Jack, it would be best if your friend were to leave at once! And as far as you're concerned, I think you should lie down in one of the guest rooms as you've become intoxicated. Barthelme will help get you to your room," Laurent said and struggled to remain calm.

"I agree with Monsieur Richelieu. I need to leave. I feel I'm not welcome here!" Stefan announced, his tone sounding agitated.

Laurent reacted triumphantly, sensing he had the upper hand, and said, "Good! Then it is settled."

"For the record, Monsieur Richelieu, you cannot prevent me from seeing Jack; that is entirely his decision. I suspect our paths will cross again. And with that, I wish you both a delightful rest of the evening. Until we meet again, Monsieur," Stefan said.

"I trust you can see yourself out, Monsieur?" Laurent replied coldly.

"Yes, by all means, Monsieur, don't bother escorting me to the door. I can tell that you and Jack need some time alone to sort through some of your issues. Good night" Stefan said as he stood up and walked out of the dining room into the long hallway and out the front door, as his footsteps faded in the distance.

Outside the estate, the sounds of dogs howling could be heard as a late-night fog had developed, making it impossible to make out any of the large oak trees that lined the pathway on either side leading to the massive estate.

Laurent turned to face Jack and said, "I forbid you to see Stefan again. If you and I are to be together, there will not be a third. Do you understand me?" Laurent said commandingly.

"Am I missing something, Laurent? Since when did we ever finalize anything about not seeing other people?" Jack answered back defiantly, continuing to slur some of his words.

Laurent had grown increasingly impatient with Jack's condition and said, "You're drunk, Jack. Go to bed and sleep it off; there is no point in discussing this now. We will talk more about this tomorrow evening, once I have returned from a day's business trip. You're welcome to stay here, collect your thoughts, and dry out before I return. There is a lot to discuss. But discussing anything with you while you're in this condition is pointless. Do we understand each other?" Laurent stated angrily.

"I guess I have no choice, Laurent," Jack said resentfully, sounding as if his ego had become deflated.

"Right this way, Master Jack," Barthelme said and walked toward Jack to assist him. At this point, Jack could barely walk on his own as he stood and muttered something under his breath, followed by a display of staggering as Barthelme locked his arm around Jack's waist. "Master Jack!" Jack said mockingly.

The exquisite ornate wooden grandfather clock struck midnight as Jack and Barthelme continued up the grand staircase to the guestroom, which awaited Jack.

Upon entering the guestroom, Jack flung himself onto the bed. Jack was unaware of Barthelme as he attempted to undress him so he would be more comfortable. Soon, Jack was stripped of all his clothes except his underwear and socks.

Barthelme opened the bedding for Jack, having rolled Jack to one side of the bed, "Your bed is ready for you, Master Jack," Barthelme said as Jack crawled carefully under the luxurious comforter and exquisite bed linens. No sooner had his head hit the pillow; than Jack passed out before Barthelme could leave the room.

He observed Jack sleeping briefly and thought about how much Jack looked like the man in the portrait hanging in his Master's bedroom. Perhaps his Master was correct in thinking that this blue-collar, uncultured man was indeed the reincarnated Fabien, as impossible as that appeared to be?

Barthelme suspected the Master would eventually offer Jack the dark gift. They would be together once more, and Jack would gain eternal life, cheat death, and recreate the past with Master Laurent in the present, and the future.

Perhaps that plan would be challenged due to Stefan's arrival, as he learned this evening that he ended Laurent and Fabien's dreams of eternal existence together back in Paris.

Barthelme quietly slipped out the door and gently closed the heavy wooden door behind him so as not to disturb Jack's sleep.

Outside, the howling dogs had started again, this time more intensely than before. Barthelme knew that meant another of the Master's kind was nearby. Only the undead caused the dogs to howl loudly, sounding as if they were being tortured.

Barthelme had left the window to Jack's bedroom wide open as a thick mist began to swirl outside. Suddenly trails of the dense fog spilled over the windowsill and onto the floor as it began to take shape.

The deep-set red eyes stared intensely at Jack and studied his every movement. A telepathic voice entered Jack's mind telling him to awaken and rise and come towards the image, still enshrouded with fog. It was enormously thick and filled the entire bedroom.

Jack tossed and turned, unable to fight the voice in his head, which repeatedly commanded him to rise and walk toward it!

"Come to me, Jack!" The figure commanded.

Jack had difficulty identifying the voice and felt powerless, unable to deny the figure's command. Jack answered, "yes, I hear you, and I shall obey."

He got out of bed, walked over in a hypnotic trance closer to the figure, and struggled to regain consciousness, still unable to form words in his mouth other than his initial reply.

Finally finding the strength deep within him, he managed to cry out, "Laurent!"

In the neighboring bedroom, Laurent had just begun his undead slumber once the sun had risen; he opened his eyes as he heard Jack scream out his name and quickly climbed off the bed and rushed to the room, sensing Jack was in danger.

Laurent forcefully opened Jack's bedroom door and saw firsthand what had frightened and disturbed Jack; seeing the image enshrouded in fog, yet able to detect the figure using his vampire vision, he recognized the mysterious figure as Stefan. The vampire hissed at Laurent and bore his fangs.

Summoning all of his vampire rages, Laurent screamed in a powerfully supernatural voice that reverberated throughout the grand estate: "Get out! I command you! You are not welcome here!"

Jack came out of the trance and covered his ears as his knees buckled from shaking and finally collapsed on the floor.

CHAPTER 13

Confession time

Instantly, Stefan disappeared into the night air. "You saw him too! Didn't you?" Jack asked, his voice trembling with fear.

"Yes, Jack, I commanded him to leave. I am your protector, Jack; it is me who you should trust, not Stefan!" Laurent said passionately.

"I have to leave Laurent; I can't think clearly!" Jack said as he struggled to stand up, still visibly shaken from what had just occurred.

"But it's late, Jack, and you're not safe without me!" Laurent pleaded, but it was no use; Jack had made his mind up and sobered up from last night's drunkenness.

"No, I can't stay! "I need some sleep, Laurent! Something strange happens every time I stay at your place, and besides that, I never get laid. Plus, tonight's spectacle took the cake! What did I witness in the bedroom just now? How did Stefan get into my bedroom, why would he want to harm me, and what was that mighty opera-like voice you have?" Jack asked, sounding frustrated and scared.

It was clear to Laurent that Jack hadn't been able to see Stefan's long incisors; it was too dark; naturally, Laurent's vampire abilities allowed him to see in the dark; as he made out Stefan's twisted and rage-filled face, which included his menacing fangs.

Jack, I think you had better sit back on the bed," Laurent suggested.

"What is it, Laurent? Jack asked and looked at him with concern in his eyes. Laurent returned Jack's gaze lovingly.

"Jack, I have something to tell you; this goes against everything in my being to tell you what I am about to share," Laurent said, yet Jack sensed his hesitation.

As he sat down on the bed, Jack tried to prepare himself for whatever Laurent was about to share with him. "For Christ's sake, Laurent, just come out and say it!" Jack shouted, sounding agitated.

"Jack, I am not who I appear to be. I may appear to look human, but I'm not. I am one of the living dead, in other words, I'm a vampire." Laurent confessed; his voice sounded full of agony and despair.

What followed was a long silence; then Jack rose from the bed and walked over to the window, as he pulled the curtain halfway open and stood there observing the sky as it began to get light as the dawn approached.

"Laurent? Vampires don't exist; that's just fiction!" Jack said as he struggled to believe his love interest's confession.

"Why would I make up such a story, Jack?"

"Well, if this is true, give me some proof?"

"Jack, please! Don't make this any more difficult than it already is," Laurent said in an agonizing tone. "Alright, if you insist, but I warn you, Jack, prepare yourself for what you are about to witness; it may come as quite a shock!" Laurent said ominously.

Instantly, faster than any mortal eye could detect, Laurent moved across the room and stood in back of Jack, separated only by inches. Jack could feel Laurent's breath on his neck.

He turned to face Laurent and quite suddenly witnessed, Laurent's face had begun to contort; his eyes turned from their pleasingly attractive blue color into blood-red; Jack instantly recognized those were the same color eyes that had stared at him in the bedroom earlier that evening. Laurent opened his mouth to reveal two large incisors as he reached his arms towards the ceiling, and commanded the weather to respond violently, followed by a spectacular thunder and lightning display as the wind began to howl. As Laurent lowered his arms, the weather quickly turned calm.

"Would you like any other proof? Or does that satisfy your curiosity?" Laurent said, his voice sounded exhausted and filled with despair.

Laurent's display of immortal abilities visibly shook Jack.

"It's late; you had better return to your bedroom Laurent. If you are what you say you are, then you'll need to shield yourself from the sun," Jack said as his voice began to tremble. "Jack, did you hear what I asked? You witnessed everything I showed you as proof that I am who I say I am," Laurent said, starting to sound irritated.

"Yes, I believe you. How could I not from what you just showed me? Truthfully, I'm shocked to find out that creatures like you and Stefan actually exist! I'm finding it difficult to absorb. It's all so incredible," Jack said and looked at Laurent. "But why me, Laurent? I don't understand?"

"Jack, if you would follow me to my bedroom, there is something I need to show you; it will undoubtedly answer your question," Laurent said, sounding mysterious, as Jack nodded and followed Laurent into his room.

As they walked toward Laurent's room in silence Jack thought, *now it all makes sense. This is why Laurent never ate food, why he could never be seen during the daylight hours, and why his touch always seemed to remind me of touching ice or what it must be like to touch a dead body.*

As Jack entered Laurent's bedroom, he was surrounded by darkness, with the heavy burgundy velvet drapes drawn to prevent any trace of sunlight from entering the bedroom. A single candelabra burned on the dresser.

Laurent walked over to pick it up and held it close to the wall, which illuminated the painting. There, on the wall, hung the portrait of Laurent's beloved Fabien, Jack's counterpart.

Jack couldn't contain his shock as he gazed upon the portrait and released an audible gasp, "Oh my God! He looks identical to me!" Jack exclaimed as the color left his face.

"Yes, he does. His name was Fabien. He was my love and eternal soulmate and my vampire maker. He was taken from me over two hundred and fifty years ago. I've mourned his destruction ever since," Laurent confided, as a single blood tear ran down his cheek.

"So you're trying to turn me into him, is that it?" Jack asked innocently.

Laurent turned to face Jack and said, "Don't you see Jack? From the moment I met you at the Jazz club, I knew that my Fabien had returned to me, in another body, namely yours. We are destined to be together. Don't you feel that as well?"

"I need to leave here; I can't think clearly; none of this makes sense to me!" Jack said dismissively.

"Doesn't anything I've said hold any importance for you, Jack? Even now, as I bear my soul and share my dark secret with you?" Laurent said as another blood tear ran down his pallid cheek.

"I didn't say that it didn't matter. I never said that, Laurent. As I told you, I need to leave; I have a lot of thinking to do about you and me and Stefan," Jack said and tried to exit the bedroom.

He had difficulty getting past Laurent when suddenly, the vampire took ahold of his arm in a vice-like grip.

"We haven't finished our discussion yet, Jack!" Laurent commanded as the vampire's sadness turned toward anger.

"Let go of my arm, Laurent; you're hurting me!" He shouted. Laurent reluctantly released his arm as Jack rushed over to the bedroom window and ripped open a panel of the velvet drapes, hoping that the sun, which had risen, would stream through the window, causing Laurent to stop his advances. As the curtains were violently pulled open the sun's rays streamed into the window temporarily blinding Laurent; a bloodcurdling scream was heard with the vampire protesting, "Close it! I command you to close it!"

"I will, under one condition," Jack said, feeling like he had the upper hand and noticed that Laurent's arm, having been exposed to the sun, had begun to ignite into a small flame that caused smoke to fill the room.

"Yes, anything, just do it!" Laurent replied angrily as he continued to hold his arm up to shield his face.

"That you will allow me to leave here safely. I need some time away from you to sort out my feelings, especially given the fact you shared something with me that is unbelievably incomprehensible," Jack said anxiously.

"Alright, I shall let you leave in peace, Jack, but understand this. It has taken me over two hundred and fifty years to find you; I cannot lose you again! I feel it's our destiny to be together once more, Jack; I need you to realize this", Laurent pleaded.

Jack finally closed the heavy velvet drapes, which filled the room with darkness once more, except for the light from the candelabra sitting on the dresser as Jack started to leave.

"When will I see you again, Jack?" Laurent asked timidly.

"I'll be in touch, Laurent; give me some time," Jack replied.

"Jack, one word of caution before you leave," Laurent said, sounding mysterious.

"What's that?" Jack asked coldly as he turned to face the vampire.

"Stay as far away from Stefan as possible. I don't have time to tell you the entire story. I need rest with the daylight outside; however, Stefan is evil. There are those vampires that cling desperately to any ounce of humanness, who desperately hold onto what it feels like to love and be loved and long for companionship. I am one of those. Yet others have ignored their former human traits, turning them into wild, bloodthirsty, rabid animals; Stefan possesses all these undesirable and dangerous characteristics. He has his designs on you and, unlike me, will not give you a choice," Laurent warned.

Jack hesitated before answering and then said, "Thanks for the warning, Laurent, I have no doubt that what you're telling me is true. I'll take it under advisement," and turned to leave as he walked out of the bedroom.

Laurent suddenly found himself alone as he walked over to the canopy bed draped with the finest silks and laid down and remained motionless. Before entering his undead slumber, he reflected on the terse exchange of words he'd had with Jack which left him feeling hurt and confused, as a single blood tear formed in his eye and ran down his cheek as he wiped it away with his handkerchief. He wondered if he would ever see Jack again.

Shortly after he entered the realm of deep slumber Laurent started to dream. Stefan appeared before him, but he was not alone; there was another present, it was Jack. Both appeared to be laughing at him as they held hands.

Downstairs, Jack approached the last few remaining steps of the long staircase which lead to the foyer; Barthelme greeted his arrival at the bottom of the staircase.

"You're up early Master Jack," he said.

"Yes. Call it another sleepless night at Laurent's," Jack sarcastically replied.

"Where would you like me to take you, Master Jack?" Barthelme asked.

"I would like you to drive me to the City Park Barthelme; I need to do some thinking," Jack answered back politely.

"Right away, Master Jack, I will fetch the car and meet you in the front." Barthelme said and headed toward the garage to retrieve the car.

For a brief moment, Jack was alone to process his thoughts and what he'd witnessed and heard as he opened the door and made his way outside. He looked up at the sun, as it nearly blinded him, thinking how good the warmth felt on his skin and hearing the birds chirping their morning song as if they were welcoming him into the start of another day.

His thoughts turned to both vampires, and he thought to himself, what a pity Laurent, and Stefan, couldn't enjoy the sunlight, and its warming rays and see the splendor of the trees and grass with their rich colors. Jack wondered if he were to become a vampire, whether he would miss everything he currently enjoys as a human. If he were to become as they, he would only be able to come out at night, essentially becoming a night creature destined to face eternity in the darkness. Jack had much thinking to do; the complex and nearly impossible decision to either accept Laurent's offer and live as one of the living dead or to stay as he was, rejecting Laurent and continuing along a path of unhappiness and loneliness. Jack thought *Laurent must love me; otherwise, why would he be giving me a choice? He could have attacked me and turned me back at the house.* Jack's thoughts were interrupted as Barthelme pulled up with the Rolls Royce and stepped out to open the back passenger door. As he entered, he gave Barthelme a polite smile. Barthelme closed the door, and the car sped away.

Jack remained silent for much of the ride, trying desperately to comprehend what Laurent had revealed. Barthelme didn't initiate any conversation at first; he knew Master Jack had been told the truth about his Master and that Master Jack might be shocked. Barthelme had stood outside his Master's bedroom and overheard their entire conversation.

Twenty minutes into the ride, the silence between both men became palpable and increasingly awkward until Barthelme finally broke the silence and said, "You know Master Laurent cares for you very deeply, Master Jack. It's not easy for me to say this to you; I don't understand two men together in a sexual way, but I do understand love. Master Laurent seems to have fallen in love with you. I've seen the way he looks at you; he believes you to be his long-lost soulmate, Fabien brought back to him from the dead," Barthelme said and continued to look at Jack in the mirror and tried to gauge Jack's reaction.

"So you know what he is, don't you?" Jack asked, their eyes met and locked in the driver's mirror.

"Yes, I know what Master Laurent is; I've known that for a very long time, since he arrived at the estate over two hundred years ago. You might say I am the Master's gatekeeper," Barthelme admitted.

"I don't understand; you've been with him since the beginning, two hundred years ago? How can you have lived for so long if you're not a vampire?" Jack asked looking confused.

"You don't need to concern yourself with that, Master Jack. However, Master Laurent shared some of his past with me. You saw the portrait of the Master's dead lover, didn't you? I'm sure you noticed the uncanny resemblance between you and Fabien?" Barthelme asked.

After a considerable pause, Jack replied, "Yes, I did. Fabien and I could be twin brothers. But I'm not Fabien. At least, I don't think I am?"

"There are many mysteries in life, Master Jack; we don't know all there is to know. Many unanswered questions lay ahead of us all on our journey through life," Barthelme said.

"I don't know; maybe I've been reincarnated? What I do know is that my head is swimming with all these thoughts; I need time to think, as I told Laurent," Jack said.

The Rolls made its way into the city limits of New Orleans and soon arrived at its destination, The City Park.

"Thank you, Barthelme," Jack said humbly.

"For what, Master Jack? Barthelme asked.

"For listening and being the voice of reason."

"All in a day's work, Master Jack. Keep this in mind. You are two souls bound together; Master Laurent loves you very much and will always be your protector and companion. Now is that so bad?" Barthelme asked as Jack got out of the vehicle as it sped off.

Jack felt the sun's warmth and heard the birds singing their morning songs once more and glanced at his watch; it read seven-thirty.

Jack walked into City Park and looked for a bench to sit on and collect his thoughts. He quickly spotted one with someone seated there. He'd hoped to find one to himself, unable to; he reluctantly walked over. The bench was in a prime location directly across from a pond with magnificent old oak trees and hanging moss; the majestic trees lined the banks of the pond.

CHAPTER 14

A queen intervenes

An elegantly dressed black woman with a head scarf sat on a park bench, reading a newspaper as Jack approached.

"Excuse me, do you mind if I sit here?" Jack politely asked with a smile. The woman looked up at Jack and saw a vision of another standing beside him; the image looked identical to Jack, except that his hair was longer, and his clothing appeared to be from a different period. She couldn't hide the astonishment on her face; her eyes narrowed as she continued to stare at Jack.

"Excuse me?" She asked.

This time Jack didn't sound so polite, annoyed that he needed to ask her the question again, "I said, do you mind if I sit here as well?"

"No, I don't mind. Please join me; there is certainly enough room for the two of us. I'm sorry I was lost in my thoughts." She admitted.

"Yeah, I know the feeling," Jack replied with a sigh. He focused his attention on the pond and the trees in the distance, hoping that the beauty of it would distract him from his troubled thoughts. An awkward silence ensued.

Finally, the woman dropped her newspaper and sighed loudly. Jack looked over at her; she returned his gaze with a smile. "We both appear to be troubled by something," she offered as an icebreaker opening the way for further conversation.

"Yes, I've just been made aware of something that's beyond belief."

She stared at him in amazement. "Would you like to share your thoughts with me? I'm an excellent listener," She said and sounded genuinely concerned.

"Why? Are you a shrink of some sort?" Jack asked sarcastically.

"Heaven's no, my child!" as the woman laughed uncontrollably.

"What's so funny?" Jack asked and felt confused.

"Everything and nothing at all, forgive me, allow me to introduce myself to you; my name is Queen Raphaella. I own a Voodoo shop on St Ann just inside the French quarter," she said proudly.

"Nice to meet you. I'm Jack Devereaux, a queen who runs a Voodoo shop. Do you come from royalty?" Jack asked timidly, realizing at once how ridiculous that sounded.

The mysterious woman broke out in a boisterous laugh, "No, my parents gave me that nickname when I was young; they said I acted as if I'd come from royalty!"

"Are you a Psychic?" Jack asked; the woman abruptly ended her laughing. "Not only am I a psychic, but a medium as well!" She confided.

"A medium?" He asked.

"It means I can speak with ghosts, meaning dead people," she clarified. This time it was Jack who laughed.

"Excuse me! You doubt me?" Raphaella retorted.

"No, not at the rate I'm going; anything is possible!" Jack said and shook his head.

"So, you, believe me, Jack?" Raphaella asked.

"Yeah! Perhaps you can see into the future?" Jack said apologetically, feeling bad and as if he'd offended her.

"Do you want to know why I looked at you so oddly when you asked me if you could join me on the park bench?" Raphaella asked with a sense of urgency.

"I was kind of wondering that myself," Jack said.

"I'll take that as a yes, Jack," Raphaella turned away from him, sounding annoyed.

"I apologize. Yes, please tell me more," Jack replied.

Her gaze focused intensely on Jack as she looked him over and said, "First, let me tell you a little about myself. I'm originally from Haiti, and I've experienced all sorts of phenomena, from raising a corpse to seeing and conversing with the dearly departed, more commonly known as ghosts. When I saw you for the first time, I also saw another standing beside you; he appeared to look just like you, only he was dressed differently than you and wore period clothing. His hair was tied back in a ponytail", Raphaella shared. "You mean I have a twin?" Jack asked as he immediately thought of the portrait hanging in Laurent's bedroom.

"Yes, Jack," Raphaella replied.

"You say he looks identical to me, except for his clothing?" Jack asked.

"Yes, identical in every way," Raphaella confirmed.

Jack suddenly felt a rush of coldness wash over him as all the color left his face. He thought back to being escorted into Laurent's bedroom, seeing the portrait of his beloved Fabien, Laurent's destroyed vampire maker. Could this be the image Raphaella saw?

"What's wrong, Jack? You look like you've seen a ghost!" Raphaella said and started to laugh.

"This is no laughing matter," Jack retorted.

"I'm sorry. Please tell me what's troubling you?" Raphaella asked as she tried to regain Jack's trust.

"I've met someone; I've been seeing him romantically for over a month." Jack confided.

"Go on," Raphaella replied, appearing interested in hearing all the details.

"At first, I didn't know what was going on; his hand felt like ice every time we touched. I never saw him during the daylight hours; he told me he traveled a lot on business." He said as Raphaella held his gaze and watched him intensely.

"Whenever we got together for dinner, I never saw him eat anything; usually, he would drink a glass of some red substance, which I knew wasn't wine; he even admitted that he couldn't drink alcohol. At first, I tried thinking of what he might be drinking, whether it was a protein shake or tomato juice, or something else.

Then finally, he came out and admitted he was a vampire; and even demonstrated his powers when I asked for proof!" Jack admitted and was visibly shaken.

"I see; go on," Raphaella said.

"There is another vampire far more dangerous than the one I have been dating; I met him recently at a club. His name is Stefan, and he and the vampire I had been seeing, Laurent, have known each other for a very long time; they strike me as being enemies. I believe each has their plan to turn me into a vampire", Jack said, his breathing becoming shaky.

"Jack, I need you to come to see me at my shop; I can perform an in-depth reading for you and perhaps call on the spirit of your counterpart and get him to confirm your suspicions. I believe everything you've told me. I think you are in mortal danger! Are you available this evening, say seven o'clock?" she said frantically.

"Yeah, I'm available, Jack replied.

"Excellent! My address is 709 St Ann, in the French Quarter; do you know where that is?" Raphaella said.

"Yes, I've lived in New Orleans a little over ten years; I know the location exactly; I'll find your shop," Jack assured her.

"Good! I'll see you later this evening, Jack, I must go, but before I do, I want to give you something." She reached into her bag and pulled out a family heirloom. "This was given to me by my late parents. It's always provided me with comfort and good luck", Raphaella said as she handed him a beautifully ornate crucifix.

"That only works in vampire movies and on television," Jack defiantly said.

"Don't be a fool, Jack, take it! It symbolizes goodness, purity, and love; it is a powerful weapon against evil!" Raphaella warned him.

"Jack reached out his hand as she gently placed the crucifix in his hand and stood up to leave.

"Wait! I don't even know the name of your shop?" Jack asked in a panic.

"Why, it's Queen Raphaella's voodoo shop!" She answered him with a shout.

"Of course! I should have guessed that", Jack said to himself.

"Until this evening Jack Devereux! Be safe and walk with the light. And don't let that crucifix out of your sight!" she instructed and hurriedly left the park.

Jack watched as she made her exit and felt safer having met the mysterious Voodoo queen and the object she had given him.

Jack sat and stared at the crucifix, touching and examining it, completely lost in thought. He finally looked down at his watch, thinking he'd lost all track of time. It had been an entire hour since he and Raphaella had met.

A wave of exhaustion suddenly consumed Jack. He struggled to stand up and staggered, reflecting on having seen Laurent's incredible abilities and how the vampire's face had transformed. He recalled Laurent's blood-red eyes and two large fangs. *Is that what I am to become?* He thought.

Jack figured his exhaustion was because he hadn't gotten enough sleep and the shock of what Laurent had confessed. In addition to not getting enough sleep, having just met a woman who claimed to communicate with the dead!

He thought, was it any wonder why I'm struggling to find the strength to walk? Despite that, Jack somehow managed to stand up and left the park, and there at the entrance, he spotted a taxicab. Jack used his remaining strength, quickly walked to the cab, and opened the door. "Are you available?" He asked.

"Sure, get in. Where to Mac?" The driver asked with a heavy East Coast accent.

"Take me to the Stardust motel. And do me a favor, stop calling me Mac; that's not my name, Jack said, sounding annoyed.

The cab driver scowled and said, "Whatever you say," as the cab bobbed, wove its way through the rush hour traffic, and arrived at the motel in under twenty minutes.

"That will be Five dollars," he said.

"Wow, I'm impressed; no one else has been able to get me around town as quickly!" Jack admitted.

"Yeah, you can probably tell I'm not from around here; I learned to maneuver much harder streets than these back in New York!" the cab driver said proudly.

Jack seemed disinterested and paid him.

"Thanks, Mac!" the driver said and sped away.

Jack shook his head and quickly dismissed the rude driver. There was only one thing on his mind. Getting some much-needed rest. Jack felt safe that he had the crucifix in his possession and could rest a little easier, knowing it would help render Laurent and Stefan powerless if either chose to attack him.

Jack climbed the staircase to the second floor, where he knew a comfortable bed awaited his weary and aching body.

He opened the door and had only enough strength to remove his shoes before he threw himself onto the bed.

Jack was so exhausted that sleep soon followed. Although he felt the nightmares would haunt him again, he felt safe in his room, at least temporarily.

Jack slept the entire day, waking up once or twice to go to the bathroom. As night approached, the nightmares returned with a vengeance as he tossed and turned in bed and dreamt that he was in a wide-open field with someone he didn't recognize at first, as a thick layer of fog enveloped the mysterious figure.

As he made his way over, its facial features became more apparent to Jack. The man's hair was dark, and his eyes were deep-set and cruel-looking.

He recognized it to be Stefan. Somehow he managed to infiltrate Jack's dream! But what did he want from me? Jack wondered.

At once, a loud, almost eardrum-bursting tone of laughter erupted from Stefan's mouth, followed by his hand as it reached out, drawing him nearer and nearer until he grasped Jack's arm in a vice-like grip drawing him ever closer.

"Did you think you could escape me, Fabien?" Stefan asked and continued his boisterous, sinister laugh, and suddenly stopped. The face that had appeared to be laughing only seconds earlier had become a menacing grimace. It twisted and contorted the facial features looking more like a bloodthirsty animal, complete with his mouth open to reveal two large fangs and blood-red eyes.

"I'm not Fabien! I'm Jack!" He awakened himself by screaming as his entire body became drenched in sweat. Jack wondered if this dream was perhaps a foretelling of what was to come. Jack sat in bed, still feeling drained from the night before, and glanced out the window only to find that day had turned to night.

"My God! How long have I been asleep?" Jack said and looked at his watch; it was seven o'clock. Jack had slept the entire day away and now was late for his reading with Raphaella.

He quickly got out of bed, decided he needed to shower, and thought that would reinvigorate him.

Jack quickly undressed and showered in record time; he didn't want to be later than he already was. As he dressed, Jack heard a scratching sound coming from the window. Jack froze, becoming motionless with fear, thinking the sound was quite unusual. It almost sounded as if an animal were making scratching sounds or something attempting to get into his room.

Instinctively, Jack picked up the crucifix Raphaella had given him earlier that morning and cautiously walked over to the window. He was met with the levitating figure of a man who wasn't a man at all. It was Stefan!

"I want you to leave here, Stefan; you're not welcome!" Jack defiantly shouted through the closed window.

Stefan ignored his command and said, "I command you to open this window at once and welcome me in!" Stefan's booming voice was heard and echoed in the night. A voice so overpowering it felt like Jack was about to go into a trance; Jack thought he had little choice but to obey Stefan's demands and began to lose his will to resist.

Jack reached for the window latch, unlocked it, and opened the window; Stefan asked, "Are you inviting me in?" the vampire asked as Jack concealed the crucifix tightly in the palm of his left hand.

"Yes. I hear you, and I obey you, Stefan. You may enter," Jack replied, his voice sounding flat and emotionless.

Instantly, Stefan made his way through the window and stood only a few feet away from Jack. He looked at Jack scornfully and said, "Did you think you could escape me, Jack?" Immediately Jack had a feeling of déjà vu and thought, *those were the exact words Stefan had asked me in my nightmare; the only difference was the name he called me, Fabien.*

As Stefan uttered those words, it temporarily jolted Jack out of Stefan's trance. Jack decided it was best he try and appear as if he were still in Stefan's hypnotic trance.

"Jack, I hope you realize you are the chosen one; you know what Laurent and I are. We want the same thing. Both of us want you to return to us as Fabien. Your special friend Laurent most likely failed to mention that I was the one who turned Fabien into what he was, not Laurent. So, it appears that history is trying to repeat itself; however, this time, you will be mine and will stay with me for eternity!" Stefan said in a guttural growl.

Jack quickly remembered all the vampire-themed movies he had seen in his lifetime, never imagining these creatures existed and finding himself in this sort of unbelievable predicament! He remembered how the crucifix had helped defend the victim from the vampire's attack and remembered Raphaella's words "It symbolizes goodness, purity, and love; it is a powerful weapon against evil!" He briefly prayed that it would work.

Jack slowly took a step toward Stefan with the crucifix still hidden in his palm as he came face to face with Stefan. "I am yours for the taking, Stefan," as Stefan smiled triumphantly and came close to Jack's neck. Jack suddenly thrust the cross directly into one of Stefan's eyes. A blood-curdling scream erupted from Stefan. The crucifix was embedded deep in his eye as flames and smoke erupted causing the mighty vampire to stagger back toward the window as he disappeared into the darkened night with a trail of smoke along with the vampire's screams that were heard in the distance.

Feeling relief, at least temporarily, Jack knew he would encounter Stefan soon. He knew the vampire was older and wiser and more potent than Laurent, making it more challenging, if not impossible, to destroy him.

Jack immediately thought of Raphaella and how he needed her help more than ever. He glanced at his watch, it read eight o'clock. *I'm an hour late!* Jack thought, *she probably has given up on me; I'll prove her wrong and allow her to show me, beyond just a crucifix, how she plans to help me.*

A sense of dread had come over Raphaella. Just now, she'd had a blurred vision of a struggle between two men but couldn't quite make out who they were. She immediately thought of Jack and hoped that he was okay, and if it had been him involved in a struggle with one of the vampires, she hoped he would have remembered to use the crucifix she had given him.

Raphaella had spent the day cleaning her shop in preparation for Jack's session with her, which included arranging various artifacts that adorned her shop. She'd owned it for a little over a year. Despite being open that long, she hadn't developed many customers, likely due to the numerous other Voodoo shops in the French Quarter.

How exactly would any passerby be able to tell the difference between a legitimate shop and something that was merely a tourist attraction? She hated calling her shop a Voodoo shop; she felt it diminished her natural born talents in being able to communicate with dead people. Raphaella wondered if any of the other supposed Voodoo shops had any as gifted as she in being able to contact spirits.

Naturally, she had experimented with actual Voodoo back in her native Haiti as a teenager but then quickly lost interest and decided to devote her time to being the bridge between the world of the living and the dead. She was much more than simply a "Voodoo queen." First and foremost, she was a powerful psychic and medium.

She asked herself, how many others who ran "Voodoo shops" had the same success rate of communicating with the dead?

While Raphaella possessed psychic abilities, her talents didn't involve her being able to foresee her future. Those visions were left for others. She felt that was odd, and over time perhaps her abilities would strengthen so that she could see not only everyone else's future but hers as well.

Had she been able to foresee her future, she would have been able to see how her business would fail and how dismal the return upon her investment would have been.

While she genuinely wanted to help Jack, naturally, he would need to pay her handsomely for her services. After all, she had a mortgage payment to make to the bank, along with feeding and caring for herself. Despite the apartment being directly above the shop, which eliminated commuting costs, the rent was pricey for being in the heart of New Orleans, in the desirable and famed "French quarter."

The clock on the wall struck eight-thirty, an hour and a half after the scheduled appointment reading with Jack. Raphaella had sadly given up any hope he would show. Perhaps it was Jack she had seen in her visions struggling with another, thinking he was injured or worse? But if he had died, unquestionably, his spirit would have come to her? Just as other ghosts had appeared to her.

Raphaella put the thought out of her head and sensed Jack wasn't dead, although perhaps injured.

She decided a drink would help calm her nerves as she opened a bottle of vintage rum she had brought from Haiti. Maybe the entire evening wouldn't be a total loss.

Raphaella was known to enjoy her spirits, not only those that appeared before her but equally those that came in a bottle.

As she walked over to the small kitchenette directly adjacent to her shop's private reading room, she heard what appeared to be footsteps outside. She quickly dismissed it as mere tourists walking by. She thought, doubtful they would stop in, as the window looked too ominously decorated with skull heads, shrunken heads, and frightening-looking masks, which could be why customers avoided her shop.

As Raphaella opened the bottle of rum, she toasted herself to soothe her nerves a bit. The rum hit the back of her throat as an audible "Ah!" came from her mouth.

A bell rang above her front door, indicating someone's arrival.

"I'm closed!" Raphaella protested, wishing not to be interrupted.

Now that she finally had a potential customer come into her shop, she felt uninspired and wanted nothing more than to enjoy the rest of her rum.

Raphaella reluctantly walked out towards the front of her shop and repeated what she had said only minutes before, "I'm closed, come back another day!"

"I hope not. I had a lot of trouble getting here." she heard a man say as he walked back to greet her. Much to her astonishment, it was Jack as he stood there heavily breathing as if he had run over.

"Jack! You made it!" She said as she came close to tears. She was overjoyed seeing him. Her joyful mood quickly switched to business as she said, "We need to get started right away."

He nodded and led him through the shop as he trailed behind her noticing the shrunken heads, the many candles, and books that dealt with various subjects such as Witchcraft, Santeria, and Voodoo until they reached the back.

"I'm impressed," he uttered.

"Thanks, Jack. But too much time has passed; we need to start immediately!" she said.

They walked into a cozy room with a round table covered by a tablecloth and a candelabra in the center of the table, with the candles not yet lit.

As Jack gazed at the candelabra, his thoughts returned to Laurent's bedroom. Having seen a similar one gave him a chill making him feel slightly uncomfortable.

CHAPTER 15

Calling long distance

Raphaella told Jack to sit at the table opposite her and instructed him to clear his thoughts from his mind and join hands with her. "It is important that whatever you experience, you must not break the bond, do not let go of my hands at any cost Jack, do you understand?" She asked intensely.

Yes, I understand," Jack replied.

"Before we begin, give me the crucifix Jack," she asked.

"I don't have it," he answered back.

"What do you mean you don't have it?" Raphaella said, sounding annoyed.

"I used it against Stefan in a life-or-death struggle before I came over here. The last time I saw it, I used it to fight him off; by sticking it into one of his eyes. If I didn't have that crucifix, I wouldn't be here, or if I were, I'd be a spirit that you claim to have a connection with telling you I've been murdered."

"My god that must have been the vision that I had. But we are wasting precious time having this discussion. We need to begin!" Raphaella said anxiously.

"Sorry!" Jack replied.

"Apology accepted. Now, please, clear your mind, and let's focus on the candles so that you are open to receiving whichever spirits appear."

Jack wondered if the spirits she had mentioned were inside a bottle or those she claimed appeared to her. The thought of that made Jack grin. Instinctively as if she could read his mind, she glanced at him disapprovingly. He quickly composed himself.

Jack had doubts about Raphaella's ability to contact any spirits, much less Jack's counterpart ghost; however, at this point,

Jack was open to anything or anyone that offered their help against the two vampires as Raphaella had done.

After reflecting briefly on the incredible spectacle that unfolded back at the grand estate and Laurent's confession about being one of the undead, he thought, well, why not? If vampires exist, ghosts could exist as well. It was like Barthelme had said to me earlier we don't know all there is to know in life.

"Now, before we begin, please give me the full names of both vampires," Raphaella said. Jack thought for a moment and struggled to remember Stefan's last name.

"The one I've been dating, his full name is Laurent Richelieu, the other's name is Stefan… damn it! Why can't I think of his last name? It's very French sounding, Vita?" Jack said.

Raphaella took a deep breath, exhaled, and said, "Alright, calm down. Focus, Jack.

"Vita, Viter, Vitré! That's it!" Jack answered excitedly.

Raphaella smiled, closed her eyes, and instantly slipped into a trance.

"If there are any spirits here who have come into contact with either of the two vampires known as Laurent Richelieu and Stefan Vitré, please come to us and let your presence be known," Raphaella pleaded.

At once, the flames of the candles began to flicker as Raphaella started to moan and sway from side to side. "Ooooh," in a female voice that sounded much different than hers.

"Why have you called me out of my slumber?" The voice asked.

"Who are you?" Jack asked. He knew he had to take over if Raphaella had temporarily been overtaken by a spirit using her body as a vessel to communicate with them. It would be up to him to find out exactly who this spirit was.

"I repeat, who are you?" he asked once more.

"My name is Anne; I died over three hundred years ago."

"Why have you come to us?" Jack demanded.

"I was summoned by the one seated across from you. I will share this with you; there are those attempting to remake the past! You are in grave danger!" the spirit of Anne said. Jack figured the entity had referred to Laurent and Stefan when she said mentioned remaking the past.

Raphaella suddenly came out of her trance as her moaning ceased. Both of them peered at the corner of her store and saw what appeared to be that of Anne.

Anne stood in the corner with a hand outstretched; she appeared gaunt and dressed in period clothing. Somehow the ghost no longer needed Raphaella as a vessel.

"One looks to restore the past and seeks power over others. He has rarely, if ever, felt love for someone.

The other also seeks to restore the past, yet feels like he has met the one that can take the place of his long-destroyed lover. Only you, Jack, can determine which of them is truly evil." And as suddenly as Anne appeared, she vanished.

Jack is stunned by what he's just witnessed. However, the warning was nothing new to Jack. Laurent had warned him of Stefan's intentions back at the estate.

There was a momentary silence between them until Jack broke the silence by saying, "Laurent was right about Stefan; he tried to warn me about him, but I wouldn't listen! Stefan is pure evil. He tried to turn me before I came over here this evening!" Jack shared with Raphaella.

No sooner had he said this; another figure appeared in the shadows which Raphaella noticed immediately as she said commandingly, "Spirit, speak to me. Tell me your name?"

"My name is Fabien," the entity answered.

"Tell us, Fabien, why have you come here? And what do you want?" Raphaella asked the mysterious ghost. The spirit once again answered her, "I want him!"

Suddenly, Fabien's ghost flew out of the shadows and appeared alongside Jack, making it nearly impossible for Raphaella to distinguish between them.

"You will never take over my body Fabien!" Jack shouted.

"We shall see about that, Jack Devereaux!" The spirit warned his counterpart.

At once, various objects toward the front of the shop began to fall off their shelves violently and came crashing down to the floor, making a mess of Raphaella's neatly organized merchandise.

"Stop this at once! I command you to stop this destructive behavior!" Raphaella demanded as the spirit continued to wreak havoc as books and artifacts were violently thrown about.

Suddenly, the store went silent except for the voice of Fabien, who warned, "I need a body to inhabit, and Jack shall provide me a vessel into this world," as the entity came face-to-face with Jack, as the spirit's face became as distorted as Laurent's had earlier.

"I've been observing you for quite some time. Laurent offered you a gift, one that is sacred, and you dare to contemplate this? Look at yourself and your pathetic existence. You were a lost, desperate soul, unable to exist romantically with either woman or man. You hate your true desires and loathe yourself. My beloved saved you from your agonizing loneliness and despair!" Fabien said scoldingly.

"Don't listen to him, Jack!" Raphaella yelled.

"I witnessed how awkward you always felt, feeling inferior, drinking yourself half-blind every time you two were together." Fabien's spirit said scornfully. "Give me your body, and I shall gladly receive his dark gift so that he and I can reunite again for eternity!" Fabien said.

"Stop it!" Raphaella shouted as Fabien's ghost turned his attention toward her.

"You're a poor excuse for a woman and nothing more than a drunk! You claim to be a psychic, although had you truly been one, you would have foreseen how miserable your life and business would turn out! Not to mention your parents ending up with a fatal disease, killing them!" Fabien's spirit said cruelly.

Suddenly the spirit of Anne appeared once more and confronted the ghost of Fabien.

"You must leave. Go back to your eternal resting place." The spirit of Anne said. Somehow it appeared she had a hold over Fabien, which neither Raphaella nor Jack understood. Her command caused the ghost of Fabien to disappear. Knowing her work was done, Anne vanished from sight.

"That was close. It's nice to know we have an ally in Anne, whoever she might be," Raphaella said and sighed.

"Yes, to your point, who exactly is Anne, and what does she want in return?" Jack said.

"Obviously Anne has some connection to either Laurent or Stefan; otherwise, she would not have appeared to us when I called out to all who crossed paths with either vampire. But to which vampire is she connected that's the most important question."

"Only time will tell. Well, I guess we're done here for the evening? Unless, of course, you want to try and conjure up some other spirits tonight?" Jack said, attempting to lighten the mood as prepared to leave.

Raphaella disapproved of his comments and wasn't amused by the look she had on her face as the conversation turned serious. "Jack, aren't you forgetting something?" Raphaella asked.

"What would that be?" Jack asked, sounding confused.

"Payment for tonight's session." She replied.

"Payment? For what? Endangering my life this evening?" Jack answered angrily.

"Endangering your life? Why, you ungrateful bastard! How dare you! I reached out to help you to see if any spirits would come to us and help enlighten us about Laurent and Stefan's motives. And Anne, whoever she is, answered!" Raphaella retorted.

"Yeah, well, another spirit answered your call, Fabien. He is attempting to take over my body so that Laurent will turn him so that the two of them are reunited. Where exactly does that leave me?" Jack shouted and paced her shop. Finally, he stopped, glanced at her, and asked, "Alright, you win. How much do I owe you?"

"One hundred and fifty dollars Jack," she answered defiantly.

"You think I carry that much cash around with me?" Jack scoffed.

"I accept credit cards as well," Raphaella answered him coldly.

"Send me a bill!" Jack said and walked toward the door.

"Jack! Come back! Don't leave; it's not safe for you. Listen, we can negotiate the price!" Raphaella shouted.

Yet it was no use; Jack had already left her shop as she heard the bell and the slamming of the door, which announced his departure.

Despite her anger, Raphaella was genuinely concerned for Jack's well-being and thought *that man will get himself killed without my help.*

Feeling guilty about how she had left things with Jack and his seething anger and riddled with anxiety, she remembered the bottle of rum she'd been enjoying before Jack's arrival. She decided to finish the bottle, thinking it might soothe her nerves as she walked over to the cabinet, got herself a big glass, and filled it to the top. She thought the rest of the evening wouldn't be a total waste. The thought of that made her chuckle.

Jack walked the darkened streets of the city, wondering where to go. His mind was racing after the series of events played out throughout the evening. Jack thought, *let's see, I fought off a vampire stabbing him with a crucifix. I went to a crazy woman's voodoo shop, only for her to conjure up not one but two ghosts. One whose motives are questionable, and the other threatening to possess and inhabit my body so he can reunite with his vampire lover!*

Jack decided he could use a drink and perhaps a little company. He thought it'd been a while since he'd had sex with anyone. Stefan ruined everything only to reveal his true self, a monster, and even a worse one than Laurent! He shook his head as he entered the Rawhide.

Right away, Jack sensed something wasn't right; and had a strong feeling he would likely run into Stefan.

His suspicions were confirmed as he glanced over toward the back of the bar as Stefan stood there wearing an eye patch over the one Jack had thrust the crucifix in earlier that evening.

Stefan's one eye met Jack's gaze, and in an instant, Stefan appeared beside him. "How do you like my eye patch, Jack? By the way, that wasn't a very nice thing you did to me back at your motel. I thought you liked me? You even invited me on a date to have dinner with your friend Laurent, not that he or I ever eat food," he said sarcastically, with a tone of anger.

"So, I guess the old crucifix does work just as in all the vampire movies?" Jack answered coldly, careful not to meet Stefan's intense gaze.

Stefan began to laugh, and instantly his mood shifted from laughter to a fit of seething anger followed by a warning. "You are funny, but understand this, I could kill you right here, and there wouldn't be anyone to help you," Stefan said softly under his breath.

"Well, then, why don't you do it? Why don't you kill me and end this torture?" Jack said, appearing to challenge the powerful vampire with the eye patch as he gazed deeply into Stefan's eye.

"Because much like your friend Laurent, I believe you are the reincarnation of Fabien, my vampire minion. As you recall, he disobeyed me and left me to create his vampire fledgling, which would be your special friend Laurent. I destroyed Fabien by accident. It was Laurent I was coming to destroy. Now that I have found you, I have my second chance, and you will be mine this time. And you will stay mine for all eternity. I will let you think about that. I'm in no rush; I have all the time in the world. One bit of advice, if you think you can run to your friend Laurent for help, realize there's nothing he can do. I'm much older and much more powerful than he. I will destroy Laurent this time, as I meant to do over two hundred and fifty years ago," Stefan said as Bauhaus's "Lugosi's Dead" began playing in the background.

Jack thought of the irony that this song referring to the classic actor of the 1930s made famous by his portrayal of "Dracula" should begin playing at that exact moment. "God, I need a drink!" Jack muttered.

"Stefan, I'm going to go to the bar and get a drink, I would offer you one, but they don't serve blood here," Jack said sarcastically and glanced at Stefan and gave him a wink. Stefan responded with a scowl.

Jack walked over to the bar and noticed the oddly dressed bartender, who couldn't have been more than twenty, dressed entirely in Goth-style clothing, including eyeliner and a nose ring. Something about this young man struck Jack as odd.

He had the blackest hair Jack had ever seen; its color was much like a raven's. The darkness of his hair made his skin color much more pallid, like Laurent and Stefan's. Jack thought if I didn't know any better? Suddenly, his thoughts were interrupted by Stefan's commanding voice from across the bar, "Say hello to the bartender," as Jack turned to look back at Stefan, catching a wink from Stefan's eye.

Jack focused his attention on the young bartender dressed in black. The bartender didn't speak and merely scowled at Jack.

Jack said, "Gee, thanks for asking; I'll have a Jack and coke and make it double, will ya?" as his eyes shifted to the bartender's neck, which appeared to have two puncture wounds.

As the bartender returned with Jack's drink, he caught a glimpse of Jack and how he seemed preoccupied with those marks on his neck. The bartender suddenly asked, "Do you like them? I could give you the same if you'd like?" the bartender said and smiled, revealing two long incisors.

"That's okay; I'll take my drink for now. By the way, I'm supposed to tell you hello from Stefan," Jack said calmly.

"Cool! He sure is mighty fine. His eye patch makes him that much hotter. Don't you agree? I heard you attacked him," the bartender said as he continued to scowl at Jack.

"Yeah. Cool. It gives Stefan a bit of character, wouldn't you say? The only thing missing from your cool look is an eye patch like your friends. I could give you the same if you'd like?" Jack sarcastically replied. The young Goth bartender slammed Jack's drink down, and some spilled on the counter.

"There you go, Jack," he said as he addressed Jack by his name, much to his surprise.

"How do you know my name?" Jack asked as his eyes squinted.

"I'm a friend of Stefan's; he told me all about you. If I'm being honest, I don't see what he sees in you!" The young bartender sarcastically replied and walked away to serve another patron.

Jack looked across the bar to where Stefan had been only minutes before and was suddenly nowhere to be seen.

Jack downed his drink with one gulp. Instantly the bartender in black returned and stood directly in front of Jack.

"Pour you another? Somehow, I feel you're going to need it, Jack. You have a very long night ahead of you", the young man said in a threatening tone.

"No, thanks, I'm good; something tells me I will need all my wits about me. You never know who I might come into contact with." Jack turned to leave and stopped and turned back to face the young bartender, "Oh, and by the way, kid, go to hell!" Jack smugly said.

The young bartender's face instantly twisted into a snarl with teeth barred and eyes that burned red.

Jack's cockiness melted away and was replaced by a feeling of unease, knowing that Stefan had created another vampire that Jack would undoubtedly need to deal with at some point.

As Jack walked away from the bar, he listened to the song in the background, "Like a Virgin." He listened to some of the lyrics while standing there, making him cringe. Maybe I will take that other drink; he thought as Jack returned to the bar looking for the Goth bartender, who was nowhere to be seen. There was another bartender in his place. A guy dressed similarly to the bar patrons, complete with a flannel shirt, tight jeans, and cowboy boots.

"What'll you have?" asked the normal-looking bartender.

"Jack and coke, make it a double," Jack replied.

"Coming right up," the bartender replied.

Jack thought, *where did this cocky son of a bitch go? Maybe he's with Stefan.* Jack downed his drink in a couple of gulps and quickly finished his second drink. He thought *this ought to help me sleep tonight, provided I don't have any unexpected company!*

Having had two drinks and looking around at the slim pickings of men standing around, he decided he would forego trying to hook up with someone for the night and instead, decided it was time for him to head back to the motel and attempt to get some much-needed rest.

As he made his way through the crowd, he thought he'd caught a glimpse of the Goth vampire. But after a second glance, he determined it was another bar patron dressed similarly.

The humid Louisiana night air felt heavy and pregnant with rain. The rumble of thunder in the distance confirmed that a storm was approaching. Jack suddenly thought of Raphaella and felt terrible about how he had walked out of her shop without paying her a stitch of money and checked his wallet, counting the cash, and discovered there were two hundred dollars in cash. Jack's Catholic guilt set in, and he decided to make things right by visiting her shop and paying her for the services she had provided earlier.

Jack thought it would appear she did possess a talent for communicating with ghosts. Jack realized he had no other tools to use against all three vampires. He figured if he stopped by and offered to pay, perhaps she would have a change of heart and provide him with something more to use as protection.

Jack suddenly began to feel as if he were being watched and followed as he hurriedly walked along the streets of the French Quarter until he found himself in front of Raphaella's shop.

Jack began to knock at first with no reply and quickly switched to pounding on the door with his fists as he shouted in a panic, "Raphaella, let me in. I need to talk to you!"

"Go away. I'm closed for the night!" Raphaella answered from inside.

"Please! It's urgent!" Jack screamed.

The door suddenly opened, as Raphaella appeared with a smug look on her face. "Back so soon, Jack? Are you here for another reading?" She bitterly said.

"No, I'm here to apologize and pay you for your services. I'm sorry, here." He said as he took out two crisp one-hundred-dollar bills and handed them to her. There's a little extra for you," he said, sounding embarrassed and avoided asking her to give him fifty dollars back.

Raphaella looked at Jack as if he'd gone mad, as her demeanor changed. She reflected on his words and how Jack had sounded sincere. "Jack, what's gotten into you? What changed your mind?" She asked.

"I've just come from The Rawhide; I thought I would stop in and have a nightcap before returning to the motel. Guess who I should run into?" He asked, sounding mysterious.

Her reply was a shrug and blank expression.

"Stefan! That's where I met him originally about a month or so ago. Guess what he was wearing?" She shrugged once more. "An eye patch, where I stabbed him with the crucifix you gave me! But that's not all; Stefan made a vampire minion. This young guy was pretending to be a bartender at the bar. Now I have three vampires after me. So, I'm back and thought I would again ask you for your help. You're the only one I could think of", he said anxiously.

"My help?" She said with a grin.

Jack could smell that Raphaella had been drinking, but then again, so had he.

Raphaella, this is all so unbelievable! I never dreamed any of this could exist," He said.

"Jack, you must accept what's happening. I know it's terrifying, but you and I must have a clear mind if we're going to deal with these creatures," She said and attempted to encourage him to remain strong.

"We?" Jack asked with a surprised look on his face.

She held out her hand.

"What?" He asked once again, sounding irritated.

"The money Jack. If I am going to offer you any more of my time, then you need to pay me!" She explained, sounding agitated.

"Of course, I don't expect you to do this for free. Listen, I'll stop by tomorrow and pay you, I promise. But for now I need some other form of protection. I no longer have the crucifix you gave me which managed to only take out one of Stefan's eyes. I need something much more powerful to fight off these bloodthirsty monsters," Jack explained.

"I have just the thing! Follow me, Jack," as they walked to the back of the shop where the séances were held and over to a dresser as Raphaella opened the top drawer. Inside, a glass vial appeared containing a clear liquid.

"What is it?" Jack asked, looking confused.

"Haven't you ever seen holy water before? What kind of Catholic are you, Jack?" She said, sounding as if she were scolding a child.

"I thought you were supposed to be some Voodoo queen or something?" He replied.

"Jack! I was brought up a Roman Catholic on the island of Haiti. Do you even know where Haiti is, boy?" and gave him a look of disapproval.

"Would you believe me if I said I did?" He answered.

"Never mind, Jack! We don't have time for this. I thought you were in trouble with just the two vampires. Now you're telling me there's a third?" She said excitedly.

At that moment, the front door opened as a cold breeze rushed in. The young vampire stood at the threshold of the front door. He knew he couldn't enter the shop unless he was invited to. Hearing

Jack's voice in the back confirmed that he was here with the store's owner and decided he would need to hypnotize Jack to have him suggest to the owner to invite him in. He focused on Jack's image in his mind and began to instruct him telepathically, "Jack, I command you to tell the owner to let me in." Jack heard the young vampire's command and told Raphaella, "I think someone is at the front door and wants to come in. You should let him." Jack said.

"Come in! I wonder who it could be at this late hour," Raphaella said, looking perplexed.

"Perhaps it's a customer looking to connect with a dearly departed family member," Jack replied.

"Well, at least I can schedule the reading for another day," she said excitedly. The two of them moved toward the front of the store to greet the unexpected guest and were shocked to discover it wasn't a customer out for a late stroll looking to connect with a spirit of a loved one but rather the young vampire. Jack recognized him instantly as a look of shock came over his face.

"Well, Jack, fancy meeting you here in a place like this; nice to see you again!" The Goth Punk sarcastically said.

"I wish I could say the same," Jack answered back. The young vampire appeared amused by Jack's cockiness and chuckled. "Jack, is that any way to talk to a new friend?" he said as he turned his attention toward Raphaella. "And who do we have here?" The Goth Punk asked as he stared at Raphaella intensely.

"My name is Raphaella; I own this store," She replied defiantly.

"Ah! A lively one. I like that! Tell me, what does one do in a Voodoo shop, if you don't mind my asking? Can you turn me into a Zombie? Or perhaps cast a spell on me? Or are you just a sorry ass phony like every other Voodoo shop in this wretched city!" The Goth vampire said in a taunting manner.

"Don't mess with me, Boy! I can summon any number of spirits willing to assist me at any time!" Raphaella replied, seeming to challenge the young vampire.

"Is that right? Now just who might that be?" He asked as he began to stroll toward them, leaving a path of destruction along the way with an arm outstretched as he began to knock several items off their shelves. A single book dropped at his feet, and he read the title, which sparked his amusement: "Vampires, the Myth, and the Reality." He said. "Oh, look! One of my favorite subjects!" he scoffed, kicking the book away from his feet as he laughed and displayed his fangs.

Instantly he lunged toward Jack.

Seeing that Raphaella reacted quickly, despite consuming a considerable portion of her rum before Jack's return as she reached for the glass vial, which contained the holy water, and tossed it into the face of the young Punk vampire. "Take that demon! Be gone from here. You are not welcome in my shop!" Raphaella shouted.

The young vampire screamed, "Bitch, you'll pay for this!" as Jack and Raphaella looked on in horror. Instantly, the holy water had transformed the vampire's milk-white complexion into a red, blister-covered face.

"The two of you haven't seen the last of me," he threatened and disappeared instantly, leaving behind a trail of smoke.

CHAPTER 16

Possession

Laurent appeared transfixed by the flames as they danced and flickered in the fireplace of the drawing room. He seemed consumed by many disturbing thoughts involving Jack and Stefan. *Has Stefan finally tracked me down, only to fulfill his vision of restoring the past and making Jack his Fabien? Will Stefan attempt to make good on his promise and destroy me, as he had intended to do over two hundred and fifty years ago? Is Jack the reincarnated version of Fabien? If not, how will I transform Jack from a blue-collar, uncultured man with so many bad habits into the romantic, witty, and well-spoken beloved Fabien? Or is it enough that Jack is identical to Fabien in appearance in every way?*

Laurent was so engrossed by his thoughts he was unaware of Barthelme, who had entered the room and said, "Is there something on your mind Master Laurent?"

His question went unanswered, "Master Laurent?" Barthelme asked once more as he tried desperately to capture the attention of his Master.

Finally, Laurent replied, "Yes? Is there something you need, Barthelme?"

"I'm not certain you heard what I asked you, Master Laurent."

"Yes, I heard you, Barthelme. I would rather not discuss that with you. Barthelme, I feel the hunger coming on. Bring me a glass of nourishment," as Laurent turned to face his trusted servant. His face had taken on a ghastly shade of white, with eyes as red as rubies.

"Right away, Master Laurent," he replied and quickly exited the drawing room.

Alone once more with his thoughts, Laurent was unaware of the translucent figure as it appeared.

"Laurent, I'm here!" The spirit of Fabien said as he captured the attention of his undead lover. Laurent was overcome with emotions, just as he'd been, having seen him the first time in the crypt back in Paris so many centuries ago.

"Fabien! My God, it is you! You have come back to me!" Laurent cried out as he extended his arms out towards the spirit of Fabien, sensing nothing but cold air.

"Yes, I have returned with a proposal, if you are willing to consider it?"

"Yes, please share your thoughts with me; I am listening," Laurent replied anxiously.

"The one known as Jack Devereaux is not my reincarnated self; I can assure you that I am stuck here in another realm known as the spirit world; I am a ghost."

"I don't understand, Fabien?" Laurent asked innocently.

"It's quite simple; I am without a body to host my soul. You see, I am translucent. You cannot touch me nor embrace me. I shall get right to the point; you have experienced many feelings since meeting Jack, have you not?" The ghost of Fabien asked Laurent.

"Yes," he said and turned away from the spirit as if Laurent were embarrassed having answered.

"I have been observing you for quite some time now, even though you could not see me, nor did I reveal myself to you; I was here the entire time to witness your budding romance with the mortal known as Jack and your deep disappointment in him. How shall I say this? He is a bit of a challenge, is he not?" Fabien asked.

"Yes, candidly, I'll admit, Jack has been a bit of a disappointment. He certainly doesn't have your refinement, despite my attempts," Laurent admitted.

"I have a solution for that," Fabien shared.

"What would that involve?" Laurent asked.

"It would mean that you would agree to have my soul possess the body of Jack. Once I have taken over Jack's body, and you have bitten me, we will be together for eternity. I observed how you offered Jack the dark gift and his reaction of shock, if not his distaste, and saying he would need time to think over your generous offer of immortality," the spirit of Fabien said.

Laurent looked at him with questioning eyes. "Go on."

"Do you think if Jack were me reincarnated, I would have given it even a second to consider? I want to be together with you again, only this time nothing will stop us, not even Stefan!" the spirit of Fabien proudly proclaimed.

"Stefan?" Laurent asked.

"Yes, not even Stefan. Once we have been reunited, you and I, along with the vengeful spirits whose lives he ended, will destroy him. And it all rests with the help of one who can command the spirits to appear and act!

All I need is your agreement to lure Jack back to the estate, and I shall take care of the rest. Are we in agreement?" Fabien shared.

"But how? Jack told me that he needed time to think things over; how can I get him to come back so soon against his own will?" Laurent innocently asked.

"You have the ability. I bestowed upon you many vampiric abilities so very long ago. Have you forgotten? Or are you perhaps reluctant to use them?"

Fabien asked Laurent.

"I still don't understand, Fabien," Laurent replied and looked confused.

"Through hypnotism. Your voice will carry through the wind, Jack will not only hear you, but he will obey," Fabien said.

Laurent walked over to the window, glanced out at the darkened night, and replied, "I wanted it to be Jack's choice, unlike Stefan, that forced you into this undead existence. Do you recall Fabien?" he said.

Barthelme suddenly entered the room with a glass of blood. "Your drink, Master, pardon the long delay," as he handed Laurent the glass, seemingly unaware of Fabien's spirit in the room.

"Thank you, Barthelme; that will be all for this evening."

"Excellent, Sir. I bid you a pleasant evening, Master."

As Barthelme moves past his Master, Laurent gently reaches for his arm, offering his appreciation, "And to you, my trusted servant." Each smiled at the other briefly as Barthelme exited the room.

"How touching; you still possess many humanlike emotions," Fabien asked tenderly.

"Barthelme is a good man and an extremely loyal servant. He has been with me for over two hundred years. He has provided me with a bit of companionship, however, not in a romantic way. I long for that intimacy," Laurent confided.

"As do I. That is why you must agree to my plan!" Fabien said. "What would happen if Jack rejected you and told you he does not wish to become a vampire? Would you then take him against his will?" Fabien asked, leaving Laurent to ponder the idea. There was a brief silence between them until Laurent finally answered, "Most likely not."

"Instead, you would allow Stefan to turn him and have them plot to destroy you once and for all." Fabien stated cruelly.

"No. I'm confused; I…" Laurent replied, appearing weak and indecisive.

"What are we waiting for?" Fabien asked commandingly.

Jack and Raphaella reflected on having fought off the vampire fledgling. Jack thanked Raphaella for her bravery but required additional protection before leaving.

"Before I go, do you have any more of that water? You used quite a bit of it on that punk." Jack asked. "Yes, I certainly do," Raphaella said and walked over to a chest of drawers. She opened the top drawer, which revealed another glass vial containing the liquid known as holy water.

"Here, take this; you might need it, Jack. Any one of them may wait for the right opportunity and ambush you out of nowhere; you best have some protection. You've seen this evening what affect it has on them," Raphaella instructed.

"Thanks, you truly are a lifesaver," Jack tenderly said as she handed him the all-important vial.

"It's all in a day's work." She replied, appearing to blush a bit.

"No, it's far more than that. You're also a good person and a wonderful friend," He said and wished her a good evening as he turned to leave.

"Jack, be careful out there." She said.

He turned to her and smiled, and opened the door to leave.

Once outside, Jack felt confident he had the protection he needed, and if the young vampire were foolish enough to present himself once more, Jack vowed he would destroy him at any cost.

Once again, Jack had the uncanny feeling of being watched, just as he'd felt before. He held the glass vial close to his chest and began to walk from St. Ann, crossing Dauphine and heading deeper towards the center of the French Quarter at a steady pace, thinking that if the young vampire were around, and was to appear and attempt to attack Jack that he would have the right tool to defend himself.

Instantly, Seth, the young punk vampire appeared, his face showing the damage the holy water had done earlier. "Hello again, Jack! Look what that bitch did to my face! She'll pay dearly with her life, but not before I end yours!" Seth snarled and lunged toward Jack's neck, with red eyes ablaze.

Instantly, Seth knocked Jack to the ground and appeared before him and struggled to reach Jack's jugular.

"Unlike your two other vampire lovers, I have no interest in turning you. That would be far too good for you. Instead, I think I'll drain you dry and watch as the light in your eyes fades to nothing, as I lap up your blood," Seth said. Jack kept moving his head from side to side and landed a punch right to the young vampire's nose, which stunned the creature a bit.

Suddenly another spoke saying, "Not so fast, Seth; it's not up to you to decide whether Jack lives or dies."

Jack instantly recognized the voice belonging to Stefan as he witnessed Seth being violently lifted off of Jack as Stefan hoisted the young vampire high in the air with his hand wrapped tightly around Seth's neck.

The young vampire struggled and was released by Stefan's vise-like grip and dropped to the ground with a thud. "Master, I thought you loved me?" the young vampire asked and regained his composure as he wiped the dirt from his clothing.

"You are nothing to me. Merely a toy," Stefan scoffed coldly.

"You'll regret this, Jack!" Seth threatened and took to flight as he disappeared into the darkened sky.

"I guess you owe me one, Jack, or should I refer to you as Fabien? I could have let him kill you, but had I allowed that, how could I ever have reclaimed you as mine?" Stefan said with a sinister laugh.

"What do you mean?" Jack answered, visibly shaken by his near-death encounter.

"Ah, Jack. There is so much you still must learn. Still, I consider it a challenge, and unlike your vampire lover Laurent, I have far more patience to see you as you truly are; you're nothing like Fabien; however, I shall see to it by transforming you in more ways than you can ever dream of!" Jack stood transfixed, hearing Stefan's words, unable to move.

"Go forth, Jack, and think about what your human existence is like presently. Take a good last look at the sun. Enjoy the warmth as it washes over your body, and listen to the birds singing their songs to one another. There are no birds that sing their songs at night. Drink your beloved alcohol and relish some of your favorite foods. Soon neither will be needed. Soon you will experience no light, no warmth, and dwell amongst the creatures of the night in forever darkness," Stefan shared.

"Sounds like a meager existence, Stefan," Jack replied.

"Meager? Not on your miserable mortal life, Jack. Think about the thrill of the hunt once you have been changed into what I am. How every human will be a part of your food chain, and that you will never fear illness or death. How you'll never grow old and have the ability to fly and to know no fear; how could that be described as a meager existence?" Stefan sarcastically asked. "You and I shall be kings of our kind, you will return to me as my Fabien, and we shall be together again. This time Laurent will not interfere with that plan!" Stefan warned.

"What do you mean, Stefan?" Jack asked.

"Is it not obvious, Jack? I will destroy Laurent, as I intended to do over two hundred and fifty years ago!" Stefan proudly proclaimed.

"Stefan, you can't!" Jack pleaded.

"My, my! What are you saying? Are you admitting something to me? Could it be that you have feelings for Laurent?" Stefan said as he chuckled and instantly his mood shifted from amusement to anger.

"Speak, Jack!" Stefan commanded.

"Perhaps," Jack admitted.

"Perhaps? The answer to my question is either yes or no. There is no, perhaps. I have waited too long for this. Very soon, you will be mine. Now leave here, Jack. When the time is right, I shall come for you; I will transform you, changing every aspect of your being!" Stefan said commandingly.

Jack didn't return Stefan's gaze, which had twisted into an inhuman and sinister monster. Jack began to run back toward his motel. He'd be safe there, along with his holy water. He thought *I must contact Laurent and share Stefan's diabolical plan; perhaps Laurent could help save me.*

In the distance, Jack heard Stefan's evil laughter as it grew faint with each passing city block until he finally reached the motel which had been Jack's home for nearly a year.

As he entered his room, he immediately began to undress, thinking that a hot shower might help clear his mind. Jack removed his clothes until he stood naked and entered the bathroom. Jack stood briefly in front of the mirror and said out loud, "My God! You've aged, old boy!" and noticed a few strands of his hair had gone entirely white alongside his left temple.

Jack entered the shower stall and reached for the knob as the water spewed out, soaking his entire body. The water ran down Jack's broad shoulders and muscular back and continued over his buttocks and down his leg, spilling across the floor. The sound of the water hitting the tile created an almost hypnotic sound. He became unaware of how long he had stood there, lost in the warmth of the water, which felt incredibly therapeutic. Finally, he reached for the soap and began to lather his entire body, feeling disgustingly dirty merely for having been in Stefan's presence. He turned the water off, stepped out of the shower, reached for a towel, and dried himself off.

Jack walked over to the bed and lay across it naked, not bothering with a t-shirt or underwear, as the hot, humid, Louisiana night had him drenched in sweat so soon after showering.

No sooner had Jack fallen asleep; than he was awakened by the sound of someone's voice beckoning and calling his name from the open window.

"Jack, I want you to come to me," the voice commanded eerily. He recognized the voice; it was Laurent.

"Is that you, Laurent?" Jack yelled as the voice continued to beckon him, "you must come to me. I need you, Jack!"

"Yes, I hear, and I will obey!" Jack replied and rose from the bed, and reached for his clothes. Instantly, he was dressed and out the door and down the stairs. Jack hailed a nearby cab at the corner.

He gave the driver the address in Vacherie as it sped away. During the long drive, Jack seemed to have come out of the trance Laurent had induced, wondering why he was headed out of town. The taxi arrived in under an hour and made its way up the long driveway.

"Wow! This is someplace. Whoever lives here must have a lot of money!" The cab driver said, seeming mesmerized by the size of the mansion as it loomed in the near distance. Jack ignored his remarks as the taxi came to a stop. He paid and exited the cab as it drove off. Suddenly, the massive front door opened as Barthelme appeared, as he greeted Jack and motioned for him to enter.

"Right this way, Master Jack, we have been expecting you" Jack stepped inside and saw Laurent as he descended the majestic staircase dressed in an elegant smoking jacket and dark trousers. Jack immediately felt underdressed.

"Jack, how wonderful to see you again! I have missed you," Laurent said and leaned over to kiss Jack directly on the mouth, which caused Jack to flinch ever so slightly. Laurent took note and wondered why he was avoiding his advances.

"Jack, what's the matter?" Laurent asked with a bewildered look on his face.

"Laurent, you summoned me here, I heard your voice, you called out to me, and I had no choice but to come. Don't act so surprised to see me, but now that I'm here, there is something I desperately need your help with," Jack replied.

"Before we go any further, Jack, please have a seat," Laurent said and motioned his arm toward the chaise lounge. Jack walked over and sat as Laurent had suggested.

"May I offer you something? Would you care for a drink?" Laurent asked.

"No, thanks. I didn't come here for a romantic interlude Laurent; I came because you summoned me here. And as I already mentioned, I need your help with Stefan," He said.

"Stefan?" Laurent asked, practically sneering at the name of the other vampire.

"Yes, you heard me correctly. You're not alone in your desire to remake the past, Laurent; Stefan swore to me that he would turn me and that he and I would be together, after which he intends on destroying you, most likely forcing me to help him!" Jack shared anxiously.

"But what can I do? Stefan is so much older and stronger than me," Laurent said, sounding defeated and weak.

"You forget; I have the help of a powerful and gifted medium. When I first met Raphaella, or as some call her, the Voodoo queen, I thought she was a phony. But then I witnessed as she conjured up a spirit!" Jack shared excitedly.

"How can your friend help us, Jack?" Laurent asked.

"Perhaps she can summon the spirits who died at the hands of Stefan to help us?" Jack said.

"Us?" Laurent said and reached his hand to touch Jack's, "Does that mean you are willing to be turned and become my beloved for all time and reject Stefan?" Laurent asked tenderly.

"Yes, I reject Stefan and all that he stands for. He is the very definition of evil. No, I haven't decided whether to accept your offer Laurent; I still need time to think that over; it's a huge decision," Jack said and visibly recoiled from Laurent's touch by removing his hand.

"We must gather all our resources to defeat Stefan before it's too late!" Jack said.

"What do you propose, Jack?" Laurent asked as a trace of doubt appeared on the vampire's face as Jack shared his plan.

"I will lure Stefan to Raphaella's shop on a date, pretending to have booked a reading and that it's just for fun and entertainment. You will get to the shop before we arrive and hide; once he and I are there, Raphaella will conjure up every spirit that has fallen victim to Stefan over the centuries. With all that energy and with you at the shop, combined with Raphaella's powers, we'll be able to destroy Stefan once and for all!" Jack said confidently.

"I'm afraid it won't be that easy, Jack. Let me make you a drink," Laurent said and grimaced.

"On second thought, yes. I could sure use one to calm my nerves. Thanks!"

Over at the bar, Laurent poured Jack's favorite drink, Jack Daniels and coke, walked back and handed him his drink.

"How will you lure Stefan to your friend's shop, Jack"? Laurent innocently asked.

"Well, I need to run into Stefan again; other than that, I have no way of getting in touch with him. He seems fond of a bar called The Rawhide and even turned one of the bartenders into his vampire minion. He came to my friend's shop and was intent on killing us until Raphaella fought him off." Jack shared.

"She gave me several things that you and your kind aren't particularly fond of, a crucifix, handed down from generation to generation, and some holy water." While Jack described the tools Raphaella provided him with as protection, he noticed Laurent wince as if he were in pain.

At that moment, it occurred to Jack that Laurent didn't appear to be the all-powerful vampire he prefaced to be. Jack looked at Laurent tenderly and said, "Of course, I would never use these weapons on you, Laurent."

At that moment, Laurent was overcome by emotions; a single blood tear formed in his eye and ran down his milk-white cheek.

"Never say never, Jack," Laurent uttered softly as he wiped away the blood from his face with his handkerchief and observed Jack consume his entire cocktail in two large gulps.

"I'd love another. Do you mind?" Jack asked Laurent sheepishly while he held up the empty glass for Laurent to see.

"I don't mind at all, Jack," as he took the glass from Jack's hand and walked back toward the bar to make him another drink, only this time much stronger than the first drink.

Laurent walked back from the bar and handed Jack his drink, and said, "I hope you don't mind if I join you, Jack?" and lifted the glass of blood and emptied it with two gulps to match Jack's as a tiny trace of blood trickled down his lips and onto his chin. Instantly, Jack noticed Laurent's skin color had changed. Gone was the deathly pallor, replaced by a rosy-colored complexion and eyes that had turned from their fiery red color and returned to a beautifully tranquil blue color.

Laurent was quick to refill Jack's empty glass and, after some time, lost track of exactly how many cocktails Jack had consumed.

"Wow! I just realized I hadn't eaten anything since lunchtime; these drinks are going to my head! Do you have any food in this place? But then again, why would you," Jack said as he started to slur his words and laugh uncontrollably. Jack's rude remark and lack of self-control had offended Laurent.

"Barthelme!" Laurent shouted in a commanding voice. Barthelme appeared at once, dressed in a robe and pajamas, thinking he had completed the tasks for the day.

"Prepare Master Jack something to eat, anything he desires," Laurent instructed.

"What be your pleasure, Master Jack?" Barthelme asked Jack.

"What shall it be, Jack?" Laurent asked.

"How about a hamburger?" Jack said.

"Right away, Master Jack," Barthelme replied and walked toward the kitchen to prepare Jack's late-night snack.

"I wouldn't mind another one of these while I'm waiting for my snack," he said.

"Jack, you are quite fond of your drink. I only had one of your six drinks, but who's counting?" Laurent sarcastically said.

Laurent recalled what Fabien's spirit had told him. That Jack is not the reincarnated Fabien but merely an identical twin in every sense of the word, except for the all-important mannerisms of refinement, grace, and elegance inherent in Fabien's personality.

And with that thought, Jack gave Laurent a drunken look before he staggered, fell onto the couch, and passed out. Laurent merely shook his head in disgust.

"Barthelme, cancel the hamburger," Laurent shouted and thought, *Ah, Jack, you have once again proven to me that you are not my reincarnated lover. Your actions leave a lot to be desired. I shall have no choice but to carry you to the bed where you will encounter nightmares, which may prove true!"*

Laurent bends over and picks Jack up effortlessly, as if he were light as a feather, despite Jack's six foot two inches, two-hundred-and-thirty-pound frame.

As Laurent carried Jack up the long staircase, he heard Jack mumbling in a half-asleep, drunken state. Something about a "no-good bloodsucker," which Laurent chose to ignore.

Laurent gently placed Jack on the guestroom bed, which Jack had stayed in more than once. But this night should prove to be unlike any other of Jack's previous visits.

"Now try and get some rest Jack," Laurent said. He knew the last thing in the world Jack would be experiencing was sleep. Laurent decided to stay with Jack until the transformation was complete, and should there be any complications, if Jack decided to sober up and try to escape.

Laurent felt deep disappointment over Jack. He had hoped Jack was his reincarnated Fabien returned to him as if by some miracle. That was until Fabien's spirit appeared and assured Laurent they were not the same.

Laurent sat in a chair, called out to Fabien's ghost, and patiently waited for him to reappear. "I have done just as you instructed; Jack is fast asleep and ready to be transformed. Come to me and enter Jack's body so you and I can be together again!" Laurent emphatically called out.

Suddenly, a mist filtered out of the walls as an image began to take shape. It was Fabien's entity, smiling, and pleased that Laurent's efforts were successful in luring Jack back to the mansion so that the possession may start.

"You have done well; my, what a fine specimen he is. He will do rather nicely!" Fabien said approvingly.

"But one thing puzzles me?" Laurent asked rather timidly.

"What is that?" Fabien's spirit asked.

"If Jack is not you reincarnated, why did we meet? Was it just by chance?

"Perhaps. I spotted Jack on this earthly plane and knew that the two of you would eventually meet once you ended your seclusion and left the house. It hurt me to see you fall for such a pathetic drunk," Fabien said as his facial features became more apparent, which had a look of disapproval as the two of them gazed at Jack lying on the bed.

Suddenly, he began to stir, which alarmed Fabien's spirit.

"Don't be alarmed. That is merely Jack having a nightmare or shifting his body. I have witnessed it countless times," Laurent admitted.

"I see. Are you ready to sacrifice this man to me so that the two of us can be reunited?" the spirit of Fabien asked.

"Yes! Take him, take him now!" Laurent replied with a grin.

The spirit smiled tenderly and levitated in the air as the entity moved closer to Jack. The ghost was only inches from Jack's face.

For a brief period, it was difficult for Laurent to tell the difference between Jack and Fabien's spirit as the entity covered Jack's entire body. Jack briefly awakened and began to thrash around on the bed as he opened his eyes to see Fabien's spirit hovering directly above him. Jack felt a burning sensation as if something had attempted to bore its way into his body.

Jack screamed, but only for a moment, as the images of his life flashed before his eyes. All at once, it all suddenly made sense. He had been put on this earth for one purpose to become the vessel for Fabien, as his eyes closed.

Suddenly the eyes opened once again with wonder and amazement. The awkward drunkenness which had annoyed and disappointed Laurent so many times was gone.

The body that formally belonged to Jack sat up and glanced at his outstretched hands.

"It worked! I have a body once more," Fabien declared triumphantly. Laurent instantly recognized the voice of Fabien and was overcome with emotion.

"It's you. It's truly you, Fabien. You have returned to me," as blood tears ran down Laurent's face while mortal salt tears ran down the cheeks of Fabien's face.

They embraced as memories of their time spent together in Paris flooded over them. Finally, they kissed, a long and passionate kiss, two hundred and fifty years in the making, until Fabien unlocked his lips from Laurent's.

"There is another transformation that needs to take place. Turn me so that I will become as you," Fabien pleaded. Laurent reacted with a smile and removed Fabien's shirt worn by Jack. Fabien gazed into the eyes of his handsome face, which instantly transformed into a twisted snarl, and Laurent's eyes of blue turned violently red as Laurent opened his mouth and bit his lover on the neck.

Fabien felt the searing pain as Laurent's fangs penetrated deeply into his jugular, as the rich red blood ran down his lover's neck while he lapped at it, much like a feral animal might.

"Yes, Yes!" Fabien screamed as Laurent fed on his blood. Suddenly, Laurent stopped and bit into his wrist, which released the vampire's rich lifeblood.

"Fabien?" Laurent asked, filled with tenderness, "Yes?" Fabien replied barely with a whisper as he was close to unconsciousness.

"Drink my blood, which will resurrect you to eternal life!" Laurent instructed.

Fabien followed Laurent's instructions and began to suck the blood oozing from Laurent's wrist.

Fabien finally felt satisfied and began to have seizures, known as the transition from human to immortal.

Fabien's body convulsed and heaved, with his mouth opened, gasping for air until finally, he looked at Laurent tenderly, thinking two hundred and fifty years ago, it was Fabien who had transformed Laurent and given him eternal life. The thought caused him to smile.

Outside, the wind began to moan, followed by the violent sound of thunder as the lightning illuminated the dark sky.

Fabien ceased all motion and lay entirely still; his shallow gasps for air were gone. Fabien died his mortal death. Suddenly, a jolt of Fabien's body as his eyes opened, which revealed two eyes the color of a ruby.

The transformation had been successful as Fabien began to speak. "I feel your blood course through my veins, I have been reborn, and for that, I am eternally grateful," Fabien said.

"Fabien, the crucial task at hand in defeating Stefan has come. You will help set a trap for him," Laurent instructed confidently.

"But how do I lure him here? I don't think he'll come back here. The two of you recognized the other when Jack brought him to dinner," Fabien said anxiously.

"Do you not remember the plan that Jack had shared with you only a short time ago? Instead of Jack going to the bar in search of Stefan to lure him to his friend's Voodoo shop it shall be me disguised as Jack. It will be your job to stop by her shop and hypnotize her so that she is under your control you will hide in the shop until Stefan and I arrive." Fabien said. He shook his head, "I must say despite Jack being simple minded he did devise a plan that I believe will work."

CHAPTER 17

The Plot

Once Laurent received his instructions from Fabien, he left to find Stefan. According to the Fabien's plan, he would impersonate Jack to lure Stefan to the voodoo shop, where his existence would surely end.

Fabien would replicate Jack's voice and slight southern drawl and fool Stefan into thinking he was Jack.

Fabien took to the air and, within minutes, appeared around the corner from the Rawhide. Fabien sensed he was not alone and that someone was nearby.

Suddenly, the young vampire appeared and approached Fabien, naturally thinking it was Jack.

"Hey, Pretty Boy! Where do you think you're going?"

"Why I thought I would stop in for a drink and see if my old friend Stefan were here and join him," Fabien replied, replicating Jack's southern drawl perfectly as he turned to face Seth, someone Fabien had never met before. Still, from the sounds of it, this young man and Jack had had an unpleasant encounter.

"I thought we'd have a rematch, just you and I. This time without the help of your friend Stefan. Wait! There's something different about you," the young vampire said as he took Fabien by the arm. Incensed that this young vampire dared lay his hand upon his arm caused Fabien to react violently as he ripped his arm away from the young vampire at lightning speed.

"What the hell? Hey, you're not, Jack!" Seth said in disbelief.

"That is correct!" Fabien hissed and bore his fangs as he reached out his hand and attempted to grab Seth's throat. Somehow the young vampire managed to avoid Fabien's grasp as he stood there defiantly sneering at Fabien.

"What a pathetic excuse for a vampire you are!" Fabien said and leaped onto the young vampire's chest. As he threatened Seth, Fabien's nails grew as sharp as knives, "I will end your meager existence. It will give me great pleasure to destroy what Stefan made and turn it to dust!"

The young vampire made a valiant effort to defend himself by hitting Fabien with a clean left hook. The punch landed square upon Fabien's jaw, which caused the older vampire to stagger backward, as he rubbed his mouth.

At once, he rushed Seth, tackled him to the ground, and quickly stood up with his foot on the young vampire's neck. "Not feeling so mighty now, are you?" Fabien said mockingly and removed his foot from the young vampire's neck, only to stomp on his head, which crushed the young vampire's skull. The rich blackened blood oozed out and soaked the pavement as the body convulsed uncontrollably and finally went utterly still.

"Now for that drink!" Fabien sarcastically said as he entered the bar.

Once inside, Fabien scanned the bar to see whether Stefan was anywhere to be seen. As he moved through the crowd of men, each one seemed mesmerized by Fabien, who was a vision of inhuman masculinity. Fabien made his way to the bar with the grace and agility of a panther.

"What can I get you, good-looking?" The ruggedly handsome bartender asked Fabien.

"A jack and coke," Fabien replied as he scanned the bar anxiously, hoping to spot Stefan. Despite the many hot men gathered, Stefan was nowhere to be seen.

A passerby stopped and stood directly in front of Fabien and said, "What's going on, good-looking?"

"Not now; I'm here to meet someone," Fabien replied.

"Well, now you've met someone, me," the man said and placed his hand firmly on Fabien's buttocks. Fabien turned to the man, approaching fifty, balding with a slight beer gut, and hissed at him, baring large incisors and glaring ruby red eyes, and repeated what he said just a short time ago, only more forceful, "I told you, not now. Get lost!"

The man stepped back in horror and disbelief and nearly fell over a table as he quickly ran out of the bar for his life.

Suddenly, Fabien spotted the elusive Stefan as he strolled into the bar.

Stefan scanned the room and spotted Fabien from across the bar sitting at a table thinking it was Jack; as their eyes locked. Each acknowledged the other with a slight nod. Stefan began to walk toward the bar as he drew nearer until he stood next to Fabien.

"Well, well, fancy meeting you here in a place like this," Stefan said jokingly.

"Are you happy to see me, Stefan?" Fabien asked.

"More than you'll ever know. I've thought of no one else since we last saw each other, but admittedly, I'm a little surprised not to find you half-drunk already?" Stefan rudely said.

"Yeah, I've had a couple already. I didn't want to get too drunk tonight; call it the new Jack!" Fabien said teasingly.

"The new Jack? I'm intrigued. Tell me more," Stefan said and chuckled as he joined Fabien at his table.

Fabien turned to Stefan to study his face. He saw the same old cruel soulless eyes he'd always had. However, Fabien felt relief in knowing that Stefan thought he was genuinely engaging with Jack.

Fabien decided he would need to secure Stefan's interest in him romantically once more and made him an offer. "You know Stefan, you could persuade me to spend a little more time with you if you play your cards right!" Fabien said as he nuzzled up to Stefan and took him by the arm.

"Go on, you have my full attention," Stefan replied, seeming genuinely interested.

"Lately, I've been fascinated by astrology. I've located someone here in town; she's become a friend of mine. Her name is Raphaella; she can see into the future," Fabien excitedly said as Stefan shook his head disapprovingly.

"Come on, Stefan. I would never have dreamed that you, Laurent, and others of your kind existed. I heard about the legends even having grown up watching vampires in movies and television. So if that exists, how do you know people don't possess psychic abilities?" Fabien said.

"I doubt it," Stefan replied with a grimace.

Fabien ignored his remark and asked, "So, will you?"

"Will I what?" Stefan answered back, sounding agitated.

"Will you come and do a reading with me at my friend's shop? I think you'll be amazed at the results," Fabien said.

"Let me think about it," Stefan replied with skepticism.

Fabien nuzzled Stefan once more.

"Alright, if it's that important to you. But just so you know, I remain doubtful," Stefan said and shook his head.

"Keep an open mind, Stefan; that's all I'm asking, simply show up and keep an open mind," Fabien replied excitedly; he knew he'd just set the trap.

"If it's that important to you, I'll do it," Stefan said and shrugged his shoulders.

"You don't know how important," Fabien replied with a grin.

"Now you have to do me a favor, Jack," Stefan said

"What's that?" Fabien asked.

"I want you to dance with me, just like we did the first time we met," Stefan said.

"Alright, Stefan, just one dance, and then I should get going; I still need to stop by my friend's shop and arrange the session. Shall we say tomorrow night at eight?" Fabien said.

"Of course, but how do you know if she is available for this so-called reading?" Stefan asked, with a puzzled look on his face.

"You forget, she's a friend of mine. Despite her psychic talents, she doesn't have many customers to speak of. Dare I say I'm her only one? She's a bit of an alcoholic; I think she's scared most of her customers away. I think her taste for alcohol discredits her." Fabien said

"Is that so? I know someone else that drinks pretty heavily," Fabien replied and looked at Fabien.

"Wonderful. So it's settled. I'll meet you tomorrow at eight o'clock," Fabien said excitedly.

"Shall we dance?" Stefan asked as the two of them got up from the table and made their way to the dance floor, overcrowded with men. Stefan extended his hand, which Fabien declined. He feared Stefan might become suspicious if his hand was as deathly cold as Stefan's.

"Stefan, we're not dancing the Viennese waltz," Fabien sarcastically said; Stefan laughed.

Fabien thought Stefan hadn't changed a bit in over two hundred and fifty years and searched his innermost soul for any lingering feelings he might still have for Stefan, his vampire maker and one-time lover. Fabien could quickly determine that he had no feelings for him other than contempt.

How could he possess any emotions for the monster responsible for ending his existence and who had initially intended to destroy Laurent, the only man he ever loved? No! He would follow through with their plan to lure Stefan to Raphaella's shop. There was no other way. The world would indeed rest a little easier knowing Stefan was destroyed.

As they danced, Stefan held Fabien's gaze, which began to make Fabien feel uncomfortable. He looked deep into Stefan's eyes and detected a slight redness. He wondered if Stefan could also see traces of red in his eyes. Fabien thought perhaps it was just the lights on the dance floor. Overrun by paranoia, Fabien decided it was time he and Stefan made their way off the dance floor and back to their table. Fabien would tell him he'd grown tired.

"Stefan, I need to take a rest. You have limitless energy as a vampire, which is sadly not the case for me," Fabien said. Stefan readily agreed and they left the dance floor to head back to their table.

As Fabien passed by one of the bar patrons, he could detect the beating of the man's jugular vein and heard his heart beat. It took everything in his power to resist the urge to attack the man as the blood lust had over taken Fabien and seemed uncontrollable.

Stefan noticed Fabien's pallid complexion as they sat down and said, "You don't look so good, Jack. The last time we danced, your skin color became rather red. Now you appear very different, almost deathly sick. Are you feeling okay?" Stefan said. Fabien knew he had to come up with an excuse for his pale appearance and fast.

"I think I've had too much to drink and feel nauseous. Would you excuse me while I go to the bathroom? I think I'm going to be sick," Fabien said, excusing himself as he stood up and hurriedly made his way to the bathroom. Fabien stayed in the bathroom for a bit, attempting to appear overcome with a feeling of sickness as he stood in front of the sink and glanced into the mirror, seeing no reflection other than the bathroom stalls directly behind him.

He finally returned to the table after having been gone nearly ten minutes. Stefan had eagerly awaited his return.

"Are you feeling okay, Jack? You were gone quite a while. I almost came to check on you," Stefan said as a smile appeared.

"You know me. I guess I did have too much to drink this evening, Fabien said and hoped by admitting that they would end their date early.

"I better say good night Stefan. I still need to stop by Raphaella's store and make the arrangements for our reading tomorrow night." Fabien said.

"Are you sure you're okay to do that? You look very pale, Jack," Stefan asked.

"Yes, I'm fine. I'm just slightly drunk and exhausted, that's all," Fabien replied.

"Alright then, until tomorrow night. And yes, you've got me intrigued about tomorrow night's session. It should prove to be an interesting evening," Stefan said.

"Good night, Stefan," Fabien said. Suddenly, Stefan grabbed Fabien by the arm; he had forgotten how strong Stefan was, with nearly the strength of fifty men.

Fabien looked at Stefan with panic and thought Stefan might be onto him by impersonating Jack.

"Good night Jack. Until tomorrow evening," Stefan said with a sinister grin and released Fabien's arm.

"Wait," Stefan shouted. "I need to know where I'm going," Stefan said and shook his head.

"My apologies. The address is 709 St Ann; see you tomorrow evening at eight, Fabien said and waved to Stefan as he turned to leave.

"I'm certain I'll find it," Stefan muttered as he watched Fabien leave the bar.

Once outside, Fabien walked around the corner, flew high in the air over the French Quarter, and landed in front of Raphaella's shop in mere seconds.

Fabien passed the first test with Stefan, but would the gifted psychic be fooled into believing his charade?

He quickly decided to cast away any doubt he had and entered the shop. The bell above the door rang, which announced his arrival. He spotted her toward the back of the store. It was obvious to Fabien she'd been drinking as the stench of alcohol permeated the shop as she greeted him, "Jack," Raphaella shouted from across the shop as she unsteadily moved toward him, nearly knocking into a table with various occult objects for sale.

"I've missed you. How have you been? I've been worried sick!" She said, slurring her words.

"I can see that. It's good to see you, Raphaella," Fabien said and hugged her; she immediately reacted to his coldness.

"Jack, my god, you feel like a block of ice. It's such a hot and humid night out. What's wrong? Are you getting sick?" She said, sounding alarmed.

"I think I might be coming down with a cold or something. Listen, I'm here to arrange a reading for my friend and me tomorrow evening at eight; I'll pay you handsomely," Fabien said to Raphaella's delight.

"Well, let me check my appointment calendar to see if I have any availability," she said as she strolled across the room, nearly knocking over a chair as she reached her desk.

After a minute or two, she asked, "What time were you looking for?"

"Eight o'clock," Fabien answered, sounding annoyed. Fabien thought *I don't understand how mortals consume this liquid called alcohol. A substance that disables and affects an individual in such unflattering ways makes them lose control over their senses, making downright idiots of themselves!* Thinking back to when he was human, before meeting Stefan, he wondered if he had ever become intoxicated and if perhaps it was an American phenomenon, despite Raphaella being Haitian.

"Good news. Yes, I have availability at that time." She announced.

"Wonderful! With that, I need to bid you good night. I need to go home and get some rest before I get even sicker," Fabien said as he offered an excuse for his abruptness and for leaving so soon after his arrival.

As he turned to leave, she shouted, "Wait!" As Fabien cautiously turned around to face her.

"Why don't you join me for a drink, Jack?" she said and motioned toward the half-empty bottle of rum sitting on the counter. Fabien was relieved to hear her invitation but graciously declined.

"I hate to be rude, Raphaella, but I need to leave, I don't feel so well. Good night," he said and left her shop without as much as a glance back.

"Good night," She muttered to herself to a now empty store.

She thought about her interaction with Jack and said to herself, "You know, if I didn't know any better, I would say that Jack seemed different this evening as if he'd become someone else. But that's a ridiculous thought," as Raphaella poured herself another glass of rum.

"Here's to you, Jack," she said and drank the entire glass as she sighed and poured herself another.

Fabien took to flight as soon as he'd left Raphaella's shop; he needed to get back to Laurent to share how the course of the evening had gone. In a matter of seconds, he reached Laurent's estate, Le Petit Fleur.

Laurent was startled as Fabien barged in and announced the good news.

"Well, it all went according to plan. It's all arranged," Fabien proudly proclaimed.

"Please, tell me more," said Laurent excitedly.

"The trap. I met with both Stefan and Raphaella. I met Stefan at the Rawhide, the bar Jack initially met him at. After proposing the idea to attend one of Raphaella's séances, he finally agreed after some persuasion and agreed to meet me tomorrow evening at Raphaella's shop. I met with her and scheduled an eight o'clock reading. So far, the plan is working brilliantly!" Fabien said with pride.

"That truly is wonderful. I am so fortunate to have you once again! I waited so long for this moment. Soon, we'll no longer need to fear Stefan," Laurent said as Fabien nodded his agreement.

"There is one thing you must do before Stefan, and I arrive," Fabien said.

"What would that be?" Laurent asked and ceded control to Fabien.

"You must arrive before Stefan and I arrive. You have the advantage of Raphaella having never met you before. You will walk in and make her believe you are simply a passerby interested in a séance. She will inform you of a prior commitment, namely the session I booked with her this evening. Once you have her full attention, you will take control of her mind and employ your hypnotic abilities. Once she is under your command, you will instruct her that once Stefan and I arrive and are seated, she will call upon every tortured spirit that has fallen victim to Stefan to appear and help control him. You will remain hidden until I call out for your help, so Stefan doesn't become suspicious upon seeing you. With all the spirits present and Raphaella's help, you and I will be able to rid ourselves of Stefan and destroy him once and for all." Fabien instructed in a commanding voice.

"Brilliant," Laurent replied.

CHAPTER 18

Showdown

Both vampires heard the sound of the booming thunder in the distance as a brilliant display of lightning lit up the night sky.

"The skies sound angry this evening," Laurent noted.

"Yes, they do," Fabien replied and walked over to the drawing-room window as he glanced out at the mighty, majestic oak trees as the branches swayed with the wind. These trees were as ancient as the two vampires themselves.

"I sense you're feeling a bit of apprehension about what we are about to do?" Laurent asked Fabien as he walked over to join him at the window.

"I do; however, I'm comforted by an image of Stefan's destruction in my mind. It can't come too soon. He terrorized France with death and destruction and will continue that here. Tomorrow evening, his reign of terror will end with the spilling of his blood and his destruction," Fabien said with such intensity.

Laurent couldn't help but notice a change in Fabien. Perhaps he had grown angrier, having been a spirit for so long?

Since Fabien took over Jack's body, he seemed consumed with rage, with little of the other emotions initially attracting him to Fabien in the first place. He wondered if Fabien would ever regain those emotions other than rage.

Everything Laurent treasured about his beloved, his gentleness yet immeasurable strength and strong convictions about right versus wrong, seemed not to be present, at least for the moment.

Laurent wondered whether he had started to miss Jack and perhaps regretted having lured him back to the estate only to have him become the vessel for Fabien.

Fabien reached his hand out and placed it on Laurent's shoulder as they stood side by side gazing out the window. "I love you with all my heart and soul," Fabien said tenderly. Upon hearing those words, the doubts that Laurent had only seconds ago seemed to vanish.

Laurent felt drawn to Fabien and knew he was not only his soulmate but also gave him eternal life as his vampire maker with the darkest gift imaginable. He had also been responsible for ending Laurent's loneliness and for someone Laurent grew to love immeasurably.

"I love you as well, Fabien; I'm eternally yours!" Laurent said with a smile.

The antique wooden clock on the fireplace mantle struck five in the morning, which announced the impending dawn.

"It's been a very long evening, even for us, where time passes in a blink of an eye. It's getting late. Shall we retire upstairs?" Fabien asked. Laurent nodded and took Fabien's hand as they ascended the majestic staircase and gazed periodically into each other's eyes.

Once they had entered their bedroom, Laurent walked over to the large window that looked out upon the majestic live oak trees and weeping willow trees; he gazed at the sky and saw the first rays of light in the distance as it struggled to break through the darkness. Laurent grabbed the heavy velour bedroom drapes and pulled them closed, shielding them from the daylight.

They heard a rooster crow near the servant's quarters, which announced that the sunrise would be only moments away. They quickly undressed, got under the fine silk sheets, and were locked in an embrace. Soon, each of them fell into a deep slumber.

Laurent began to dream. He pictured Raphaella's shop enshrouded in a heavy fog as he entered. The dense fog enveloped the entire inside of the shop. Raphaella was nowhere to be seen, yet several figures stood there until one emerged from the mist, his features becoming distinguishable; it was Jack as he began to shout.

"How could you do this to me, Laurent? I thought you cared for me? How dare you plot to have your vampire maker Fabien take over my body?"

"I'm sorry, Jack, you could never have replaced Fabien; that became more obvious each time we spent together," Laurent answered and carefully avoided looking at Jack directly.

"Here's someone that loves me for who I am!" Jack replied. Another figure stepped out of the dense fog; it was Stefan. As he smiled and displayed his fangs to Laurent.

"That's right, Laurent, your plan has failed. Now it is you, who will be destroyed, as that was my original intention. This time, there will be no Fabien to save you!" Stefan said with a snarl.

Laurent instantly awakened with a jolt, lying there attempting to interpret the nightmare he'd just had, thinking, what was Jack doing alongside Stefan when Fabien overtook Jack's body? This doesn't make any sense! Was it just a dream? Or does Stefan have the ability to enter my dreams? Laurent decided he would need the help of his servant to assist with Stefan's destruction.

Still shaken from his nightmare, Laurent tried to calm himself, closed his eyes tightly, and held the hand of his beloved Fabien for the rest of the daylight hours.

That evening, Laurent told Barthelme they needed to speak privately.

"What do you want to discuss with me, Master Laurent?" Barthelme asked with a puzzled look on his face.

"Barthelme, my loyal and trusted servant, I had a horrible nightmare while I rested. In some ways, I feel I had a premonition of sorts."

"A what?" Barthelme asked.

"I will explain that later; I will need you as a driver and an accomplice. Before we leave for Raphaella's shop, I need you to construct a razor-sharp stake which you will bring along with you. Should Fabien and I fail in our attempt to destroy Stefan, you will need to be our backup. Once the Voodoo queen has summoned all the ghosts that perished at the hands of Stefan, you will be in hiding along with your stake; Fabien and I will attempt to destroy Stefan with the help of the spirits. Should our plan fail, you will come up behind Stefan and plunge the stake as far into him as possible. Is that clear?" Laurent instructed anxiously.

"Yes, of course. I would do anything for you, Master Laurent," Barthelme replied.

"Good. Then go and make the ultimate weapon of destruction!" Laurent instructed.

Laurent was reminded of the time by the clock on the fireplace mantle, which chimed and read six o'clock.

"We'll leave here in half an hour. It is an hour's drive from here to the shop, meaning we should arrive by seven-thirty. I prefer to arrive by car rather than by flight," Laurent said.

"Yes, Master Laurent," Barthelme replied as he turned to leave and embark on creating the stake.

Fabien walked into the drawing room to join Laurent.

"Did you have a restful slumber?" Fabien asked as he kissed Laurent on the cheek.

"Not exactly, but it was very enlightening," Laurent replied grimly.

"You sound mysterious. I don't understand?" Fabien asked, looking confused.

"Let's say I either had a nightmare or a look into the future. I've decided to plan accordingly," Laurent replied.

"Were you going to share that with me? We have planned this entire thing out together?" Fabien asked as Laurent walked toward the window before answering Fabien. In the near distance, Laurent saw Barthelme carving a significant wooden stake.

"Don't you trust me?" Fabien said as he grew agitated.

"Yes, of course I do! However, if Stefan got a hold of you and were to ask you what's planned, at the very least, you wouldn't be able to tell him as you're not privy to it?" Laurent explained.

"I don't appreciate not knowing what's going on. What sort of dream would place doubt in your mind about my love and loyalty to you?" Fabien retorted.

"Fabien, please. Don't ask; there is a reason for this; call it a backup plan," Laurent pleaded.

"When do we leave for Raphaella's shop?" Fabien asked coldly and chose to ignore Laurent's explanation. The tone of his voice revealed his displeasure.

Laurent looked over at the antique clock and said, "We leave in half an hour." Fabien wasn't used to Laurent taking control, nor did he appreciate the commanding tone Laurent had used.

Suddenly, the front door opened as Barthelme entered carrying the wooden stake Laurent instructed him to make.

"Why is he carrying that thing?" Fabien gasped.

"You will find that out in due time; until then, that is between Barthelme and me" Once again, Laurent used a commanding tone with Fabien.

"I'm not sure I like all of this, Laurent. Let me remind you of something. I devised this plan to trap and destroy Stefan. You have added something to that plan, yet you are unwilling to share that with me?" Fabien said and appeared to be growing increasingly agitated.

"Well, for the record, it was Jack who had come up with this plan we are about to embark on," Laurent answered and immediately felt awkward for mentioning it.

Laurent decided he needed to soothe Fabien's ego and defuse the rising tension in the room; Laurent softened his approach to Fabien and chose the path of least resistance.

"I'm sorry, Fabien; I'm extremely anxious about what we are about to do. There are so many things that could go wrong this evening. One misstep from either of us could prove fatal."

"Do you trust me?" Fabien asked.

Laurent hesitated for a moment before he answered and then looked Fabien directly in the eyes.

"Yes, unequivocally!" Laurent answered.

"Then stop playing games and tell me what this backup plan is and what Barthelme is doing with a wooden stake?" Fabien pleaded.

"Alright, if all else fails, should the spirits fail to materialize, and if together we cannot destroy Stefan, Barthelme will be in hiding and will attack Stefan from behind with the wooden stake," Laurent revealed.

"How can Barthelme save us? He's a mere human?" Fabien replied, sounding dismissive.

"Barthelme is not merely mortal. Centuries ago, when I first inherited this estate, I drank a small portion of his blood and told him to drink some of mine. I needed a gatekeeper and a servant who wouldn't wither away and die but one that could live for eternity as you and I; still, he is not one of our kind. Since that day, he has remained my loyal and trusted servant and guardian." Laurent confided.

"But why would you need to retain him as your guardian when I have returned my love? Haven't I always been your protector?"

"Yes, until Stefan destroyed you. Then I no longer had a protector and guardian, did I? Yet I managed to survive on my own and look out for myself until I arrived here and enlisted the help of Barthelme back in the late eighteenth century.

Meanwhile, you had become a spirit and only appeared to me once in the crypt long ago. Every night, I mourned my loss! Until I met Jack, who later became your body vessel! So, you see, dear Fabien, without me, you wouldn't have a body, nor would you again be a vampire. I gave you the dark gift this time, making you my fledgling!" Laurent yelled and left the drawing room using his vampire speed.

"Laurent, wait!" Fabien cried out, ran after Laurent using his immortal speed, and stood at their bedroom door as he knocked, awaiting Laurent's reply.

"Enter," Laurent said.

The door opened, and Fabien stood there with a look of tenderness and love.

"Laurent, why must we argue this way? You and I are not enemies?" Fabien said as a single blood tear fell from his azure blue eyes and ran down his pallid cheek.

Laurent turned to face Fabien, smiled, and remained silent. Until he finally spoke, "Fabien, you mean everything to me; you are the one that took me under your wing so very long ago and transformed my very existence; I owe you everything. I love you more than you will ever realize. However, you must not think me the same man that fell deeply in love with you so long ago; I was young, human, and impressionable," Laurent confessed to Fabien.

"So, what are you telling me? I don't understand; I thought this was what we both wanted. To destroy Stefan, if you wish, we can call off this plan and allow things to return to how they were," Fabien's mood instantly turned from tenderness to irritation.

"Except for one thing, Jack is deep within you. I will admit there is something about Jack that I miss. Dare I say I started to have feelings for him?" Laurent confided.

"How dare you admit that to me? I observed this man, this pathetic excuse for a human being! Arrogant and lacking intelligence, not to mention his addiction to alcohol, namely a drunk!" Fabien shouted.

Suddenly, a knock on the bedroom door. "Master Laurent and Master Fabien, it's time to leave if we are to arrive at Raphaella's shop before Stefan," Barthelme advised.

"Give us a moment, Barthelme; go pull the car out front; we will be down in a moment!" Laurent shouted.

"Are you committed to this plan?" Fabien asked gently. There was a brief pause until Laurent answered, "Yes, I am!" Laurent looked at Fabien, seeing a trace of the blood tear that had run down Fabien's cheek earlier. The two vampires embraced and shared a brief kiss.

"Forgive me for ever doubting you. You are my one true love. Now let's end this bastard's existence once and for all!" Laurent said.

They left the bedroom and walked down the grand staircase hand in hand as Barthelme met them below.

"The car is out front, Master Laurent," Barthelme said as they exited the estate and walked towards the rolls; once Barthelme had opened and closed the door for both, the car sped off.

"We're off!" Barthelme announced.

The two vampires sat silently in the backseat while Barthelme remained equally silent. To Barthelme, each of them seemed preoccupied with their thoughts.

The rolls made good time, encountering very little traffic as they arrived at the city limits in an hour. The car continued to make its way through the wide boulevards of the downtown area until it reached Royal Street and parked. They were immediately around the corner from Raphaella's shop.

The night air brought in the fog, which appeared to be as thick as anything in London.

Laurent stepped out of the vehicle and into the dense fog while Fabien and Barthelme waited in the car. Barthelme quickly lost sight of Laurent as Fabien's vampire eyes cut right through it as he saw Laurent turn the corner as he approached the shop.

Laurent appeared in front of Raphaella's door and knocked.

"Just a minute!" a female's voice replied. The door swiftly opened as a black woman who seemed to be in her early thirties, wearing a decorative turban and a colorful African-looking vest, stood before him.

"Yes, may I help you?" Raphaella asked, sounding annoyed by the sudden and unexpected visitor. Laurent replied, "I was walking past and looked through your window. My curiosity got the better of me. I had to come in and see if perhaps you were available for a session?"

"Why?" The Voodoo queen replied, sounding disinterested.

"You see, I recently lost someone very dear to me, and I was wondering if you would be able to make contact," Laurent replied.

"Well, I have a reading at eight o'clock, but we have half an hour. It will have to be a quick reading if that's acceptable to you?" Raphaella said as she thought about the additional income, which would buy many things, including more rum.

"Right this way. I'm sorry I didn't catch your name?" Raphaella asked respectfully; Laurent could immediately detect a change in her attitude.

"That is quite alright. I never gave you my name," he said and chuckled. He could immediately tell her mind would offer little to no resistance from his hypnosis.

"My name is Laurent, and you must be Queen Raphaella?" he said; she had a puzzled look on her face.

"How did you know that?" She asked.

"By the sign on your window," Laurent replied with a half-grin on his face.

"It only says Raphaella's Voodoo Shop on the window." She responded with one eyebrow raised.

Laurent glanced at the clock on her wall, read the time, and said, "Please, may we get started? It's already seven-forty, and we only have twenty minutes until your next appointment arrives. I don't want to be inconsiderate of your other customers and have my appointment run late for your next one. May I enter?"

"Yes, by all means but let's be quick about this," she replied.

Laurent ushered her toward the rear of the shop until they reached a section separated by a curtain and a round wooden table with several chairs placed around. Each of them sat down.

"Now, give me the name of the spirit you are trying to communicate with?" She asked, unaware she would soon lose the ability to control her thinking.

"Look at me, Raphaella. From now on, you will be under my control; you will lose the ability to maintain control over your thoughts. Is that understood?" Laurent asked as his eyes switched from azure blue to a deep red.

Raphaella nodded, "I hear, and I shall obey."

"Excellent. In exactly twenty minutes, you will receive a visit from someone claiming to be Jack Devereaux, along with someone known as Stefan Vitré. Once they have been seated, and I say the word, *now*, you will summon all the spirits that lost their lives to Stefan, you will do this willingly and without hesitation, and you will do this quickly! Once the spirits have appeared, you will command them to attack Stefan, hold him, and prevent him from escaping. Do you understand my instructions?" Laurent asked forcefully.

"Yes, I understand, and I will obey!" Raphaella replied.

"Good," Laurent said and snapped his fingers as she came out of his trance. He quickly transformed himself into a rat and hid under a table in the corner of the room to observe the arrival of Fabien and Stefan.

Barthelme reminded Fabien the time had come for him to leave the car so that he would appear at precisely the moment of Stefan's arrival. Fabien heeded Barthelme's advice and exited.

Shortly after that, Barthelme left the vehicle with his trusted wooden stake and quickly made his way to Raphaella's shop. He came across an open window in the back of the building as he scanned the area for anyone that could have seen him and climbed through. Once inside the shop, he quickly located a place to hide.

Fabien avoided using his vampire speed; instead, he casually strolled to the front of the shop and appeared as human as possible. He figured Stefan may be observing him from somewhere nearby.

Fabien stood in front of the shop and checked the time. The watch read seven fifty-nine, with only one minute to spare as Stefan suddenly appeared out of nowhere.

"There you are, Jack. Look at this fog. It reminds me so much of London. You could almost hide anything out there!" Stefan said and broke into a burst of hideous-sounding laughter.

"Hello Stefan, you're right on time. What did you mean by that? Hide what?" Fabien asked, as he suddenly felt paranoid about their plan to trap Stefan.

"Jack, can't you tell when I'm joking? As you Americans say, lighten up!" Once again, he laughed that sinister laugh that made Fabien cringe.

"Shall we go in?" Stefan asked.

"Gladly. This session is going to be fascinating! I know you have doubts, but she is truly gifted. She can even conjure up spirits!" Fabien shared as if to tease him with what was yet to take place.

"There are many that claim the ability to do that; we'll see about that," Stefan said, still sounding skeptical.

"I'm one hundred percent convinced of her abilities, Stefan. You'll see!" Fabien said with a grin as he reached for the door and said, "Hello! It's Jack, and I've brought a friend. May we come in?" Fabien said as Stefan looked at him strangely. "You said you're her friend. Why don't you go inside? Why do you need to wait to be invited in?" Stefan said with a confused look. Fabien panicked until suddenly Raphaella appeared, much to Fabien's relief.

"Jack, you made it. Of course, both of you may enter," Raphaella said, pleased that her old friend had shown up as promised.

Stefan noticed Raphaella giving him the once-over as she shifted her focus on his eye patch.

"It happened as a result of an accident, didn't it, Jack?" Stefan said and, at first, looked at Fabien, then at Raphaella.

"I see, follow me," she said.

Laurent, who had observed all of this, was amazed at how natural she sounded, perfectly normal as if she had never undergone hypnosis.

"Please sit, make yourselves comfortable," She said as she held back the curtain that separated the room where she conducted her séances from the rest of her shop and motioned them towards the chairs.

"What brings you here for this reading?" She asked both.

"Well, I wanted to show my friend Stefan how truly gifted you are, Raphaella," Fabien said.

"Why, thank you, Jack! I must say I'm flattered! Stefan, is there anyone you would like to contact?" She asked the dark, brooding, mysterious stranger.

"Yes! My mother, Anne Vitré, she died quite some time ago when I was just a child," Stefan shared.

"I'm sorry to hear that, but I don't know if that's such a good idea. The longer the dead are away from us, the angrier they appear to us when summoned to return," Raphaella warned.

"If you want to know the truth, I think you're a fake and that you can't call on anything to return, much less my mother!" Stefan rudely admitted.

Raphaella, raised one of her eyebrows and said, "Well, Stefan, allow me to prove to you how utterly wrong you are."

Instantly she heard Laurent's telepathic command deep within her mind to call on Stefan's victims; *Raphaella, I **now** command you to summon every spirit that lost their lives at the hands of Stefan Vitré!*

CHAPTER 19

Reunited at last

As commanded, Raphaella called upon all the spirits that lost their lives to Stefan Vitré. "What is she doing, Jack? Has she gone mad?" Stefan asked, visibly shaken by her words.

Fabien didn't reply, remained silent, and looked toward the front of the shop. A dense fog had suddenly formed outside and slipped underneath the shop's front door, enveloping the entire inside.

Instantly, various indistinguishable figures appeared and stood there in silence until one finally spoke, "You monster! I died at the hands of your ruthlessness and cruelty back in Paris in the 18th century! Do you remember me, you evil bastard?" Stefan turned and gazed at the twisted and contorted shape of Jacques's ghost, Fabien's servant at the turn of the century that he had killed in front of Fabien so long ago.

"What the hell is going on?" Stefan said, feeling bewildered as his eyes grew wide in disbelief.

"Your undoing monster!" Fabien retorted.

"Jack! What are you saying?" Stefan asked in disbelief.

Instantly, all of the spirits levitated over toward Stefan in an attempt to hold the almighty vampire down.

"Welcome to the end of your existence, monster!" said the spirit of Jacques.

Stefan realized at that moment that a trap had been set. A plot designed to lure him to his destruction so Jack and Laurent could be together; he wondered if Laurent were present and called out to him.

"Laurent, I know you're here; show yourself, you coward!" Stefan commanded.

In a rage, Laurent transformed himself back and came out from behind the curtain to say, "Yes, I'm here, not only to witness your destruction but to participate in it as well. All of us will destroy you. For clarity, that is not Jack seated across from you, but rather Fabien!" Laurent triumphantly proclaimed as Stefan looked on in horror.

"Yes, that is correct; it's me, Fabien; he stopped speaking in Jack's voice with its hint of southern drawl and returned to his French accent. The spirits continued to hold Stefan rendering him helpless and unable to move.

As quick as lightning, Laurent displayed the Martial Arts talents he had trained so hard at with a roundhouse kick to Stefan's face that propelled the mighty vampire backward, landing on the floor a few feet from where he'd been sitting. Laurent suspected his hand-to-hand combat training might come in handy against Stefan, and the time had come to prove it.

Raphaella commanded, "Quickly, go hold him down!" as the spirits Fabien and Laurent combined forces to confront Stefan.

"Well, Stefan, how does it feel to be the hunted and experience the same terror you inflicted on so many?" Laurent asked as he held Stefan down by the neck with his foot firmly planted. Fabien bent over near Stefan's face and spit on it.

"Take that, you son of a bitch! I'm not Jack, as Laurent mentioned; I'm Fabien; do you remember me? The one you destroyed over two hundred fifty years ago. Well, now it's your turn. Prepare to meet your maker. May he pity your wretched soul if you have one?" Fabien snarled his words.

Without warning, Stefan turned himself into a bat and escaped Laurent's hold and away from the clutches of the vengeful spirits.

As the bat flew toward the front of the shop and attempted to escape, Fabien and Laurent took to flight and grabbed the creature each taking one of its wings. During their struggle, Stefan transformed himself back into the shape of a man, as Fabien and Laurent found it impossible for Stefan to be contained, his strength far exceeded theirs.

The ancient vampire grabbed Laurent by the collar and tossed him aside as he was merely an article of clothing as he flew through the air and landed against a bookshelf. Stefan lifted Fabien and threw him across the store as he crashed through the storefront's window. Both vampires were shaken but unscathed as they rose and lunged toward Stefan, each determined to defeat Stefan.

"Wait! There's a spirit here that I didn't call," Raphaella shouted while everyone focused their attention on her.

The uninvited spirit materialized, Anne Vitré, the ghost of Stefan's mother, as he locked eyes with someone he hadn't seen in over three hundred years. His mother, the one who loved and accepted him, despite his cruelty.

"Stefan, you must stop this! "Anne commanded.

"Mother, I can't help myself! I have such bitterness inside me. I can't control myself!" Stefan admitted.

"I am the one who loved you unconditionally while others vilified you, while you brought physical and emotional torment to others. However, I can no longer witness your continued destructive path. These two other vampires are different from you. They retained human traits such as love, compassion, and emotions besides anger, blood lust, and evil. All they want is to be together. Tell me, son, what do you love besides power and destroying everything in your path? Are you even able to feel love at all?" Anne asked.

Stefan appeared stunned to be hearing these words from his very own mother. "Mother, I have longed to see you again, dreaming of this very moment; despite my many vampire powers, I could never get you to materialize in front of me as much as I wanted and tried. You asked me if I could feel love. Yes, for you and one other. I've missed you for so long, until this day," as the mighty vampire broke down and cried. His cheeks quickly became stained with his blood tears as they ran down his face as he offered his confession.

"You do feel something?" Anne asked her son as she levitated toward him with a white glow that encompassed her figure.

"Then, for my sake, join me; we shall exist together in perfect bliss and harmony with our family. In a world known as the spiritual realm," Anne emphatically said.

"I don't understand, mother?" he asked her softly.

"Free yourself, go in peace, for the sake of God and all of humanity, and all that is decent, let yourself go. For once in your existence, do what is right, Stefan," Anne pleaded.

"Yes, mother, I realize what you're saying is true, but I'm fearful of laying eyes upon my maker; surely he will condemn me to the deepest pits of hell for all my evil deeds. I shall dwell there with the other tortured souls, with the devil himself presiding over us!" Stefan said passionately.

"My son, the fact you've admitted this, and have seen the errors of your ways and the remorse you feel, makes you different from all others that dwell in the underworld. You are different; you have a soul. Surely our maker will take mercy on you," Anne said reassuringly.

"Yes, I hear what you're saying, mother," Stefan uttered.

"Stefan, the time has come. Are you ready?" Anne asked him.

Stefan ceased struggling against the other vampires and spirits and realized he must do what was right and accept his fate.

"Yes, mother, I accept this as truth; take from me this tortured existence. However, before I leave, know this, Fabien, I never meant to harm you nor make your existence with me so miserable. In my way, I cared for you. When you insisted on leaving me to return to Paris, I felt heartbroken and enraged! All I wanted was for us to be together, to revel in what we are, powerful vampires, writing our own rules, existing the way we saw fit. I believed you when you swore that you would never make an immortal fledgling of your own. And yet you deceived me. My love for you turned into jealousy and rage. I felt I had no choice but to avenge my feelings of betrayal. Fabien, do you recall why I came to Paris that night? It was not to destroy you but this fledgling you created! I had no intention of harming you; how could I destroy what I had made, the one who captured my attention and heart when we first met at the Procope café in Paris so long ago? How could I ever destroy you willingly and end your existence?" Stefan confessed.

"That's all very touching, Stefan. But you forget one essential fact. I had fallen out of love with you. You made me do unspeakable things, forcing me to use human beings as a food chain, killing indiscriminately, and causing me to hate myself. Above all else, I hated you, and I hated myself. Do you remember? I begged and pleaded for you to release me! I couldn't stand to exist with you in this way!" Fabien retorted.

Stefan's display of tenderness and compassion during his confession to his mother and Fabien quickly turned to rage.

"You ungrateful bastard!" Stefan said, almost spitting out the words. Stefan suddenly had a change of heart, sensing a betrayal by the spirit of his mother and the two vampires.

Barthelme rushed over to Stefan and lifted the stake high in the air to thrust it into the evil one's heart; Anne appeared in front of Stefan to shield him from sudden destruction and commanded Barthelme to stop.

"Drop the stake! Allow me, the mother of this creature, to rid you and the world of my son's evil presence," Anne lifted her arms to the ceiling as the store began to rumble, and the floor broke open, exposing a fiery red glow below.

"Son, take my hand!" Anne commanded Stefan.

"Are you certain, mother?" Stefan asked with an anxious look on his face.

"It is the only thing that can make right everything you have done wrong in both your human and vampire existence," Anne replied as she reached for her son's hand.

Everyone seemed mesmerized by what they witnessed as Stefan slowly reached out his hand.

"You are willing to do this, my son?" Anne asked Stefan tenderly.

"Yes, I have thought about everything I have done and reflected on everything that's been said. I am ready to atone for my sins and transgressions and face whatever judgment to whoever awaits me, as long as you and I are together. I realize your undying love for me is the only thing that matters to me," Stefan said as he looked at Anne.

She took his hand, and instantly they descended downward as Stefan screamed.

For several minutes, the room remained silent; having witnessed what had happened left everyone temporarily speechless. Laurent was the first to speak as he broke the silence.

"Is it finally over?" Laurent asked and reached for the hand of the one he'd always loved, Fabien.

"Yes, I believe it is. Let's return with Barthelme so we may celebrate the destruction of Stefan," Fabien suggested.

"Alright, but first, give me a moment so I can thank someone who rightly deserves it," Laurent tenderly replied and walked over to a corner of the shop where Raphaella was huddled in a corner and appeared to be trembling.

"Raphaella, I would like to thank you for all that you have done; if it had not been for you, Fabien and I would still be under constant threat of attack from Stefan," Laurent said softly.

Raphaella looked up at Laurent with wild eyes after having witnessed the spectacular series of events; and replied angrily, "The two of you took the only friend I ever had, Jack, and used him as a vessel for your diabolical scheme to be reunited. I don't need your thanks, and I certainly don't need any vampires in my life! The only thing I long for is that someday, my friend Jack will somehow find his way back and return," as she broke down and cried uncontrollably.

Fabien walked over to where Raphaella was and said coldly, "We did what we felt we needed to do!"

"How are the two of you so different from Stefan? You're all evil. I condemn both of you to hell," Raphaella retorted and turned away from Laurent's intense gaze. She no longer felt concerned for her safety.

"I understand you're upset, Raphaella, but Fabien and I belong together, and nothing and no one could ever interfere with that," Laurent said, as he desperately attempted to sound sympathetic.

As Laurent turned to leave, she warned him, "This isn't over," For a moment, he stood motionless, and reflected on what she had just said, as he slowly turned to face her.

"What do you mean?" Laurent asked as he felt the anxiety building inside of him.

"You shall see monster!" she said and began to laugh.

Laurent was rarely shaken by mere words, especially from a human. However, Raphaella was different. She was no mere mortal, and her warning felt ominous, downright sinister.

"Are you coming, Laurent?" Fabien asked, which prompted him to take Fabien's hand as they left Raphaella's shop for the last time.

Raphaella heard the front door close, stood up, and walked to the drawer where her rum was stored. She poured herself a full glass and made a toast, "To my friend Jack, wherever you are. I toast the friendship we once had. I miss you," She said and took a large gulp of her rum, walked over to the round table where she had sat many times before, and decided she needed to contact a spirit as the tears rolled down her cheeks.

The Rolls arrived back at the estate, with everyone feeling exhausted from their battle, as they entered the mansion.

"Shall I pour you both some nourishment?" Barthelme asked.

"Yes, I think that is in order, Barthelme," Laurent replied.

"Right away, Master Laurent," Barthelme said and exited the drawing room.

"I cannot believe Stefan is gone for good," Fabien said and felt a sense of relief as he reached for Laurent's hand.

"Is he?" Laurent replied, released his hand from Fabien's, and walked over to the window as he peered into the darkness expecting at any minute for Stefan to reappear.

Fabien walked to the window to join his lover and replied, "What do you mean? You saw for yourself; his mother lied to him and lured him to the bowels of hell. The flames naturally consumed him. Didn't you hear his screams? How can there be any doubt, Laurent?"

"Fabien, before we left, Raphaella said something that deeply disturbed me; it was as if to say that Stefan might return!" He said, his voice filled with anxiety. Fabien gave Laurent a puzzled look.

"Tonight, we witnessed first-hand how powerful some spirits are, what extraordinary abilities they possess, not unlike our abilities. It would appear the angrier the spirit, the more powers they possess. Stefan's rage was endless; it was all-consuming; that energy doesn't simply vanish into thin air. What if it can return?" Laurent confided to Fabien.

"You don't think?" before Fabien could complete his sentence, Barthelme returned to the drawing room with an antique silver tray carrying two wine goblets and a carafe filled with blood.

"Here we are," Barthelme said as he held the tray out for both vampires.

"Thank you, Barthelme," Laurent said as each of them sat in front of the roaring fireplace that Barthelme had prepared for them upon their return as the fog remained and brought in cooler temperatures.

Both seemed mesmerized by the orange and yellow flames that flickered in the fireplace.

Fabien turned to Laurent and said, "I would like to make a toast to you," as he raised his goblet. "May we never again be separated, not even for a second; here's to our union for now and forever."

Laurent was visibly touched by his lover's toast and answered him with, "here, here!" as both drank from their goblets.

"Would you care for a refill?" Fabien asked.

"Yes, that would be lovely," Laurent answered as Barthelme replenished his goblet.

Both immortals, satisfied and adequately fed with the carafe of the blood, left the drawing room as the antique clock announced the impending daylight. Each hurriedly walked up the long staircase, hand in hand, until they finally reached the master bedroom.

Upon entering, Fabien glanced at his portrait as he appeared back in the late eighteenth century.

"I certainly was a fine-looking man," Fabien said proudly.

"You still are; you haven't changed a bit," Laurent replied as each of them began to laugh.

"Come lay beside me on the bed and let me stroke your hair the way I always used to," Fabien suggested tenderly.

Raphaella had attempted several times to summon a spirit without any luck and had fallen asleep at the table. As she awakened, she thought *perhaps my abilities had been weakened due to consuming an entire bottle of rum.* She looked at her watch. The time read five-thirty. She had been asleep at the table since the two vampires left her shop; that was nearly eight hours ago!

As Raphaella laid her head down and began to rest, she was suddenly awakened by an entity enveloped in a red mist. "You've finally come!" Raphaella greeted the spirit as it nodded, "Where are they?" the entity asked.

"They went back to their estate!" Raphaella replied, and as suddenly as the spirit appeared, it vanished.

In their bedroom, both vampires felt nourished and satisfied. Feeling Fabien's body next to his, Laurent felt safe and secure and questioned how he could be led to believe Stefan would return. Indeed that was simply the rantings of a deranged woman as he chuckled at the thought of it and closed his eyes once more. Suddenly, a red mist appeared near the bedroom window, followed by a figure's appearance! It was too faint to make out from the bed, even with his vampire eyesight.

Laurent arose from the bed, careful not to awaken Fabien. As he walked cautiously closer to the figure, some red mist seemed to surround and envelop Laurent; as if it were attempting to drown him. The red mist had developed tentacles, wrapped themselves around his body, and drew him ever closer until the figure's face finally appeared before Laurent. It was Stefan! Laurent opened his mouth to scream but couldn't. The figure in front of him instantly became a liquid mass that entered Laurent's mouth entirely.

Laurent stood motionless by the window; the red mist had entirely disappeared inside him. He turned slowly to see Fabien lying on the bed in his undead slumber and walked over and laid back down, careful not to awaken him, and closed his eyes.

Shortly after the sun had set, Fabien awakened from his slumber and noticed the empty bed next to him. Sensing something was amiss, he exited the room using his vampire speed and raced down the staircase and into the drawing room as Laurent stood there, draining the blood from their trusted servant's neck.

Laurent turned his attention to Fabien and greeted him mockingly. Fabien stood motionless and stared at the spectacle in shock and horror.

"Good evening, my love. You've finally awakened. So sorry, but I decided; I've never truly cared for the taste of dog's blood and thought I might upgrade to something human."

Instantly, Laurent's face transformed into Stefan's as Fabien reacted in horror and disbelief. For a moment, Fabien could not speak and finally found the strength to cry out, "No!"

"Did you truly think you could get rid of me so easily?" Stefan said and quickly morphed back to Laurent, yet still speaking in Stefan's voice.

"I don't understand?" Fabien barely managed to utter and began to tremble.

"Come now, did you think you were the only one to perfect the art of spirit possession?" Stefan sarcastically asked. "No, I let you go once, but now you will never be rid of me! From the beginning, you and I were meant to be together for all eternity. Now be a good sport and help me say goodbye to our trusty servant Barthelme!"

From outside the stately mansion named "Le Petit Fleur," the bloodcurdling screams of Fabien and Barthelme were heard.

ABOUT THE AUTHOR

(Len Handeland)

Len Handeland's creativity took him from attending FIT (Fashion Institute of Technology) in Manhattan to hair. He studied fashion illustration, then years later to a long and successful 27-year career in the hair industry as a sought-after hair stylist, hair colorist, and salon owner. Len owned a salon in San Francisco's Union Square for nine years and two salons in the town of Sonoma, Wine Country; for eight years; now fully retired from hair, Len became a full-time writer in the spring of 2021. Len is an award winning writer specializing in fiction, specifically horror, paranormal, and crime drama novels. Len has enjoyed writing as far back as middle school. To further enhance and better his writing, Len has taken many creative writing classes and, in 2017, attended The San Francisco International Writer's Conference, which inspired him to write his first book, "The Darkest Gift," based on his love of vampires. He credits the late Anne Rice for being the author that inspired him the most to write his own dark vampire story. His first book earned him 5-star reviews from readers and professional book reviewers. His first novel became a finalist in the American book fest contest in the fall of 2021.

Last spring, Len's novel "The Darkest Gift" was awarded first place in the Bookfest 2022 awards in the category of Fiction/Horror. In addition, Len's book and author interview were featured in the fall literature issue of "DeMode" magazine, with Len's book named one of 10 must-read books of 2021. With the completion of Len's second novel "Requiem for Miriam," and his third based on his 27 years in the hair industry, "Tales from the Chair," he's writing his fourth book ("Transplant – The evil that lurks deep within") to release in the spring of 2023.